Broken Angel

∘ Book One ∘

Holly Huntress

Copyright © 2022 by Holly Huntress
Published by Kindle Direct Publishing

All rights reserved. No part of this book may be reproduced or used in any manner without written permission of the copyright owner except for the use of quotations in a book review.

Second edition: March 2022

Broken Angel by Holly Huntress
Cover design by Emily Lewis & Holly Huntress

This is a work of fiction. Names, characters, places, and incidents either are the product of the author's imagination or are used fictitiously. Any resemblance to actual persons, living or dead, events, or locales is entirely coincidental.

This one is for my parents who have supported me in all my endeavors…I wouldn't have made it this far without you.

Prologue

Ephram's eyes flickered as sleep threatened to overtake him. He couldn't remember the last time he'd slept for more than a few hours straight. His head bobbed forward while he sat at his desk. A soft whisper floated past his ear, catching him off guard, as it always did. It brought him back to full awareness. Whipping around to see who was there, Ephram realized he was alone. He could feel someone there beside him, giving off a familiar aroma of floral perfume. The presence seemed to fade into the abyss. He tried to hold onto it, breathing in deeply, but the scent faded too quickly.

Ephram turned his attention back to the book laying open in front of him, continuing to scan the pages. It was written thousands of years ago, and age had taken its toll. The pages were fading and frayed along the edges. He squinted, trying to decipher a particularly ragged page, and found himself drifting off again.

He didn't know how long he'd been asleep, but as he woke, darkness engulfed him. Something had roused him from his sleep. Lighting a candle on the table before him, he peered around to find nothing amiss.

"*Ephram...*" he heard the whisper of the voice again. That time he was sure it belonged to Amelia, even though she had been gone for over a decade. He shook off the chills that had settled into his bones. He would never become accustomed to hearing her voice, as if she were still there with him. Not all angels could communicate through the veil that separated heaven and Earth, but Amelia had always been exceptional and of course she'd found a way. Her presence faded, leaving Ephram to continue scanning the ancient book on his desk.

Suddenly, a pure white light replaced the darkness surrounding him. An even more luminous figure appeared before Ephram, forcing him to avert his gaze. Ephram went down on one knee, bowing before his dominion, Jeremiah.

"Ephram, I have a task of great importance to bestow upon you and your followers." Jeremiah's voice boomed around Ephram and echoed through the night. "There is a young woman on her way to you and she requires your guidance. You must protect her at *all* costs. Lucifer wants her for himself, and you must do everything within your power to make sure she does not fall into his hands."

"Yes, Jeremiah. If I may ask, what is her name?" Ephram stayed in his bowed position and did not dare glance up at Jeremiah.

"Andromeda." Jeremiah's voice and figure faded out as he spoke the name, and he was gone. The darkness returned and Ephram was left alone, kneeling before the night.

I

The Neighbors

"Andy, can you come help me with this?" Andy turned to see her dad, Wayne, struggling to move the tower of boxes they piled in front of the door. He had the build of a lumberjack and could have probably handled the box tower easily on his own if it weren't awkwardly stacked.

Andy hurried over and helped him finish disassembling the tower so they could get outside into the fresh air. In her current state, she knew she would not have been able to move the tower on her own. She had lost a significant amount of weight since leaving home and was glad she did not have a mirror to balk at her sharp angles and diminishing outline.

"Ahh there we go." Wayne opened the door and took a

deep breath. The wind ruffled his disheveled brown hair, and the sun glinted off his dark brown eyes. Neither Andy nor her brother inherited these traits, instead they took after their mother. They both had her bright blue eyes with gold flecks, and blonde hair. "It's always nice to get outside after being cooped up all night." Andy grinned, taking in her own breath of fresh air. The mornings were still cool enough that her jeans and t shirt weren't too overbearing, but in the middle of the day, the heat became a bit more intense and made Andy wish she could cut off the bottom half of her pants. But, as her dad had warned her, then she'd be cold at night.

They'd been lucky enough to stumble across a few abandoned clothing stores along their journey, so she had been able to swap out her clothes a couple times, but they became dirty so easily on the road.

Temporarily, Andy and Wayne were staying in an old shed somewhere in southern Vermont. On one side of the shed, about two acres of bare fields stretched out, full of unkempt grass, flanked on all sides by a forest of spruce and pine. In New England there were always woods within a mile of you. Only when you went deeper into the big cities, trees were a little harder to find.

The small size of the shed made it easier for Andy and Wayne to protect themselves from any demons who might happen upon them, or worse, one of their pets. Their pets were werewolf-like in shape and hairless. They had elongated, razor-like fangs, claws as sharp as kitchen knives, and were generally horrifying. The sunlight kept them away, and Andy assumed it burned them or they were sensitive to the light. Thankfully, she had never been near one long enough to find out.

They were living in a world that had been turned upside down as it played host to war. There were two distinct sides in the war: angels and demons. All the humans had been caught somewhere in between, either joining in the fight, or watching the world crumble around them. The President, as well as all the other leaders of the world, went into hiding, leaving the remaining humans in chaos.

For the time being, Andy and Wayne were hiding out, pretending to be as human as possible, which was easy for him since he *was* human. Andy's mom, Angeline, was an angel, a fact hidden from the whole family until after the war began. Andy and Wayne hadn't been hiding because they were afraid, though Andy was *definitely* afraid. They were biding their time until they found an angel camp, that was supposedly not too far from where they were now. They planned to head for the camp in hopes they could finally feel somewhat safe again and possibly be of use in the war waging around them.

"Look, Andy." Wayne's voice broke Andy out of her reverie, and she glanced in the direction her father indicated. Squinting, she put her hand above her eyes to block out the sun and finally saw what he did. The small family who they had seen reinforcing a small garage up the hill the night before, had stepped outside. There used to be a house to accompany the shed and the garage on the property, but all that remained of it was ruins. It appeared to have been burned down. Andy tried her best not to think about the people who may have lived there when it happened.

Wayne waved politely to the couple up the hill and turned back inside the shed. Most people had flocked to larger towns and big cities when the war became serious. It was uncommon to see other people out and about that far from the main hubs. But her dad acted so nonchalant about it, Andy could *almost* forget they were living in a world filled with monsters who only used to live in her nightmares.

"Is it time for breakfast?" She hoped they still had some food leftover from yesterday. Wayne was not the best hunter, but he sure knew how to fish. They almost always had fish for their meals, as well as berries and other edible things they could scrounge up. Yesterday, Andy found a whole group of berry bushes past the tree line beyond their shed.

"We have enough food left for breakfast and lunch today. I think we should get some more berries for the night, though." His eyebrows furrowed in worry. "We shouldn't stay here another night, your mom said to try our best to always be in a group…" His eyes glazed over as he mentioned Angeline. Andy knew the exact moment he was remembering, the day Angeline forced them to run while she fought off a demon who had broken into their home. That was the same day she had revealed her secret to Andy. It seemed ages ago, but Andy knew it had only been a couple of weeks. Thinking of her mom left her with an unbearable ache in her chest, and a sense of hopelessness.

Andy rolled her shoulders back, taking a deep breath, and pulled herself back together. "I'll go get the berries now while you get the fish ready. Do you think I should get some for the people up the hill?" She figured they probably did not know where to find food yet since they arrived about an hour before dark the night before.

"Why don't I go with you to meet them? We can't be too careful when it comes to strangers." Wayne grabbed his pistol off the one shelf in the shed and stuck it in the back of his jeans. Andy copied her dad, grabbing her own pistol and putting it in the waistband of her pants. Andy kept wondering if maybe her angel side granted her some special angel powers or something, but for now, all they had were their guns to keep them safe.

Walking up the hill, Andy pulled her tangled hair that trailed halfway down her back into a ponytail. She wanted to make a good impression on the family who may be able to help them, or at the very least, add to their numbers. There wasn't much she could do about her torn, dirt and grass-stained clothes, though. She'd have to find a new set of clothes to replace them as soon as she could.

The couple had started bustling around inside their garage as the two approached. The young man who Andy had seen with them before was out of sight. Andy wondered where he had gone off to. It seemed the family planned to stay for a little while longer because Andy saw they were rearranging the furniture as she and her dad walked up.

As they grew closer, Wayne cleared his throat so as not to startle the couple. They knew what could happen in the new world when you startled someone who was constantly on edge. The two people in the garage were a man and a woman about her dad's age. They seemed beat down and tired. *Just like us*, Andy thought.

"I'm sorry to intrude," Wayne said. The man and woman both glanced up quickly, realizing they were no longer alone. "I'm Wayne Brooks, and this is my daughter, Andy. We wanted to ask if you need any assistance getting settled in." Wayne had a knack for calming nerves. Andy thought it was his deep voice. It always soothed her as a child, and still did to that day. Relief washed over their faces.

"Phillip Windham, and this is my wife Eleanor," the man said.

"We hate to impose ourselves on anyone these days." Eleanor spoke in a light and squeaky manner. "But we would greatly appreciate it if you have any food to share. We had to leave ours behind yesterday when another group invaded our shelter."

"Of course, we can share. I was about to head into the forest to pick some berries." Andy smiled gently at Eleanor. Searching her face for anything that may give her away as either angel or demon, she concluded Eleanor was fully human. There were certain tells Andy knew that could give demons away, like their black irises, the fluidity of their movements, or their abnormal strength. From a human's point of view, these were simply little quirks or oddities.

Andy had also deduced that Angels and demons didn't age once they reached adulthood, considering every description of a demon she had received had been that they appeared no older than thirty. Also, her mom still looked twenty-nine, and could pull off telling them that every year. Before then, Andy had assumed her mom was simply aging well.

"You shouldn't go into the woods alone!" Phillip spoke up. "There are beasts in there. You never know when one will pop up." He shuddered, as Andy guessed they all did at the thought of coming face to face with a demon or one of their pets.

"It's fine, I've done it before. The berries are not too far past the tree line anyway," Andy tried to ease his mind. He nodded. He needed food more than he worried about a stranger's safety. She started back down the hill and broke out into a run. The wind rushing past Andy's face gave her the feeling of freedom; like she could fly away from her life of hiding and go back to the way things were before the war. She kept running into the forest until she spotted the patch of berry bushes. Scanning the area first to make sure no surprises lurked behind the trees, she began to gather berries.

Andy had a small backpack she always kept with her

for occasions when she came across food or other supplies. The front compartment of her backpack was almost full from her haul, when she heard a small cracking of a twig. On instinct, she dropped to the ground and held her breath. She heard demons had keener eyesight and a stronger sense of smell than humans, so staying as hidden and silent as possible was safest. After scanning her surroundings, Andy saw nothing amiss. It could have been an animal, likely a squirrel, but she stayed on the ground. She had also heard about how stealthy demons could be and she worried if she moved, even an inch, one would see the movement and kill her before she could scream.

    She stayed in the same position on the ground for a couple of minutes and decided to make a run for it. If whatever made the noise wasn't gone, it would be far enough away that she could probably make it out of the forest before it caught her. If it even *was* a demon or their pet… she was being overly paranoid. *Better paranoid than dead*, Andy thought.

    Taking a deep breath, Andy jumped to her feet and sprinted back towards the shed and garage. She didn't even glance back, not wanting to know if there was anything behind her worth running from. If not, great, if so, looking back would have only slowed her down. As she reached the edge of the forest, she paused, trying to catch her breath. Out of the corner of her eye she saw a shadow. Her heart jumped into her throat, and she turned too quickly away from the potential threat. Tripping over herself, she fell to the ground with a thud. It knocked the wind out of her, and she sealed her eyes shut, waiting for whatever came next.

"Um, hello? Are you okay?" someone said from behind her. Andy slowly brought her breathing back to normal and opened her eyes. Squinting up at the shadowed figure, she held up her hand to block the sun. "Oh, good you're alive. I thought I scared you to death for a second there!" The guy laughed at his joke but stopped when he saw her frown. Death was not a joking matter. Andy had seen too much of it in the past few months; on the news, and in person.

"I'll be okay when you move out of my way so I can get up," Andy snapped at him. He moved back a few steps so she could stand. She brushed the leaves and dirt off her front, only to find she had dumped all the berries into the grass. "Crap." She started picking them up, one by one, and putting them back into her backpack.

"So... I guess I'll go back to the garage." The stranger started to walk away. Andy stared after him incredulously. *He* knocked *her* down and yet didn't feel the need to help pick up his mess?

"Eh-hem," she cleared her throat. "If you mean *that* garage on top of the hill, these berries are for you, and if you don't help me pick them up, you're not getting any of them," she snapped at him again, not caring what he thought of her at that point. She wanted him to take responsibility for scaring her half to death and making a mess of the blueberries.

"Right, yeah." He turned back and knelt beside her.

Broken Angel

Andy had a fleeting sense of triumph as he bent down. She noticed the young man appeared around her age, eighteen. He was also muscular, not buff like he worked out all the time, but his muscles were clearly defined. His hair was blonde and shaggy; resembling the man who Andy had met earlier, whom she assumed was his father.

"So why were you picking berries in the forest?" he asked, curiosity sparking in his chocolate brown eyes.

"That's where the berries are," Andy said.

"Right. So why were you running before?" he asked another question. Andy rolled her eyes.

"I don't know. It was probably nothing. But I don't take chances out there." She picked up the last berry off the ground and stood up, slinging her backpack over her shoulder. Now that they were both standing, she noticed he stood a few inches taller than her five foot six inches, probably about five nine or ten. His height would be an asset for the nights they had to climb trees. "I know what happens when you're not careful. Now come on, let's bring these berries to your…parents?"

"Yeah, they're my parents. And I'm Bo, by the way." He put out his hand for Andy to shake, but she kept walking right past him. She'd never liked shaking hands with anyone.

"I'm Andromeda, but you can call me Andy. You may have met my dad; he's been helping your parents get the garage ready for the night," she said as they climbed the hill. "We'll be leaving in the morning, and I advise your family to do the same." They needed to keep moving if they wanted to reach the angel camp Angeline had told Wayne about, and this family shouldn't stay out here by themselves.

"Why would your dad be helping us set up a shelter for us to leave it in the morning?" Bo caught up to her. Andy shook her head.

"You must have led a pretty easy life till now if you don't understand how this works yet." Andy could tell from the blush creeping up his neck that she was right.

"We had been living with my aunt and uncle until a week ago. They were survivalists, so we were set, until…" He gulped and turned away. Andy knew that look.

"I get it," she cut in to save him from recounting whatever horror he had faced. "But these days you need to stick together in groups. Fighting off one demon is hard enough with a couple of people, but if two or three, or even more demons come along, you're done for. So, we need to keep moving until we find a bigger group, got it?" Bo nodded slowly. Andy thought her words were beginning to sink in.

"But we're human, what would the demons want with us?" His brow furrowed. "I thought their war was with the angels?"

"The war may be between the angels and demons, but a demon won't hesitate to kill a human that gets in their way," she explained to him.

"So… how do I know you're not a demon trying to prey on my family then?" He smirked.

"You don't. But I'm not. Trust me, any demon would have killed you by now with all these questions," Andy joked. Bo's grin grew a bit wider, and they both started towards the garage again.

"I was beginning to worry about you." Wayne glanced up from the fish he was eating. "Did you have any trouble getting the berries?" Andy decided to keep her little fright to herself, not wanting to worry him over something that had probably been nothing.

"Nope." She forced a smile. "In and out as always." Bo glanced at her, but kept his mouth shut.

After they ate, Andy and her dad finished helping Bo's parents fortify their garage. While they worked, everyone kept to themselves, except for a few comments here and there about how something should be done. Andy showed Bo how to best arrange furniture in front of the door for maximum hold. By the time the sun began to set, they had done the best they could to make sure they would be safe for the night. Andy and Wayne decided to walk back to their shed.

"Do you think they'll be okay?" Andy asked, thinking her dad knew more about the strength of the garage's walls.

"I sure hope so because we'll be in there with them. Eleanor asked if we would join them for the night since it's better to stay in groups." Andy saw the true fear in her dad's eyes then. He had been suppressing it all day, keeping his mind off it by helping the others.

"Why didn't we leave today?" Andy asked him. Since

they left home three weeks ago, they had only been staying one or two nights in each shelter. They both knew they needed to reach the angel camp as soon as possible. It was unlike her dad to allow them to stay in a place this long, especially a place as exposed as a shed or a garage. Houses tended to be much safer and easier to hide in.

"I'm not even sure where the camp is," Wayne admitted. He had never been unsure of what to do…or at least he had never admitted it. If Andy wasn't worried before, she was now. She helped her dad grab their few belongings, and they went back to the garage.

All five of them settled in quickly and hours of silence followed. Eleanor fell asleep on Phillip's shoulder and Andy longed for the ability to fall asleep so easily. She hadn't slept well since leaving home, nightmares plaguing her almost every night. A bone chilling growl in the distance broke their silence.

"Here," Wayne said, handing Andy two of the guns off the floor. One was her pistol that she stuck in the back of her belt. She held the other in her hands, ready to defend herself, if it came to that. Her dad held a gun in one hand and a hunting knife in the other. His weapon of choice was a knife because he hated the idea of wasting bullets, but if there were too many demons or pets…the gun would be necessary. It was like that every night, preparing for a fight that may never happen. Her dad had given a gun to Phillip as well, who clutched it so tightly, his knuckles turned white.

Guttural choking noises came from the direction of the forest. Andy had told her dad they reminded her of when she used to gargle mouthwash, to try and make the noises seem less scary. She realized she was holding her breath, and she let it go in a rush. She gazed over at Bo who could be mistaken for a ghost in the glow of the one candle they had lit. She reached over and gently put a hand on his arm.

It's okay, she mouthed silently to him. He failed at trying to smile and it came out as a grimace. A loud thud shook the wall behind Andy, causing her to jump in surprise. Eleanor let out a faint squeak but pulled herself together quickly. It came again, and again. Andy buried her head in her lap. She knew a creature stood on the other side of the wall, itching to kill her. That time Bo touched her arm, trying to reassure her it would be okay. She lifted her head to see her dad standing beside the furniture pile. He positioned himself to fight in case anything broke through. Thankfully the thudding stopped, and Andy let out a sigh of relief, finally able to breathe again. The sounds moved on to what Andy assumed was the shed. The sound of shredding metal and creaking wood echoed, and she thanked her lucky stars they had decided to stay in the garage.

A wolf-like howl sounded off in the distance and the creatures bounded away, crashing through the woods. No one dared speak again in the following silence.

Morning finally came, and they emerged from the

garage to an incredibly vivid sunrise Andy couldn't believe existed in the same world as those creatures. It reminded her of a work of art, the way the orange and pink colors were painted across the sky. Andy stretched her whole body, and her limbs began to uncramp. The day was already hot and humid, and Andy could feel her clothes and hair clinging to her. She was about to offer to go get some berries for breakfast when her dad took her arm gently, but firmly.

"Andy, we're leaving now," he stated. She knew they would leave today, but she thought they would at least be able to relax, maybe sleep a little first. "Phillip, Eleanor, you are welcome to come with us, but if you do, you have ten minutes to get your essentials together and then we are gone." Andy had never heard her dad be so stern, probably because it was usually just the two of them. She did anything he told her to, no questions asked.

"I will run and get some berries for the road," Andy offered, pulling away from her dad, but he held fast to her.

"No. The sun is not all the way up yet. Those creatures are still roaming, it's not safe." His voice softened. "We will find food on the way."

Andy assented, but Bo butt in. "I'll go. Just tell me where they are. I want to help." He stood straighter.

"Don't be silly, Bo." Eleanor grasped his hand. "You heard Wayne, it's too dangerous."

"But what if we can't find food on the way to wherever we're going?" he protested. Andy knew he had a point, but it was stupid to risk their lives for berries.

"We will find food," Andy said. "You need to know when to play it smart. Right now, we all need to get out of here and find a new shelter as soon as possible." Bo remained silent. Andy strode past him and back into the garage, grabbing her weapons and putting them in her backpack. She still had a gun in her belt, and she left it there. It may have been daytime, but the creatures weren't the only monsters they needed to worry about when they were on the move.

2

The Farmhouse

As they walked, Andy noticed the trees on either side of the road began to change from spruce and pine to more maple and ash trees. There were also dirt roads spidering off into the woods leading to God knew where.

They all kept their eyes out for any food or water source. What they had left would barely last them the day, especially in the heat. Andy walked side by side with her dad for a while. Eventually she slowed down and fell into step with Bo, who brought up the rear. Andy didn't want to make any enemies today, so she apologized to him.

"Sorry I snapped earlier…I just wanted you to realize you shouldn't get the berries." She knew he was only trying to be helpful.

"I get it. You think I don't realize how dangerous those *things* are. You think I'm just some guy trying to be the hero." Bo locked eyes with Andy. "And maybe you're right. I haven't seen any demons firsthand, and I am trying to be brave, but I am also trying to live a little. We could die any day, and if I want berries, I'm gonna eat berries. That's how I see it, anyway." A shadow came over his face. Andy had unfairly assumed he'd had it easy, when she knew *no one* had had it easy these past few months.

"Okay. I guess that's one way to look at it." Andy blushed. "Like I said, I'm sorry."

"Don't worry, I'm over it. Let's talk about something else." Bo's face shifted back to his normal casual demeanor, making Andy relax a little as well.

"Like what?" Andy wasn't good at small talk, which was probably why she had few friends back before the war began.

"I don't know… how did you get your name?" It was a question she received frequently. She didn't mind it as much as she used to. In school the question was more *like what kind of name is that?*

"Have you never heard the story of Andromeda and Perseus?" Andy glanced at Bo, and he shook his head. "Well, as I've learned from my mom and google," she smirked, "Andromeda was the beautiful daughter of Cepheus and Cassiopeia in Greek mythology. She was saved by the hero Perseus after being chained to a rock as a sacrifice for a monster." As much as Andy always thought her name was a mouthful, she loved that it had a story behind it.

"Wow. That's quite the name you've got there. I inherited my name from my uncle. Not quite as exciting." They both laughed, and it felt nice for Andy to finally have someone she could laugh with.

"My mom was into Greek mythology, I guess, and she loved the name. My brother's name was Jason." She stopped suddenly, her heart clenching as tears sprung into her eyes. Andy bit down hard on her lip and fought back against the grief that threatened to take over, as it always did whenever she thought about Jason. She shoved it back into its tightly sealed compartment.

"I think your mom did a great job naming you. I mean, you're clearly beautiful, like this Andromeda you've told me so much about." Bo tried to cheer her up.

"Thank you," Andy whispered. The lump in her throat cleared, but she was still afraid to talk and lose her grip on the grief that slowly subsided. A part of her wondered how Bo truly saw her. She had not looked in a mirror in over a week, and she could only imagine the kinds of knots her hair had worked itself into.

"Hey, kiddos!" Andy rolled her eyes as her dad called them over to him. He insisted on calling her 'kiddo' even though she was clearly not a kid anymore. "I found some food!" Hearing that, they all hurried over to Wayne to see another berry bush, but it was better than nothing.

They picked the blackberry bush clean, but Andy could still hear her stomach grumbling. She needed something more substantial, but she had grown used to going without any food for a while. "Sorry I couldn't find anything else yet." Wayne rubbed the back of his neck, and Andy recognized his frustration that he could not provide more for everyone.

"Wayne, we are thankful you have even found this. Once we get settled in a new place, I will find a way to repay you for all of the help you have given us," Phillip promised. That seemed to remind them all they still needed to find a place to stay for the night, and it was nearly midday. They set out on the road again.

Once the trees cleared, they came across a small farmhouse sitting atop a hill, surrounded by fields filled with yellow flowers and weeds on all sides. Being higher up would give them a perfect view if anyone approached the house from either direction. But first, they had to make sure it was not already claimed by another group.

Wayne knocked on the door before he entered, and once he finished searching the whole house, he waved the rest of them inside. He always insisted on going in alone, to scout for any demons or strangers. If things went south, Andy would be able to get away.

Inside, the house was a mess. Furniture laid on its side, dirt covered the floors, trash littered the corners, and dust coated every square inch. It had definitely already been scavenged by people searching for food and other supplies.

Andy and the others went around and made sure all the windows and doors were locked before they started to search for any leftover supplies. Andy found one can of peas that had rolled under a cabinet. They opened it and divided it equally between the five of them. Wayne found a few knives and stowed them in his backpack.

After they ate their miniscule meal, Bo, Eleanor, and Andy headed upstairs to get some sleep. Phillip offered to take the first watch while the rest of them each found a bed and passed out. It had been two days since Andy last slept, and she was out like a light as soon as her head hit the pillow. She dreamed of Jason and her mom.

"Andromeda," Andy heard her mom's voice calling to her. "Andromeda, why did you leave us?" Grief thickened her voice, and it cut Andy deeply. Her mom hardly ever used Andy's full name, but it sounded so beautiful as she said it. Andy tried to reach out to her, but she moved further away. Andy strained herself, pushing forward and closer to her.

"Mom!" Andy called out. Silence enveloped her for a moment until a snarl came from directly behind Andy. She spun around, but all she could see was Jason. He reached out to her, and she tried to hug him, but he slipped away. "Jason, please stay with me," she begged him, but he chuckled, as if he were playing a game with her, and faded into nothing.

Andy woke with tears streaming down her face,

wishing she could be with her mom and Jason. She let herself wallow for a moment but pulled herself together after a few minutes. She was all her dad had left, and she had to stay strong.

"Hey, Andy." She wiped away her tears quickly as Wayne came into the room. "I heard you saying Jason's name in your sleep." He sat beside her on the bed, stroking her hair once, like her mom used to do when she was upset, and he kissed her forehead. "It's going to be okay, kiddo. We're going to be okay." He smiled half-heartedly and she hugged him, letting her tears soak into his shirt. Andy felt like a child, but she didn't care. She gazed out the window at the darkness which had fallen and let go of her dad.

"We should be watching the fields, if one of those creatures caught our scent last night..." she stopped because her dad understood what she was trying to say. She hurried to the window and peered outside; nothing seemed out of place. There was no movement, and she could hear no growling as she opened the window to let in some air.

"It's pretty quiet tonight." Her dad came up beside her and placed his hand on her shoulder. "Go back to bed, kiddo. I'll wake you if I see anything. I promise."

Andy laid back down and fell asleep again within seconds. The next time she woke up, sunlight streamed in through her window. She hurried downstairs to find everyone sitting around the table.

"I think we should stay here one more night..." Phillip

was saying as Andy entered the room, his eyes filled with determination. Wayne sat opposite him at the table, seemingly wary.

"It may seem safe now, but we have no idea if that creature the other night caught our scent. If it did and it finds out we are in here, it will take them all of two seconds to find a way inside." Wayne was clearly not keen on the idea of staying put, and Andy could understand why.

"There was no sign of anything last night. I think we would be safe staying here, and we can leave tomorrow morning," Phillip argued. "I found three cans of beans in the basement, and Eleanor saved some berries from the bush we found yesterday. It's not a lot, but it will sustain us until tomorrow." Wayne sighed heavily, he did not like being told what to do; he usually made the decisions.

"I can go out and see if I can catch us a rabbit or something," Andy offered. She had hunted many times before with her dad, even before the war began, and she was getting pretty good at it, probably better than him, though that wasn't saying much.

"I'll go with you; I think it's about time I learn to catch my own food." Bo stood from his chair. Andy debated telling him no, worried he might scare away the prey. But she decided he was right, and he ought to learn. She took the rope and some wire out of her dad's backpack and made a rabbit snare. She figured they could set it somewhere close, and come back to it before dark, or in the morning.

"Let's go." Bo and Andy set off across the field behind the house towards the woods. "I'm going to set this up, and we can go search for some other food." They approached the edge of the woods and cautiously entered. About ten feet in, Andy set up the snare, tying it to a low hanging branch of a spruce tree. They usually needed to set them at least a day in advance if they hoped to catch anything, but it was worth a shot.

Bo watched Andy's every move. She knew he wanted to learn how to do it for himself, but it made her feel self-conscious and nervous.

"Well, that should do it. Let's get out of here." Andy scanned the woods surrounding them and noticed some leaves rustling in the wind. She shivered, hoping nothing lurked behind the trees. Andy led the way out of the woods and back into the clearing. Out in the open again, the sense of foreboding lifted.

"You're good at all this surviving stuff," Bo commented. Andy tried to give him a smile, but it was hard knowing the truth about *why* she had to learn all these things. It haunted her, wondering if she had known how to fight back and survive sooner, maybe it would not be just her and her dad.

"I can teach you how to survive too, but, so far, you seem to be doing a pretty good job yourself," Andy told Bo, and that made *him* smile at least. Andy sat in the little clearing, feeling the need to take the world in for a while. She was working on reminding herself to enjoy the little things while she still could. Bo sat beside her, facing the trees while Andy faced the house. He at least knew they always needed to keep an eye in every direction.

"I wonder," Bo began. "Sometimes I wonder what it's like. To be a demon, or an angel. How did they stay undetected all these years…" Bo mused, and Andy laughed inwardly. "They must have superpowers, right?"

"Like Superman?" Andy scoffed, and Bo laughed.

"No, not like Superman." He nudged her from behind with his elbow. "I mean like, gifts, I guess." Andy had nothing to say to that, she honestly had no idea if angels had any gifts, she didn't have any she knew of. "And why did they suddenly decide to start a war *now*?" Bo only voiced the thoughts Andy figured all humans must have. She wondered about it all too. Of course, she was an angel, but she didn't even know what that meant yet. Andy had been told in the last few weeks that angels and demons had always been around, living undetected among the humans. The angels and demons were *never* civil with each other, always butting heads over territory, or souls. Only recently did the demons decide to declare war on the angels. Andy didn't know why the demons waited so long to openly fight the angels, but it didn't matter now. All that mattered was which side you were on, versus the person standing next to you.

Andy's side had been chosen for her. She could have, technically, chosen not to side with either the angels or the demons and pretend nothing was happening for a while, which some people did. Everyone noticed the whole world changing around them but could not bring themselves to accept that a war had begun.

People kept trying to place the blame elsewhere, mostly on other countries. People would say, "Look over at that country, they have the *most* horrific things happening, so it must be their fault." Or, "What a terrible accident," as if the three separate airport explosions in one day were not planned attacks by the demons. Of course, after that attack, the angels made sure all other airports were shut down indefinitely for the safety of humans.

As the war raged on, it became clear to most everyone that angels and demons were more than religious symbols, but actual entities causing the global strife. People had either gone into hiding, like the leaders, or tried their damned hardest to go about their normal lives. The latter became harder and harder by the day. The angels took care to have as few human casualties as possible, but as could be imagined, the demons could not care less whether one human died, or one million. The war was about as close to the biblical apocalypse as it got.

Humans were hoarding food and weapons, staying safe for as long as possible, and only venturing out for more provisions. If they saw anyone out on the streets, it was safe to assume they were not human.

Andy wondered how Bo would feel if he knew the truth about her. She considered telling him, but only for a moment.

"I wish I knew," Andy finally responded to Bo's question, shifting slightly so her back touched his. It was nice to not feel so alone; to have someone else here with her.

They both sat in silence, leaning against each other as they were lost in their own thoughts. Andy started plucking blades of grass from the ground and when she glanced up, she noticed her dad walking towards them. He gave her a small wave and Andy returned it. After standing up, she wiped the dirt off her pants and started towards him.

"I wanted to let you know Phillip and his family are definitely staying here tonight. I'm a little hesitant…I don't want to stay here too much longer." Wayne spoke quietly so Bo would not overhear him. Andy peeked over her shoulder at Bo, still sitting in the grass, picking at the blades, and inspecting them.

"I think we should stick together," Andy whispered back. "There were no signs of the creatures last night, I think we can assume the ones from the other night didn't get our scent," she reasoned with him.

"If you want to stay, I will stay." He gripped her shoulder and pulled her in for a hug. Andy knew he was only worrying about her safety. He had said on more than one occasion she was the only thing he lived for anymore. Andy worried about what he would do if anything ever happened to her. She shook her head and gave him her best reassuring smile.

"I want to stay," she said definitively.

"Phillip told me he has heard of a safe place not too far from here. I think he may be talking about the angel camp, but I didn't want to come out and ask in case he wasn't, and I gave us away." Wayne seemed hopeful. "Why don't you kiddos come inside and I'll show you the map Phillip has. I think you should know where we're headed; just in case." He meant in case they were separated, or worse. Andy assented and Bo suddenly stepped up by her side.

Observing the map, Wayne pointed to where they were now, somewhere near Middlebury, Vermont. On the map, it seemed like a short trip to Philadelphia, which is the place she used to call home. However, after the amount of time they had spent moving from place to place, never staying anywhere for more than a day, she knew it was much farther than it seemed.

"So, we're here," Wayne spoke, breaking into Andy's thoughts. "The safe place Phillip was talking about is closer to Syracuse, which is here." Andy let her eyes wander to where he pointed. "It will take at least a week to get there on foot, but we would have to walk all day, every day. There would be no staying anywhere for more than one night," Wayne explained. That was how it had been for them so far anyway. It would be worth it if that was where the angel camp was.

"So, when do we leave?" Bo asked, ready to take on the formidable journey ahead of them. There was no telling what they may come across along the way.

"Tomorrow morning," Phillip announced as he walked into the room with Eleanor following closely behind. "I'm glad you two decided to wait another day for us to join you." Phillip inclined his head towards Andy, acknowledging she was the reason her dad had decided to stay one more night.

"Want to take a walk with me, kiddo?" Wayne asked Andy, as Bo and his parents headed upstairs.

Andy followed her dad outside and down the dirt driveway, back towards the road that led them there. Andy kicked at the rocks as they walked, watching them bounce and skid off into the grass. She noticed the grass had started to grow in patches within the driveway.

"How are you doing?" Wayne asked. Andy turned to him and put on a fake smile.

"I'm fine," Andy lied. Her emotions ate away at her on the inside, threatening to devour her, but she had to keep a brave face on for her dad. She didn't want him to know how much she hurt, because then *he* would be hurting more than he already was.

"I know. You're always fine." Seeing him happy, even for a moment, made Andy feel a little better. "You've become such a strong young woman. I am so proud of you." Her cheeks burned; they'd never had a conversation like this before.

"Thank you. You taught me well, I guess." In the few weeks since they lost the rest of their family, he had taught her everything he knew about survival. Andy never had the time to learn any of the skills before, but when it was just the two of them, it seemed like all they had was time. Except at night, when the creatures came out and it seemed as if their time was up.

"You seem to like these people," he said. Andy realized what the talk was *really* about. "I don't want you getting too attached to anyone right now. We may have to separate, and I don't want it to be any harder on you than it needs to be. Keep in mind, it's you and me, Andy. If it ever comes down to a choice of saving them or you, it will always be you. I will leave everyone behind to keep you safe." Wayne's face was grave.

"I know," Andy whispered, staring at the ground again. "I thought it might be nice to have some company for a little while." Andy knew she would leave them in a heartbeat as well if it meant saving her dad. "It's still you and me," Andy assured him she was on the same page. "No attachments, and nothing holds us back."

"Exactly. Don't look back and keep moving," he sighed. "I wish it didn't have to be this way; I need you to know that."

"I know, Dad." She could see the sadness and guilt shadowing his face. They'd had that talk before, about leaving people behind, because their goal was the angel camp. Andy hoped it did not come to that because she was starting to like Bo and his family.

They walked around for a while, until the sun began to set, and they hurried back to the house. Phillip and Eleanor had made a makeshift dinner. They had eaten the beans for lunch, so for dinner they had some berries and a rabbit. It appeared Andy's trap had worked after all. She beamed in satisfaction.

"I went back to check the trap and I found that!" Bo reported to Andy excitedly. "It worked! I mean, I never doubted you." Bo nudged her, and she nudged him back. Andy noticed Wayne's wary expression and stepped away from Bo. She could guess what he was thinking; she was getting too close.

They sat around the kitchen table in an assortment of chairs: a desk chair, an armchair and three precarious dining chairs. The meal was decent, not much, but it filled Andy's stomach enough that it wasn't gnawing at her anymore.

After they ate, Andy went to the bedroom she had slept in the night before and gazed out the window. The sun had set, and the stars twinkled overhead. The moon shone on the fields and made them glow. Nothing moved outside, and the stillness of the night unnerved Andy. It seemed like the calm before the storm, but she hoped the storm never came. Someone knocked on the door, causing Andy to nearly jump out of her skin.

"Come in," she called out but stayed by the window. She could see Bo open the door in the reflection. "What's up?" she asked, turning towards him.

"Nothing, I just wanted to check in with you. Anything out there?" He motioned to the window and Andy shook her head.

"Not yet," she sighed. "It's still early though." She sat on her bed and motioned for Bo to sit too. "How are you doing?"

"I'm good," he laughed. "I mean, as good as I can be in these circumstances." They watched out the window in silence for a while. It was nice not to be alone, even if they weren't talking. Andy had been alone with her dad for so long, she had started to crave a new interaction. She loved her dad, but he was not much of a talker.

"Eh-hem." Andy noticed Wayne standing in the doorway. "I think you should be getting to bed, Andromeda." He hardly ever used her full name, which made her realize he was upset because she was getting too close to the family he expected her to be able to ditch when things went south. "You too, Bo." Bo glanced back at Andy.

"Goodnight, Andy." Bo stood and left the room.

"What was that about?" Wayne asked, still leaning against the door frame with his arms crossed.

"Relax, Dad. I won't forget the plan. I figured I should get to know the people we will be traveling with." He should know better that she never went back on her word with him. "We probably won't even have to separate, and we'll have worried for nothing." Andy hoped what she said was true, but it was unlikely for them to get to the camp unscathed.

"Alright, I trust you to know what you're doing. Goodnight, kiddo." Wayne shut the door as he left. Andy figured she should get some sleep. They had a lot of walking ahead of them.

If they were lucky, they would find an abandoned car with some gas left. The angels and demons had commandeered most of the spare vehicles, but sometimes they left them behind. Andy and her dad had to abandon their own car merely twenty miles from their home because someone had siphoned all the gas; probably the demon who had broken into their home.

Andy always tried to keep some hope, though, or else she would fall into that pit of despair that always threatened to swallow her whole every time she thought about what she had lost, and the horrors that awaited her.

3

The Trees

As soon as the sun started to rise, they left the farmhouse. It was risky to leave so soon after dawn, but they needed to take advantage of as much daylight as possible. There was never the promise they would find another place to stay before night fell again, so covering more ground increased their chances.

"I spy with my little eye…" Bo broke the silence after they had been walking for nearly an hour. "Something… brown," he smirked. Andy couldn't believe he thought this was the time for games. She tried to ignore him, but he nudged her arm. "Come on, we need to pass the time somehow."

"How about keeping an eye out for danger? Or food.

That's a good use of my time." Andy rolled her eyes.

"Something brown," Bo repeated. Wayne, Phillip, and Eleanor were a little farther ahead, so they were lucky enough not to be expected to participate.

"Fine. A tree?" Andy decided it was better for her sanity to play along with Bo's road trip game.

"Nope." Bo grinned and Andy tried to spot something else brown.

"That rock." Andy pointed to a rock in the shade of a tree that appeared to be brown, and Bo shook his head. "The dirt?" Bo laughed and shook his head again. "I give up," Andy grumbled.

"That bird." Bo pointed, and off in the distance Andy could see a small brown bird perched on the highest branch of a tall oak tree. "Your turn," Bo announced, and Andy groaned.

"No way." She crossed her arms trying to convey the fact that the game held no appeal for her whatsoever, but he did not take the hint.

"Come on, Andy. You have to admit this is a little boring, walking all day. I need something to help pass the time." Bo gave her puppy dog eyes.

"Fine," she caved. "I spy with my little eye, something blue." Bo glanced around dramatically, which made Andy laugh.

"The sky!" he guessed, and Andy shook her head. "Hmm, okay... let me see. What about..." he was cut off by an eerie howl in the distance. They all stopped dead in their tracks staring in the direction of the noise. Wayne whipped his head around to Andy and she ran to catch up to him. Bo was still rooted to his spot, she tried waving him on, but he seemed frozen.

"Bo! Let's go!" his dad yelled. Bo seemed to snap out of his stupor and ran to catch up with the rest of the group. They all moved to the side of the road, towards the trees that provided more cover, and slowly began walking forward again. There was no point going back, they would only waste time. Whatever was ahead would probably have moved on by the time they reached that area. The sun was fully up and there was a slim chance one of those creatures was still out, but the demons could always be out and about.

None of them dared to speak as they trudged onward, every one of them on edge. Andy and her dad had been through this before, and they knew to react immediately to any kind of threat. They also knew the threat was not always inhuman… the new world had changed many people. As Wayne often reminded Andy, everyone had darkness within, though some people gave into it more willingly than others.

Hours seemed to pass before any of them spoke again. It was nearly sunset, and they had not yet come across a safe place to stay for the night. Andy and Wayne didn't panic, it had happened before, and they survived, but Andy could see the fear beginning to surface on Bo and his parents' faces. Contrary to the daytime, the woods were safer at night because the creatures were no longer confined to them.

"We should think about picking a spot to hole up for the night," Wayne broke the silence. Sheer panic overcame Eleanor's face.

"We can't stay out here!" she shrieked. Phillip took her hand and tried to calm her down.

"I know it isn't ideal, honey, but we need to listen to Wayne. He has more experience with this new world, and we need to trust him." Eleanor still trembled but she kept her mouth shut. Phillip nodded to Wayne, and they started into the forest. Andy could feel the tension in the air, and everyone had a firm grip on their weapons as they crept slowly into the trees. Every breath sounded like a roar in the silence.

"From what we have experienced, not all the creatures can climb, but we try to get as high as possible and make sure there is at least one tree close enough to escape down if one of the climbers comes up our tree. They're agile on the ground, but clumsy and can't maneuver as easily as humans in trees," Wayne explained in a whisper. "No more than two people in a tree, it makes it too hard to get away quickly if you need to, you get in each other's way."

"We're not experienced in climbing trees," Eleanor's voice wavered, and she hugged her arms around herself. "I would feel better if Bo was with one of you…" Wayne would gladly let Bo go with him, but that would leave Andy alone.

"He can come with me," Andy offered, reading her dad's thoughts. "Then neither of us have to be alone." She knew he would respect Eleanor's need for her son to be as safe as possible.

"Fine," is all Wayne said.

"Thank you so much, dear." Eleanor squeezed Andy's hand and turned to Phillip. "Pick a tree, honey. We best get started." Andy turned to Bo and led him to the maple tree she had already selected. It had branches low enough to the ground that they would easily be able to hoist themselves up. It was a good starter for Bo.

"This is the easy part; getting up the tree," Andy told Bo. She grabbed the lowest branch and, using the trunk as leverage, hauled herself up. "We have to get at least thirty feet up, but higher is better." After climbing each branch, Andy waited for Bo to be right below her before moving up again. Wayne climbed another maple that abutted Andy's tree. He wanted to be close in case anything went wrong.

Once Andy arrived at a point she believed to be safe, or safe enough, about thirty-five feet up, she stopped and settled in against the tree. The rough bark pressed into her back, but comfort was not an option when spending the night in a tree.

"This should be good," she whispered to Bo. The sun had set now, and it was only a matter of time before the creatures started their hunt.

"Do you think we will see any of them?" Bo asked, fear filling his eyes, and Andy debated lying to save him the anxiety, but that wouldn't help him.

"Probably," she answered honestly. "Usually, they run by without a second glance at us up here, but sometimes…

they linger. We've only had one incident, out of the three times we've had to stay in trees, where one started to climb the tree. We were able to get to the next tree and the creature seemed to lose interest. They usually have specific targets they're on the hunt for, mostly angels, sometimes humans, but they don't like to spend a lot of time getting sidetracked."

"You and your dad seem like pro's compared to my family," Bo sighed. "I feel so helpless."

"I've been climbing trees my whole life. It was something my brother and I liked to do outside together." Andy closed her eyes and could almost see the old red oak tree in their front yard that she and Jason used to climb. "You should be grateful you haven't been out here long enough to have needed the skill. There is nothing I wish more than to have had more time with my family in our home." A lump formed in her throat.

"I know, I'm sorry." Bo reached up and took her hand. "You should know if you ever need to talk about your past, I'm a good listener." She pulled her hand away.

"We should be quiet now. We don't want anything to hear us." Andy could feel slight resentment building inside her for Bo. He still had his whole family. Andy pushed her anger back down to save for later when she had time to sort it out.

After a few hours, Andy heard a rustle in the undergrowth beneath them. The same fear seized her heart that always did, and she knew what was about to appear. She held her breath and watched as a thin, milky white paw, extended forward out of the bushes. Attached to it came the disfigured body of a hairless wolf-human. Except the creature was about five feet long, hunched over with no muscle on its bones. The body of the creature appeared almost translucent in color, but a dark fog shrouded any organs the creature had. The eyes were what haunted Andy the most. Red orbs ringed with black piercing through the darkness. The nose, or snout, seemed to be pushed up into the head, and it bared his pointed decaying teeth.

    Andy shuddered and heard Bo's sharp intake of breath as he saw the creature below them. Andy tensed as the creature's head whipped up as if it had heard his breath of surprise. A growl escaped from deep in the creature's chest. Andy slowly pulled her gun closer to her side, readying herself to stand and make the leap to the neighboring tree if the creature started to climb theirs.

    As the creature took a step towards their tree, a howl like the one they had heard earlier while walking on the road, sounded off in the distance, though much closer than before. The creature whipped around and sprinted in that direction. Andy let out the breath she still held.

    "That was close," she breathed.

    "You okay, kiddo?" Andy turned and nearly fell off her branch as she noticed her dad only about a foot away from her. He had quickly moved over to their tree when he thought the creature would start climbing.

"Yeah, I'm good." Andy peeked at Bo on the branch below her. "How about you, Bo?"

He gave them a thumbs up. "Doin' alright." He sounded as breathless as Andy felt. They stopped talking again after that for fear of accidentally drawing in another creature. Andy wondered about the howl that drew away the creature's attention. It had sounded exactly like the one they had heard before. The howls sounded more human-like than animal, but not the sound of someone being harmed or tortured. She knew those cries...those were different. Her mind flickered to the house she and her dad had almost entered one day, before they heard the screams coming from inside. She could only imagine what horrors had awaited within and she shook her head to clear away the memory.

Miraculously, Andy drifted off for a while until she felt a prod on her side. She jerked awake and realized the sun was rising. They had made it through the night. She glanced down and saw Bo smiling up at her.

"We made it," he repeated her thoughts. Andy could not help but smile back. "When do we get to climb out of this tree?" Scanning to the next tree over, Andy saw her dad watching the ground below.

"Shouldn't be too long now. We like to wait at least an hour after the sun begins to rise. Some of the creatures make it back undercover last minute. So, we're not quite in the clear yet," Andy told Bo. It was unlikely they would see anything now, but it was better to be safe.

"Alright...more waiting." Bo slumped back against the tree. "What was it you were I-spying yesterday?" Andy blinked, confused for a moment, and then she remembered what he was talking about. Their silly game of I spy. They had been interrupted by that first howl.

"Your shirt," Andy told him, smirking. She had picked the first item she saw, too annoyed with the game to actually go for something interesting. Bo peered down at himself and laughed. His t-shirt was in fact, a light blue color.

They waited out the hour, and Wayne gave the signal that it was okay to climb down. He went first, the rest of them joining him on the ground. It was a relief for them all to be on solid ground again.

Wayne led the way out of the woods. When they were back out on the road, they continued on their route. Hopefully today they would find a real place to stay before the sun went down. None of them looked forward to the possibility of having to sleep in a tree again. Andy had all kinds of aches and pains, but most noticeably, she had a crick in her neck. She kept trying to massage it out herself, but nothing helped.

"I can't believe you were actually able to fall asleep in that tree." Bo popped up beside her.

"I guess it was exhaustion from lack of sleep… I can't believe it either," Andy agreed. She noticed they were walking a little faster today. She had to pick up her pace to keep up. Her stomach grumbled as they walked. Her thoughts became a bit fuzzy from the hunger gnawing at her, they'd not eaten since the meal they'd had at the country house. They found a berry bush the day before, but it had already been picked clean by animals.

After about an hour of walking, they finally broke free from the trees. A wide-open area stretched out in front of them broken up by small hills and flowers that appeared to be Coneflowers and Black-eyed Susans. The purple and yellow flowers dotted the hillsides and all along the road that cut straight through them. Andy could not stop herself from beaming at the beautiful sight.

"What a relief," she heard Bo saying. "I was beginning to wonder if we would ever see anything but trees again."

"Let's take a break," Wayne said, followed by murmurs of agreement between the rest of them. Wayne, Eleanor, and Phillip all climbed the first hill and sat in the grass. Bo offered his hand to Andy. Instead, she ignored his hand, and said, "race me" taking off up the hill. Andy wasn't sure what Bo's intentions were when it came to their budding friendship, but a friend was all Andy hoped for with him. Bo ran after Andy and they both flopped down when they reached the top.

Andy took in the entire sight from the top of the hill. Beyond a few smaller hills, she could see a town. She knew not to get her hopes up that they would find anything there, or anyone for that matter, but she couldn't help but feel them lift anyway.

Bo and Andy were far enough away from their parents they could not hear what they were saying, but they seemed to be having a serious discussion, due to the uneasiness on Wayne's face. Andy knew her dad well enough to figure it had something to do with the plan on approaching the town.

"Do you think anyone is still living there?" Bo asked. He seemed so hopeful; Andy decided it was best to lie about what she *really* thought.

"Maybe. It's possible." She tried to sound hopeful herself, but she and her dad had already come across a couple of deserted towns; deserted of people and any other potential supplies. They were too far out from any of the bigger cities for anyone to stick around. It wasn't safe for anyone to stay and test their luck against the demons and their pets prowling the nights.

"I hope we find some food there, like some cheese doodles or something… man, I have been craving those," Bo winked, and laughed. Andy shook her head, grinning.

"Maybe some ice cream? That's what I've been craving. I bet they have some freezers still running."

"I think you're getting a little crazy there." Bo nudged her arm playfully, and she fell back onto the grass, throwing her arm over her head, and gazed up at the sky. "Ah a drama queen over here! I thought I was the dramatic one in this group!" Bo laughed and lay his head down next to Andy's. "Look, a bunny!" He pointed to one of the only clouds in the sky, which happened to look nothing like a bunny. Andy squinted trying to see what he saw.

"No way! That's a…a snake at best," she chuckled.

"That's too boring. How about a snake eating a bunny?" Bo suggested making Andy snort from laughing.

"Andy." Wayne suddenly stood over them, blocking out the sky and their cloud. Andy sat upright and smoothed out her hair. "It's time to get moving." He turned and started walking back to the road. Andy hurried to catch up with him, but he moved too swiftly, so she hung back. Phillip, Eleanor, and Bo were only a few feet behind her.

As they approached the first building in town, Wayne slowed his pace and Andy caught up with him finally. He stopped when they arrived at the intersection on the far side of the building, which happened to be a convenience store. *How convenient,* Andy thought, laughing at her own dumb pun. Bo stopped beside her.

"A convenience store… how convenient," he chuckled.

"You stole my joke." Andy turned to him and pushed his shoulder lightly. He put his hands up in mock surrender.

"It's all yours, ma' lady." They both laughed, and Wayne turned on them suddenly.

"I need you both to be quiet right now. I don't think announcing our presence to anyone who lives here before we investigate a little, is in our best interest," he said in a harsh whisper. When he turned back around, Bo stuck his tongue out at Andy, making her laugh again, but she covered her mouth. She did not want to upset her dad any further. Andy gave Bo a glare trying to convey this, but he smirked back. Andy rolled her eyes, and finally, they started moving again.

They followed Wayne as he approached the convenience store. Once inside, Andy's breath shortened, and a feeling of claustrophobia came over her. The shelves stretched nearly to the ceiling and were almost entirely empty. Cardboard boxes littered every surface, but not much else. Her heart sunk as she realized they would not find anything of use here.

"Alright. We should split up and search every aisle in case there is anything left. Andy, come with me." Andy followed her dad down the first aisle. She worried he was going to scold her some more, but he remained silent. Andy saw something glint underneath one of the shelves up ahead. Hurrying forward, she bent down to see what it might be. It was just a quarter.

"Damn it." She threw the quarter to the end of the aisle in frustration.

"Careful, Andy. It's okay." Her dad finally cracked a smile for her benefit, but almost immediately, his face fell. They heard the door of the store open as it hit the wall and a little bell jingled. Andy's whole body went rigid, and her dad grabbed her arm. He pulled her to the end of the aisle and scanned quickly to the left and right before rushing them towards the back of the store, where the shelving provided more coverage. "Stay behind me," he whispered. Andy's heart raced and she kept glancing around, wondering where Bo and his parents were.

"Helloooo? I spotted y'all walking in here. It's alright. I

won't hurt ya," a man with a thick southern accent called out. Wayne's grip on Andy's arm tightened. Andy knew he played through every scenario in his mind, as she did. Whoever the man was, he could really *not* want to hurt them, or he could rob them of whatever they might have, or worse, he could be a demon.

"There ya are," they heard the man say. "I didn't mean to frighten y'all. I'm Patrick." He must have found the others because they heard Phillip respond.

"I am Phillip, this is my wife Eleanor and my son, Bo." Andy couldn't hear any fear in his voice, and she knew Phillip hadn't encountered many people since the world changed. He didn't know enough to be afraid of what other people were capable of these days. Thankfully, from what Andy and Wayne were hearing, the man seemed to be one of the good ones.

"Nice to meet y'all. I hope you weren't expecting to find anything in here, we've pretty much wiped it clean, as you can probably tell. Anyway, where're the other two?" Wayne sighed. He and Andy both knew they had to show themselves.

"It's okay, Dad. We've made it this far, right?" Andy tried to encourage him, but she knew she was equally as terrified as him, thinking how it may end terribly. "We're here," Andy spoke loud enough that the others would hear her. She and Wayne walked towards where they thought the voices had been coming from.

Broken Angel

"Aha! I knew there were more!"

When Andy first saw Patrick, he was not what she expected. He was shorter than her by about three inches, and probably one hundred pounds heavier. His tucked in plaid shirt accentuated his stomach, and his belt seemed to be on its last leg. He had a full beard and rosy cheeks, like one of those mall Santa's. He emanated an aura of friendliness that made you want to trust him immediately, and Andy sensed her dad relax beside her.

"What are yer names?" Patrick asked cheerily.

"I'm Wayne, and this is my daughter, Andy." Wayne's voice remained tense, he would never entirely let his guard down, and neither would Andy.

"Well then, nice to meet you! Aren't y'all hungry? You look famished. Come on, let's getcha some food." Patrick turned away and started towards the door. Following behind him, Wayne caught Andy's eye. She knew what he was trying to convey: at the first sign of trouble, they would run.

4

The Safehouse

    The town may have been small, but as they walked, they passed a few shops, containing things such as furniture, clothing, and small trinkets. These made way for many older colonial style houses. For every abandoned house they passed, a pang of sorrow shot through Andy. The grass grew unruly all along the sides of the roads, and even through the pavement in some places.

    Patrick led them down a few streets, towards one of the larger houses they had seen. It was like a mansion compared to the surrounding houses. It appeared as if it had once been white but was a grayish yellow color now. As they approached the house, a woman, who looked like the female version of Patrick, came hurrying out the front door to the portico.

"Oh my, Pat! You've brought home guests again!" She grinned broadly, and her face was beet red. She had her graying hair tied back into a tight bun that pulled her face back like a makeshift face lift. Her eyes were a dark brown, and they rounded at the sight of them.

"This is my wife, Stella." Patrick introduced everyone and afterwards, Stella beckoned them all inside.

The interior of the house seemed even bigger than the outside. They stepped into a large foyer, with an elegant and carpeted staircase leading to the upper level. Inside, they could hear more voices. "We've seven people living here right now, including Stella and myself. This whole area's been safe for a few weeks since everyone else cleared out." A shadow of grief passed over Patrick's face for a moment, and then he was back to his normal self. "But we 'ave plenty of food for a few more weeks and we hope y'all want to stick around and maybe help us out with restocking and updating the house."

"Can we talk about it over lunch?" Wayne spoke, finally. "We haven't eaten a real meal in a few days and would much appreciate anything you might be able to spare."

"Of course, of course. Right this way." Patrick led them into the dining room where the rest of the household seemed to be gathered. "This is e'ryone else." Patrick introduced the people at the table and Andy peered around at their faces.

A gray-haired man, Collin, who appeared to be in his late fifties, sat next to a woman, Marie, Andy presumed to be his wife. At the head of the table sat a rugged man wearing

Carhartt pants and a red flannel. He reminded Andy of her dad but was a little younger and shorter. His name was Tim.

On the other side of the table sat a cheerful little girl with bright blue eyes and blonde pigtails who seemed to be about five years old. She wore purple leggings and a pink tank top. Beside her sat a boy who couldn't be much younger than Andy, maybe sixteen. He wore ripped jeans, a Nirvana t-shirt and ratty Converse. Everyone seemed human.

"Hi! I'm Lindy!" The little girl chirped excitedly. "And this is my brother, Ace." Ace waved halfheartedly, quickly returning his gaze to the food he hunched over. His unkempt blonde hair fell in front of his face, concealing him from unwanted attention.

"Hi Lindy, it's nice to meet you. I'm Andy." Andy smiled at Lindy and Lindy wrinkled her nose.

"Andy isn't a girl's name," Lindy said. Andy was used to that reaction from some people.

"Maybe, but I like it fine," Andy responded and that seemed to appease Lindy. Stella came into the dining room with plates of food as they finished introductions.

"Sit, sit. There's plenty of room." Stella gestured to some spare chairs in the corner. "Grab those, pull them up to the table. Don't be shy!" They all grabbed a chair and sat at the table as she placed plates in front of them. Beans, corn, and pineapple filled each plate. Andy started salivating as she regarded it all.

"It's prob'ly not what you were hoping for, but it's

better than nothing, right?" Stella beamed.

"It's more than we could have hoped for. Thank you, Stella," Phillip said as he stuffed a spoonful of corn into his mouth. They all began shoveling food into their mouths.

"This is amazing, thank you," Andy mumbled over a mouthful of pineapple. Stella nodded, satisfied, and went back into the kitchen.

"Wow. You guys were hungry," Lindy commented. The rest of her family seemed to have left the table. Andy had been so focused on eating; she hadn't even noticed.

"Yeah. We haven't eaten real food in like a week," Bo exaggerated. Lindy's eyes grew wide, and she gasped, making Andy laugh.

"That's a long time. My nana always makes sure I eat three meals a day. Everyone else only gets two," Lindy giggled.

"You are a lucky lady, aren't you?" Bo smiled at her. She giggled again and ran into the other room. Patrick came back into the dining room and cleared all the plates. Once he finished, he and Stella both stood, hovering, around them.

"Have you decided whether you'll stay here with us?" Stella asked hopefully. Andy looked at her dad and gave him a nod. Phillip spoke first.

"My family would love to stay here for a while." He leaned back in his chair and put one arm around Eleanor and the other around Bo.

"Andy and I would also like to stay, at least for the

night, if there is enough room." Wayne was always careful not to intrude on anyone's territory.

"Oh of course!" Stella clapped giddily. "We love having new guests! Patrick, show them to their rooms."

"Right this way." Patrick led them away from the dining room and up the spiral staircase. "We used to always have a full house, before all this craziness happened. Stella misses having all the activity and life in the house," he told them, stopping at the second door in the hallway. "Phillip and Eleanor, this's where y'all can bunk." They headed into the room to lie down.

"And, Wayne, you can stay in here," Patrick said, pushing open the next door, revealing a single twin bed in a room that appeared to be a master suite. "There's a nice little window over there that lets you see out towards the woods, if you don't mind keeping an eye out tonight for a while." Wayne bobbed his head grimly. "I'm putting Andy in with Lindy, right across the hall here so she won't be too far," Patrick reassured Wayne. "And Bo, you get yer own room, right here next to Lindy and Andy. Ace is across the hall if you need some company, he likes comic books and card games." Patrick turned to go back towards the staircase and paused. "If you need anything, give a holler. We all take care of each other round here."

Andy opened the door to Lindy's room and poked her head inside. Lindy laid on her stomach on the floor playing with dolls.

"Hi Lindy. Is it okay if I stay in here with you?" Andy noted bunk beds on one wall, and a twin bed on the other wall. It made her shudder, wondering if there had once been more children living here.

"Yep. You can have that bed over there." Lindy pointed to the twin bed. "I sleep on the top bunk, and Penelope sleeps on the bottom." She gestured to the doll she held, indicating that was Penelope.

"Oh, that sounds perfect." Andy stepped inside and left the door open a crack. She went over to the bed and flopped onto it. "So, Lindy, how long have you lived in this room?" Andy hoped she wasn't asking anything that would upset Lindy, but she was curious to find out any information about these people.

"A while. Nana and Papa lived here before, and then they came to live with me, Mommy and Daddy." Lindy stopped and gazed up at Andy. "Where's your Mommy?" she asked suddenly. Andy wondered what she should tell her and decided to stay as close to the truth as possible.

"She isn't with us anymore." A lump caught in Andy's throat.

"Did she get taken by one of the bad things, too? Like my mommy and daddy?" Lindy's eyes widened and Andy realized Lindy had probably seen as much horror in her life as she had. Lindy didn't wait for Andy's answer but continued. "It's okay. Nana says they're happier now they don't have to be scared. Your mommy too. It's okay." She went back to playing with her doll and Andy rolled onto her back.

A light knock on the door caused Andy to sit up, and Bo poked his head into the room. Lindy glanced up and smiled at him.

"Hi Lindy, can I steal Andy from you for a little while?" Bo crouched to be eye level with Lindy.

"I guess, she's just sleeping." Lindy remained focused on her dolls. Andy followed Bo out the door.

"I wanted to show you something." Bo led Andy into his room and over to the window seat. "Look, you can see the hills from here. It's beautiful, isn't it?" Bo sat on the seat, and Andy sat beside him. Gazing out the window through the town, she could see the hills, dotted with those purple and yellow flowers.

"It really is. This is a great spot to keep watch from too." Andy scanned the street. She kept thinking she could see movement, but she hoped her eyes were playing tricks on her.

"Come on, you can't keep thinking that way. You have to push that aside for a few minutes and admire this. Forget about everything else." That seemed impossible to Andy, but she tried anyway. She could see the other houses, empty and silent since being abandoned. Beyond that were the road signs that had been knocked over, and the grass growing long and unkempt. Tears came into her eyes. The view became less beautiful by the second as she realized what it really represented: the end of people's lives there and having to find a new way of life driven by fear.

Andy tried to wipe the tears away from her eyes, but Bo noticed.

"Oh jeez, I'm sorry. What did I do?"

"It's nothing. I … It's nothing." Andy assumed he wouldn't understand. He had not lost his parents. He had not suffered as she and Lindy had. She walked over to the queen size bed in the room and laid down with a sigh. "I wish we were actually safe here." Bo walked over and threw himself down beside her.

"What do you mean? It seems pretty safe," Bo argued. Andy regarded him and saw he gazed at the ceiling, while twirling his hair that had grown just past his ears. He actually believed the house was safe, and Andy couldn't blame him for wanting to feel that way.

"I mean, it seems safe, but nowhere is safe anymore. I don't want to fall under the illusion we are *safe* and be caught off guard by an attack," Andy told him. She knew how easy it was to truly feel safe and have everything change in an instant. "My dad and I have been in a situation where we thought the place we were staying was safe when it wasn't, because we trusted the wrong people. They invited us into their home under the impression we would be fed and given a bed to sleep in, only to have our own food reserves taken from us and we were thrown out in the middle of the night to fend for ourselves."

Andy shuddered at the memory of that night. The man holding a pistol against her head… her dad giving up everything they had because he would never risk losing her. She would never forget the desperation in that man's eyes as she glanced back before they ran. Thankfully a large maple tree stood nearby, and they were able to take shelter there for the night.

"I'm sorry that happened to you..." sadness was evident in Bo's voice. "But not all people are like that, Andy. We have to give these people a chance, or else we will end up back out on the road, unprotected and unsure of where our next meal will be coming from."

"You think I don't know that? That's why my dad and I are trying to get to the camp. They'll have more supplies and weapons than they do here. It's only a matter of time before these people run out of food, and then what?" Bo only thought of the here and now, but Andy needed to think long term.

"We'll see," Bo murmured; he was falling asleep. His breathing began to slow, and he had closed his eyes. Andy closed her eyes as well and realized she was more tired than she had thought, because she fell asleep almost instantly.

Trees surrounded her, and behind them, the eyes of the creatures. They all watched Andy. She started to run but they followed her. Hiding behind a large rock, she noticed someone else they glared at now. In the center of all the trees and eyes stood Lindy. She waved at Andy frantically, and yelled something, but Andy couldn't hear her. Andy tried to run to her, but every step she took was like trying to walk through quicksand. Andy reached out to

Lindy and Lindy pointed behind her.

"RUN ANDY!" Her words finally broke through to Andy as a scream. Turning towards where Lindy pointed. A shadow loomed over her. "Andy! Andy…"

Andy jolted awake and realized she was still in Bo's room. He was sitting up beside her.

"Are you okay? It seemed like you were having a pretty intense dream." Bo seemed worried, but Andy didn't want to tell him about her nightmare.

"I'm fine." She stood and walked to the door. "I need to get back to Lindy." Andy noticed the hall was lined with solar lights. Like the last house they had stayed in, the power was not on. The lights lit the hallway enough to be able to see if she was going to walk into anything, or anyone.

Back in Lindy's room, Lindy was getting into bed. Andy realized she must have only been asleep for a little while because the sun was just disappearing over the horizon.

"Goodnight, Andy." Lindy pulled the covers around herself.

"Goodnight, Lindy." Andy did not plan on sleeping tonight. She moved the only chair in the room over to the window and sat gazing out at the same view that could be seen from Bo's room. Andy couldn't see much past the driveway. If anything *was* out there, she wouldn't know until it was on the doorstep. She would have gone to check in with her dad, but after her nightmare, she didn't want to leave

Lindy alone in the eerily dark room.

Andy stared at the end of the driveway for a moment before a strange sensation came over her and she seemed to be *zooming in* on the spot. Distinct cracks in the tar were visible and she could see further into the dark. Shaking her head, everything returned to normal, and she rubbed her eyes. *I must be more tired that I realized,* she thought.

"Andy?" Lindy whispered and Andy turned to see Lindy peering at her over the top of her comforter, the rest of her face covered.

"Yeah?" Andy stood and moved closer to Lindy's bed.

"Can you turn on the night light? It's the candle next to the window." Andy glanced around and saw a small fake candle on the windowsill. She picked it up and flipped the little switch on the bottom. Lindy's face was visible in the pale glow that filled the area. "Are you gonna sleep?"

"Not yet." Andy sat back in the chair and inspected the outside world again.

"Do you see anything?" Lindy asked as she stifled a yawn.

"Nope. Nothing at all. So, you go to sleep and don't worry, okay?" Andy hoped Lindy could more easily forget all the danger outside the walls and get some rest. Lindy didn't respond, and Andy knew she had fallen asleep.

5

The Tiara

The next few days, Andy and the others found themselves settling in with the household. It was a nice change of pace not to be constantly on the move, and to know they would have a bed at the end of the day. They even had the ability to bathe and scrub some of the grime off their bodies, though it was cold water. The electricity had gone out a few days before their arrival. Patrick and the others had been lucky it had stayed on so long, some places had lost power when the war first began. Whether it had been the demons doing, Andy wasn't sure, but she would bet money on it.

Even with the small luxuries, Andy couldn't help but feel a little claustrophobic within the walls of the house.

Andy and Bo spent a lot of time together, either

roaming around outside, or swapping stories over tea made by Stella. They never strayed too far from the house; it wasn't worth the risk of running into any other beings.

Andy slowly grew more at ease in the house. For once, she was not itching to get moving, and thankfully her dad was content to let them rest and refuel for the time being.

On their fourth day in the house, Stella served dry cereal and fresh picked blueberries from the bushes out back. Everyone ate breakfast together and went their separate ways after, as usual, except for Andy's group. They lingered around the table, and she realized the time had come.

"We need to make a plan," Wayne said to Phillip.

"What do you mean? Why can't we stay here?" Phillip did not seem to be as keen on staying mobile as Andy and Wayne.

"Andy and I, we need to get to that safe camp. I know this place seems safe now, but it's only a matter of time before the demons find us. We need to avoid that." Andy knew Wayne had already decided on leaving but was giving Phillip a chance to include his family in that plan.

"I'm going to take a walk down the street and back," Andy announced, not wanting to become a part of the discussion, already knowing she would be leaving whenever her dad declared they must leave. She started towards the entrance of the house, and Bo hurried after her.

"I'll come with you." Andy and Bo walked out the front door and down the steps. Andy had noticed before there were quite a few houses along the street. Patrick had informed them all the houses had been searched already but Andy remained curious. She made her way to the first house with Bo trailing behind her. "What are we doing?" he asked her while gazing up to the sky and letting the sun warm his face.

"I'm going to check out this house and see if they missed anything. If my dad is planning on leaving soon, we should at least try to find some more supplies," Andy told him. Bo seemed to accept her answer and followed her into the house. It was eerie at first. All that remained was the larger furniture and appliances, which were pretty much useless now. Andy went straight to the back of the house where she assumed the kitchen would be, and she was right. She started opening cabinets.

"Patrick said they already scavenged these houses pretty thoroughly," Bo informed her, and she let out a sigh.

"They still could have missed something." *Anything*, Andy hoped. But the kitchen had been thoroughly emptied. Turning around, she walked back towards the front of the house where stairs led to the upper level. There were three bedrooms upstairs. The first two had been emptied out, but the last one appeared untouched.

"Maybe they forgot about this one." Bo peered over Andy's shoulder into the room. A twin-size bed was placed in one corner of the room and a crib in the opposite corner. Toys littered the floor. Beside the bed stood a little desk that had pieces of paper covered with drawings all over it. At the foot of the twin bed was a closet that was open a crack. Andy walked over to it and eased it open. She screamed and threw her arms up to cover her face as something came falling towards her. Bo laughed behind her as she lowered her arms slowly and realized it was a giant teddy bear.

"Oh haha. Hilarious," Andy mumbled, kicking the teddy bear with the tip of her shoe, and continuing her inspection of the closet. It was filled with little clothes and shoes and a wooden box underneath it all. Andy bent down and pulled it out. Kneeling in front of it, she lifted the lid. Inside was an array of different items. Andy figured it had once been a dress up box. On the top sat a plastic tiara, and underneath, a few princess gowns and little princess shoes and jewels.

Memories of Andy's own dress up box from when she was younger flashed through her mind. She remembered how Jason used to always play the king, while Andy played the princess who had been captured by an evil sorcerer. She stole her storyline from her favorite movie, *The Swan Princess*. The memory left her temporarily paralyzed.

"Ah, I've been missing my tiara!" Bo broke through her reverie and took it from the top of the box, placing it on his head. "Much better. I feel complete again." They both burst out laughing and Andy's grief was momentarily forgotten.

"You know, it suits you." As they laughed, they heard a crash downstairs. It sounded like a window breaking. Andy went into immediate panic mode and froze. Bo grabbed her by the hand and pulled her towards the closet, shutting the door without making a sound as they squished as far back as possible. Andy could feel her heart hammering in her chest, and she held her breath. More loud banging sounds echoed from downstairs, and they heard the creaking of the steps. Bo's hand stayed in Andy's, and she squeezed it, probably cutting off his circulation, willing herself to stay calm and quiet.

"We have to get outside," she whispered. "If it's one of the creatures… they hate the sun." She talked more to herself than Bo, it helped her ease the panic still clutching her. Through the crack in the closet, she saw a shadow pass by. Whatever, or whoever it was passed on down the hall. Andy remembered she had both of her knives tucked into her boots, and she grabbed them, handing one to Bo and keeping one for herself.

"We can't go out there. We should wait it out," Bo whispered, but Andy barely heard him over the buzzing in her brain. She went through every single exit she recalled seeing, envisioning the window in the room, and if it led out onto the roof. She started to play out every scenario in her mind.

A bang sounded right outside the room, and Andy squeezed her eyes shut, not wanting to see what came next. Bo gasped and he stiffened beside her. Andy opened one eye but saw nothing. A loud, piercing whistle resonated through the house and followed by the creak of the stairs, another crash, and at last silence.

"Do you think it's gone?" Andy asked, glancing at Bo, who still stared straight ahead. He didn't respond. "Bo? You okay?" Andy waved her hand in front of his face, and he turned to her.

"Let's get out of here." He pushed out of the closet and headed towards the hallway. Andy grabbed the tiara off the floor, putting it in her backpack and followed Bo out of the house. Bo glanced both ways before stepping back out into the open. He waited for Andy to catch up and headed back towards Patrick and Stella's house. Andy peeked back as they left, but she saw nothing following them.

"Did you see it?" Andy asked Bo, wondering if that is what made him gasp. "What was it doing in that house?"

"I have no idea, but it didn't seem to be too fazed by the daylight." They had made it back to Patrick and Stella's and Bo paused. "It was on a mission, and it was about to come into the room when it heard the whistle and left." Andy wished she had kept her eyes open so she could have seen it too.

The front door swung open, and her dad stood there. He appeared a little ruffled, like maybe the discussion with Phillip had not gone well.

"Andy! What are you doing out here? Come inside." He moved aside to let Bo and Andy enter the house. "I'm going to scope out the town a little; make an escape route for those who choose to stay behind. Do you want to join me?"

"I don't think that's such a good idea…" Andy began,

but she knew he would freak out when she told him what happened.

"What's wrong?" His eyes first went to Bo, and then to Andy.

"We decided to check out the house next door, to see if we could find anything useful, and, well, we saw one of the creatures behind the house." She decided to tell a white lie and could feel Bo glaring at her, but she didn't want to feel the full wrath of Wayne right now.

"What do you mean you saw one of the creatures? What were you doing over there? You could have been killed! You know I don't like you going off without me." He freaked out regardless, but at least that was better than what would have happened had he known the creature was *inside* the house.

"I told you I was going on a walk to check out the street. You must not have heard me over your plan-making," Andy remarked, annoyed he didn't trust her to take care of herself for more than a few minutes.

"Well, I'm going to go for a walk now and you are going to stay here, in the house. I don't want to hear about any more jaunts with Bo today, or ever." Wayne stalked out of the house in a huff.

"Sorry, he's being ridiculous," Andy grumbled, shutting the front door a little too hard.

"He's just being protective. He doesn't want you to get hurt," Bo reasoned. That was *not* what Andy wanted to hear right now.

"I'm going to go lay down," she announced and hurried upstairs to Lindy's room before Bo could say anything else. She found Lindy in the same position she usually favored, lying on the floor with her dolls.

"Hi!" Lindy greeted Andy as she walked in.

"I brought you something." Andy reached into her backpack and pulled out the tiara. "I wasn't sure if you would like it, but I thought I'd give it a try." Lindy grabbed it from her hand and put it on her head.

"It's pretty! Thanks!" Lindy smiled and twirled, then she went back to playing with her dolls. "Where did you get it?" she asked, not looking up. Andy sat beside her.

"I found it. Bo and I went to another house today," she told her, not specifying which house, in case Lindy knew who used to live there.

"Oh. Is Bo your boyfriend?" Lindy asked innocently. Andy laughed at that.

"No. We're just friends. And I don't think that will ever change," Andy said. She had no time to even consider anything deeper than that right now. Lindy didn't respond, but she appeared thoughtful.

"I don't think I want a boyfriend either," Lindy announced, making Andy laugh again.

"That's good. I think it would be safe for you to hold off on worrying about that for a long time, at least ten more years. Okay?" Andy wondered who had put the idea of boyfriends into Lindy's head.

"Okay. Ace had a girlfriend once," she told Andy, and Andy understood where it was coming from. "She was nice. Her name was Penelope. I named my doll after her because she gave it to me. Ace doesn't like it when I talk about Penelope." Lindy's eyes filled with sadness. "I don't remember a lot about her; it was right after the bad things came that she went away."

"I bet he misses Penelope. That's probably why he doesn't like to talk about her. I think it's nice you named your doll after her." Andy remembered when Jason had his first girlfriend and the memory caused tears to spring into her eyes. She wiped them away before Lindy could see them. Lindy had enough of her own burdens to carry.

"I think that's why he stays in his room all day. He misses Penelope, and Mom and Dad. I tried to tell him what Nana told me; they are happier now. But he didn't believe me." Lindy stopped and let out a big sigh. "I miss them too."

"I know you do. Why don't we do something fun to take your mind off it?" Andy had an idea that might help cheer up more than one person in the house and hopefully take their minds away from the fear in their lives for a few seconds.

"Okay!" Lindy hopped up off the floor. "What are we gonna do?"

"I was thinking this house has a lot of hiding places… how about hide and seek?" Andy offered and Lindy seemed eager. Andy had not played a game of hide and seek in about ten years, but she remembered how much fun she used to have with Jason and their friends. "I'm going to find a few more people to play with us." First, she approached the easier target: Bo. He agreed in an instant. Then, Andy approached Ace's room. She knocked, wondering if he was in there. A grunt that sounded a little like "come in" filtered through the door, so she opened it.

"Ace, it's me, Andy," she announced herself. Scanning his room, she realized it was not quite what she had expected. It was much brighter and cleaner than she had imagined. No posters tacked on the wall, and no clothes littered the floor. Ace laid in his bed with his headphones on, listening to an old portable CD player.

"What do you want?" he grumbled.

"I was wondering if you would come play hide and seek with us. Lindy would love it if you did. She needs this," Andy explained. Ace finally peered up at her.

"Hide and seek? How old are you, twelve?" Andy couldn't help but laugh on the inside at his sassiness, but she didn't want to make him hate her right away, so she held it in.

"Your sister *really* needs this right now. Please, help me out here. You have both already lost so many people, don't make her feel as if she's losing you too," she pleaded with him, and he rolled his eyes.

"Fine. I'll play your stupid game."

Andy smiled, because even though he was still being

difficult, at least she had won, and he was going to help cheer up Lindy. He may even have a little fun himself. Once they were all out in the hall, Andy offered to count first.

"I'm going to count to sixty, and then I'll come find you. Ready, set, go!" Andy covered her eyes and started counting. She heard Lindy scamper down the stairs. Bo and Ace had a little bit of a slower start. It occurred to Andy neither she nor Bo had much familiarity with the house, and she had no idea where she was going to be searching.

Once she finished counting, she opened her eyes. The hallway was empty. "Ready or not, here I come," she called to whoever might hear. She decided to check Ace's room first.

"Well, well, well." Andy found Ace 'hiding' in his bed. "Looks like you have to stick with me now. Come help me find the others." He rolled his eyes and followed her back out into the hall. "Any idea where Bo went?" Ace picked idly at his thumbnail.

Andy figured she would use the same tactic she used for Ace and checked Bo's room. At least he had taken the initiative to hide under the covers. Andy shook her head and rolled her eyes as he climbed out.

"Really, guys? You both are terrible at this game. Let's hope at least Lindy found a more creative hiding spot. Come on, I heard her go downstairs." Andy left the room with Bo and Ace trailing behind her.

"I was taking pointers from Ace on where to hide. I have no idea what's in any of these other rooms," Bo explained, and Andy understood. They had not been here long enough to know what was contained in all the rooms here.

Once they were downstairs, they heard people talking in the dining room, so Andy headed in the opposite direction, towards the living room. There was a closet in the living room, so she searched in there, and behind the curtains, but no Lindy. So, they continued to the next room which turned out to be an office. They heard a giggle coming from a trunk sitting against the wall.

"Hmmm… where could Lindy be?" Andy meandered towards the trunk. "Maybe… in here!" She lifted the lid and Lindy popped up as it hit the wall.

"You found me! My turn to search!" Lindy climbed out of the trunk, covered her eyes, and started counting. As the others turned around to go hide, Tim appeared in the doorway.

"What's going on in here?" he snarled.

"We're playing hide and seek!" Lindy piped up from behind Andy.

"Hide and seek? That's a game for children. Get out of here and go help Stella with dinner," he scowled. Andy was going to respond, but the way Ace cowered beneath Tim's gaze made her think different.

"Sorry, Sir," Ace mumbled and slinked out of the room. Bo and Andy followed, keeping their mouths shut, but giving each other a look that said, *what the hell was that about?*

"I *am* a child, Uncle Tim. I like hide and seek," Lindy

argued.

"Not in this world, you're not. We can't afford to have any children around here anymore. Go help your Nana," Tim spoke more gently with her, but he was still gruff and a little scary. It made Andy wonder if he might be a demon. But not everyone who was grumpy was a demon, and not everyone who was as good as Lindy was an angel.

"Come on, Lindy." Andy held out her hand to her and she ran to grab it. "We'll find something else to do," Andy promised her. They went to the kitchen, as Tim had suggested, to see if Stella needed any help. Ace wasn't there, so Andy assumed he had gone back to his room.

"Nana, Uncle Tim won't let us play hide and seek!" Lindy hurried over to Stella and tugged on her apron.

"Oh, I'm sorry sweetie." Stella kissed the top of Lindy's head and continued wiping down the counter. "Why don't you go play in your room?" Stella suggested and Lindy rushed off in the direction of the stairs. Andy stayed behind.

"If Tim is their uncle, does that mean he's your son? If you don't mind me asking." Andy propped herself up on a bar stool beside the island Stella was wiping with a towel. Stella gave a slight shake of her head.

"No, he's not. Lindy's father, Thomas, was my son. Tim is Lindy's mother's brother. He was living in their house with them when it all happened." She stopped wiping the counter and sat on the bar stool beside Andy. "When everything started happening, you know all of this craziness."

She waved her arms to indicate everything that was their world now. "We were staying with Thomas and his family only one town over, not too far from here. We knew this house was safer, so we packed everything into the car. We were about ready to leave when we realized Ace was missing."

"We weren't thinking we were in danger. After all, we're all human and the war is between the angels and demons… but, anyway, Thomas and Natalia ran back inside to get Ace. We waited a good ten minutes, and Tim was about to go in after them, when we heard a crash from inside the house. Tim ran in, and soon after he and Ace came running out the front door. The poor thing… he had forgotten his CD player in his room and had gone back for it. In the meantime, demons had somehow gotten into the house and killed Thomas and Natalia." She took a deep breath. "Tim, though he has always been a decent man and a good uncle, deep down blames Ace for the death of his sister and my son. Ace knows it too, and he blames himself as well." Tears glistened in Stella's eyes, and she dabbed at them with her sleeve.

"I'm so sorry," was all Andy could think to say.

"I don't blame Ace, just so you know. I love him with all my heart. But I wish he would forgive himself." Stella stood suddenly and went to the cabinet, pulling out a bottle of wine, and poured herself a glass. "Would you like some?"

"I'm all set, thank you. If you don't mind me asking, what exactly happened to their parents?" Andy wondered why the demons had attacked them.

"We're not sure. All Ace has told us is the demons killed them. He was able to escape while his parents held off the demons, but we have no idea why they were there," Stella explained, and Andy believed her.

Andy liked listening to Stella talk about her family. She had so much love in her voice, and it made Andy think of her own grandmother who died before all the 'craziness,' as Stella would put it. "How close were Lindy and Ace's girlfriend Penelope? She told me a little about her."

"Ace and Penelope grew up together, so Lindy knew her from the day she was born practically. They started dating when they were in high school before all of this. But Penelope was like an older sister to Lindy. There's hope she's still out there, which I think is what is also tugging at Ace. He hates staying here because he wants to be out there searching for her, but he knows we would never let him out there on his own," Stella said. Andy noticed Bo entering the kitchen. "Well, I should start making dinner." Stella turned to the cabinet and took out some cans.

"I have one more question, and you don't have to answer this one if you don't want to, but there are three beds in Lindy's room, and I was wondering..." Andy did not even have to finish, Stella knew where she was going.

"This house has been in my family for many generations, and Patrick and I had four kids of our own, who each gave us grandchildren." She pursed her lips for a moment and continued. "That room is where the youngest,

Lindy and her cousins, used to sleep whenever they all came over." She took a deep breath. "Ace and Lindy are my last surviving grandchildren. The rest of my children and their children have passed on." She turned back to the cans she had taken out and continued to open them. Andy decided she had pried enough information from Stella and didn't wish to stir up any more bad memories. Andy walked over to Bo.

"Where have you been? I thought you came in here," she asked him, knowing she hadn't seen him go upstairs.

"I saw my parents outside, so I went to check in with them. I guess there is some debate between your dad and my dad about whether we should leave tomorrow or not. My dad wants to stay here for as long as we can," Bo explained. Andy didn't want to separate from Bo and his family, but if her dad decided to leave, she would have to go with him.

That night at dinner, the sound of chatter filled the dining room. Three different conversations were happening, and Andy tried focusing on one, but she gave up and concentrated on her food instead.

"Andy," Wayne said, trying to get her attention. She noticed he had already finished eating. "We are leaving tomorrow." Andy knew better than to argue.

"What? You're leaving?" Lindy cried out, and everyone else stopped talking to stare at Andy's end of the table.

"*We're* not leaving," Phillip clarified. "Wayne and Andy are. We'll be staying as long as you'll have us."

"Wayne, won't you reconsider? Think about the safety of your daughter," Patrick said. Wayne's face flushed red with anger.

"I *am* thinking about the safety of my daughter. I know you all think you are safe here, and that's fine. I, however, see things differently. One place is only safe for so long, until it's not anymore. My daughter saw one of those creatures today, right next door, in the daylight. What if it had come here instead?" Wayne shook his head and calmed himself. "That is why we'll be leaving in the morning. We'll keep moving until we find somewhere that has more fortified walls and more manpower. I'm sorry, but this is not that place." Everyone turned their gazes back to their plates and continued their conversations as if nothing had happened, except Lindy.

"I can't believe you're leaving me!" She ran away from the table crying.

"It doesn't take long for her to get attached..." Patrick sighed. "Don't worry about her though. She'll be okay." Andy knew he was lying. Lindy had already lost too much, and she had finally been able to take her mind off that for a few minutes, only to find out Andy was about to leave her too. Andy left the table without finishing her dinner and hurried to Lindy's room. She knocked and opened the door. Lindy was on her bed sniffling.

"Lindy, I'm so sorry I have to leave," Andy began. Lindy turned away with a *humph*. "You don't have to be sad though, I'm not going away forever. We'll see each other again.

And you'll always have the tiara I gave you to remind you of me. Okay?" Andy sat on the edge of Lindy's bed and Lindy threw her arms around Andy.

"I'm going to miss you," she sniffled, and Andy hugged her back.

"I'm going to miss you too." Despite what she'd told Lindy, there was a slim to none chance Andy would ever see her again. It made her heart ache. Even though she had only known Lindy for a few days, she had learned so much about her and all the horrible things she'd had to endure. Andy couldn't help feeling like a terrible person for adding to the list of people that had left Lindy too abruptly.

Andy stood and left the room so Lindy could have some time to herself. Andy needed to say goodbye to Bo. She went to his room, which was empty, and walked over to the window seat. Sitting down, she gazed out into the darkness. Inside, the solar lights kept everything visible, but outside, the solar lights only lit the spot in which they were placed. Everywhere else was pitch black, leaving too many things to the imagination. Andy heard the door open and shut behind her.

"I can't believe you're leaving tomorrow," Bo groaned as he flopped onto his bed.

"I knew it would happen sooner or later." Andy kept gazing out the window. "But my dad is right. We need to keep moving so we can find a safer place."

"Yeah, but I mean, until we find out if that place even

exists, this is a pretty good home," Bo pointed out and Andy glanced over at him.

"I wish you were coming with us," she sighed.

"Why, you gonna miss me?" Bo joked, sticking his tongue out and making them both laugh. Andy laid on the bed beside him.

"I think I might. I haven't had anyone to talk to normally for… awhile. Even before we had to leave home, what little friends I had moved towards the safety of the protected cities. Now, with my dad, it's always about survival. Which I guess is important. But… I miss having friends." Bo took Andy's hand and squeezed it tight.

"I'm going to miss you too, Andy." They laid like that for a while, and Andy's eyes drifted closed. She was pulled out of her daze by a knock on the door and it opening to reveal Bo's parents.

"Bo, Andy," Phillip said as he peered at them.

Wayne appeared in the doorway with them. "What's going on here?" he asked, his eyebrows bunching as he frowned.

"Nothing, Dad. I was saying goodbye to Bo, and I fell asleep." Andy stood off the bed, stretching.

Eleanor stepped into the room. "We wanted to let you know that we've changed our mind and decided to carry on with Andy and Wayne."

Bo jumped off the bed. "What?!" He grinned as he looked to Andy.

"We thought it over and realized that Wayne may be right. Staying in one place seems like it may be dangerous, and we want to ensure your safety above all else," Eleanor explained.

Bo ran to Eleanor and hugged her, making her laugh in surprise.

"You seem excited," Phillip said, smirking.

"Well, I didn't want to have to say goodbye," Bo admitted.

"You two should be getting to bed," Wayne said. "We have a big day tomorrow."

"Right," Andy agreed.

Wayne turned and walked back to his room. Phillip and Eleanor followed suit, but before they made it back to their room, Patrick was there.

"I suppose there's nothing I can do to change your minds," he said, lifting his shoulders and hands.

"Sorry, no," Phillip responded. "We'll be leaving in the morning with Wayne and Andy."

"Very well. We'll be sure to send you off with some food for lunch at least." Patrick smiled sadly at them.

"We appreciate that, thank you," Eleanor said before they turned and headed for their room.

"Well, I guess I'm coming with you after all." Bo said, turning and flopping back on the bed. "I haven't been this relieved since I broke up with my ex-boyfriend." He laughed and Andy sat beside him.

"Oh," Andy breathed, before laughing along with him. "I didn't realize..." she started and then shook her head. It didn't matter to her anyway.

"You didn't know, did you?" he asked, poking her side. "Honestly, I kind of thought you both already knew." He blushed.

"No, but you're still Bo, it doesn't change anything," Andy said, nudging his arm. "If we're being honest, though, there's something I need to tell you too." The words practically fell out of her mouth, surprising herself, but she knew it was the right time.

"Oh my gosh, don't tell me, you're a demon?" he chuckled, and Andy shook her head, laughing at how close he had come with his guess.

"No, but I am an angel," she admitted. His eyes and his grin widened.

"Really? What does that mean exactly?"

"I'm not sure, all I know is my mom was an angel, but my dad is human," she explained, hoping that would not scare him away, which it seemed to be doing the opposite.

"That is so cool. Do you have, like, special angel powers or something? Can you sprout wings and shoot lightning?" He was getting excited now.

"I don't think so, but I mean I also haven't tried. This 'safe place' we're trying to get to, we think it's an angel camp. I could finally meet more people like me and find out what I can or can't do." It relieved Andy to finally have all of that out in the open and to have Bo be so accepting.

"That's why you needed to leave in a hurry. You should have told me sooner. I would have hated to miss you learning how to shoot lightning bolts!" He laughed and then yawned.

"I should get back to Lindy's room. We both need some sleep." Andy hugged Bo goodnight. "And, if you ever want to talk about *anything*, I'm a good listener." Andy squeezed Bo's hand.

"That means a lot, Andy." He yawned again. "But right now, I need some sleep. See you in the morning." Andy gave a small wave and headed back to Lindy's room to get some rest.

∞

Laying alone in bed, Bo stared at the ceiling. In the last few days, Andy had become a beacon of light and hope for him. After her revelation, he understood the draw of her personality. She was an angel. He should have guessed it. When she smiled it was as if she was glowing, as he imagined an angel would.

No matter what it meant now that he knew, it didn't change that he wanted to remain by her side. She had been more of friend to him than anyone else he'd ever known, besides his parents. There weren't many people who accepted him so full-heartedly and trusted him enough with their own secrets. Even after such a short amount of time of knowing her, he could safely say she was his best friend.

Broken Angel

He finally fell asleep thinking about Andy and her aura. In his dreams he saw her with wings spreading out from her back and a white halo of light surrounding her. The image left him smiling in his sleep, and it comforted him.

6

The Intruder

When the sun rose the next day, Andy, Wayne, Phillip, Eleanor, and Bo gathered their belongings and met at the front door. Stella and Patrick saw them out. No one else said goodbye, except for Lindy and Ace.

"Here." Patrick handed Wayne a paper bag. "There're some apples and some snacks in there." Patrick took a step back, putting his arm around Stella's shoulders and said nothing more.

"Thank you." Wayne put the bag under his arm and opened the front door. "Good luck to you," he added while the rest of the group filed out the door onto the front porch without a word. Patrick closed the door between them.

They made their way back to the center of town where

Patrick first picked them up, not wasting any time going through the houses along the way, since they knew the others had already cleared out anything useful.

Once they made it back to the convenience store, Wayne took out his map and laid it out on the ground. He indicated a star he made on the map the night before.

"This is where we are now. And we need to be here." He pointed to another star over the location where he believed the angel camp to be. "So, we need to go this way," he said, indicating the road leading on past the convenience store. Andy noticed the road seemed to be swallowed by trees as it stretched on.

"More trees?" she grumbled. "Well, I guess we better get moving, unless we want to be sleeping in them again." Everyone agreed by marching towards their new route. They all walked single file, no one speaking. Eventually Bo fell into step beside Andy.

They remained silent for a while longer, and Wayne seemed to remember he had a bag of food under his arm. He turned back to the rest of them and held it in the air, making them all stop.

"We may as well take a quick break and eat." Wayne walked to the side of the road where a small patch of grass grew and sat down. The rest of the group gathered around him, sitting in a little circle. Wayne passed out the apples and the small sandwich baggies filled with dry cereal.

When they had all finished, Wayne crumpled the paper

bag with all the trash inside and shoved it into his backpack. No one would have judged him for leaving the bag of trash on the side of the road these days, but it made Andy smile thinking that, even in the dystopian society, her dad still held onto his morals.

Bo and Andy walked beside each other again with their parents a few yards ahead of them.

"So, about what you told me last night, does that mean you are a part of the war?" Bo whispered so no one would overhear. Andy had known that was going to come up eventually.

"I mean, we all are technically. I guess I have a more distinct part to play in it. Like, if we come across a demon, they'd know what I am and be more likely to kill me," Andy tried to explain. Saying this, she sensed someone watching them, causing her to feel exposed. Andy surveyed the woods surrounding them and shuddered. Bo noticed and he took her hand, squeezing it to reassure her.

"How would they know what you are?" He brought her focus back to their conversation.

"Well, it's definitely easier to pick out a demon from a crowd than an angel, but a demon will have a black iris, only a slight shade lighter than their pupil, never any other color. They're eyes are not entirely black, though, they still have the white around them. They can use colored contacts to try to fool people into thinking they're human. Angels can have different colored eyes, though they are usually a goldish brown, like hazel, but distinctly more gold. Mine are blue with gold flecks, but that's probably because I'm only half angel. My dad said full blooded angels can have blue eyes too, but it's not as common."

"So, do they have, like, a handbook on all of this?" Bo asked, laughing at the thought of it. Andy knew it all sounded a little crazy to him, it did to her too.

"Maybe, but I haven't come across one yet. My dad told me everything he knows, which isn't too much. From what I've seen so far, everything has been right. The demon who...who killed my mother," Andy gulped, trying to force the tears back. "He had black eyes; they were so...cold."

"So, are the eyes the only giveaway for angels and demons?" Bo interjected. Andy shook her head.

"From what I've heard, demons move fluidly, with more ease and grace than a human would. And, they are faster and stronger, I think. They're cruel." Andy thought back to the demon who had first broken into her house, and trembled. She could not think about him now. Too many other emotions came rushing back with the memory of him. She shook her head to clear it.

"And angels, they must have goodness and light in their eyes, because I can see that in yours," Bo smirked. Andy knew he was joking, but it made her smile and she continued.

"Oh yes, they're made of gumdrops and lollipops too!" She giggled. Wayne glanced back at them, and she regained her composure. "But seriously, I don't know all the tells yet that give demons and angels away, but I'm learning. I haven't met enough of either to have too much experience, but they can't be too obvious since they've been living here with us possibly since the beginning of time and no one seemed to notice."

A grumbling sound built up behind them. It wasn't the sound of the creatures, but the sound of a car engine. Andy pulled Bo along with her to the edge of the trees and the others quickly followed.

They all watched from behind the cover of the trees as an SUV came driving up the road. Andy squinted and noticed an intense focusing happening and she could see inside the car. A scared Ace sat in the driver's seat with Lindy trembling in the backseat. Andy was baffled by this, but she stepped out from behind the trees and hurried to the side of the road, waving her arms at the SUV.

"Andy!" Confusion and warning colored Wayne's voice.

"It's Ace and Lindy!" Andy yelled back. She watched as the car swerved towards the side of the road and slowed to a stop. The driver's side door flung open, and Ace stepped out.

"What's going on?" Andy asked. Ace's legs gave out from under him, and he collapsed onto his hands and knees. Andy ran to him to help him up. He breathed as if he had run all that way instead of driving.

"The...d-demons..." He gasped. "They're...they're coming." He grabbed Andy's arm. "We have to go. Now."

Broken Angel

Andy turned back to the others who were already in motion. Everything happened so fast, it was a blur. Phillip and Eleanor opened the trunk and climbed into the way back, while Wayne headed for the driver's seat.

"You two get in the back seat with Lindy," Wayne told Ace and Andy. "Bo, get in the passenger seat. Let's go." He hopped into the driver's seat and the rest of them followed his orders. Nobody spoke again until they were back on the road driving as fast as they dared go.

Finally, Wayne broke the silence.

"Now, tell me what happened." He regarded Ace and Lindy in the rearview mirror.

"It was the bad things!" Lindy cried out. "They came back for us!" Lindy had tears streaming down her face and Andy hugged her close to her side to try to comfort her.

"About an hour and a half after you all left, we heard a scratching at the door," Ace gulped. "I told her not to open the door." He glanced at Lindy and continued. "The creature knocked her down as it came inside, but it didn't want her. It was searching for someone else. Uncle Tim came running out of the office with a gun and he shot the thing, but it only stunned it for a second. He threw the car keys at me and told me to get into the car with Lindy and drive. He said not to wait for anyone and not to come back." Ace's eyes were wide and scared as he retold the story. "I grabbed Lindy and ran for the front door. I heard someone whistle, and the creature ran back outside. I looked back at Uncle Tim, but he yelled to go and so I did." He stopped to catch his breath.

"Did you see who whistled for the creature? Was there a demon?" Wayne pushed. Andy kicked his seat, warning him.

"Give him a second, dad." Andy turned to Ace. "Take your time," she said, trying to sound as calm and soothing as possible for his and Lindy's sake.

"It's okay...yeah, there was a demon," Ace stated. "He was standing on the porch and watched as I ran past him with Lindy in my arms." Ace gritted his teeth. "He told me not to bother coming back because there would be no one and nothing to come back to," he spat out the last part, hatred came off him in waves. "I would have killed him if I didn't have Lindy crying in my arms."

Andy put her hand on his shoulder. "The demon would have killed you if you had stayed. You saved your sister."

"I didn't save anyone. He could have killed us both right there if he wanted to." Ace choked back a sob. "I don't understand why he didn't, if he was planning on killing everyone anyway." Tears began rolling down his cheeks and he turned away.

"Demons like to ruin lives, it's a game for them. There's nothing you could have done differently," Wayne said.

"There's something else..." Ace began, glancing at Andy out of the corner of his eye. "As I was getting into the car, I heard the demon yelling inside the house...he was looking for someone."

"What do you mean?" Andy asked, wary of his answer.

"He yelled 'Andromeda, I know you're here. Come out, come out wherever you are! No more hide and seek.'" Ace's imitation of the demon had Andy's skin crawling. A million thoughts started running through her mind. *How do they know my name? How did the creature get my scent? Why were they looking for me?* She could feel her heart racing and her breaths came in short gasps.

"Why?! Why do the demons want her?" Eleanor's voice was panic-stricken. "I thought they only cared about Angels!" She shrieked. Andy's head began to pound, and nausea overwhelmed her.

"Stop the car." Andy closed her eyes and pressed her hands to her head. Strange voices began bouncing around inside of it. One definitively male voice kept overpowering the other indistinct voices. She wasn't sure if she could handle all the voices that made her head feel as if it would burst at any moment. "STOP THE CAR!" Andy yelled again. That time Wayne pulled over and they came to a stop.

"Andy, what's happening?" Wayne opened his door, but before he could get out, Andy was already on the ground retching. She was able to hold her breakfast down, but her stomach still roiled. "Andy!" Wayne fell to his knees beside her, his hands on her shoulders. Bo was out of the car and running towards her as well.

"Something is wrong," Andy rasped. "I can hear voices

in my head." Tears rolled down her cheeks.

"What are they saying?" Bo asked, believing her. Andy tried to make out what any of the voices were saying, but it was all jumbled jargon. Trying to focus on them only made her head spin even more.

"I don't…" a sudden pain flared up between her eyes, and they flew open. She could see a demon standing in front of her. He seemed to see her too. The demon laughed viciously and had his pet right by his side, sitting on its haunches, waiting to strike. Andy blinked and was back on the side of the road, her head in her dad's lap. Bo knelt beside her holding her hand. "The demon is close."

"What do you mean?" Wayne stared down at her, worry and helplessness filled his eyes and shaped his features.

"I can see him…the demon and his pet. Ace was right, they're coming." Phillip and Eleanor had both gotten out of the car and hovered behind Bo.

"What is going on?" Phillip tried to sound stern, but Andy heard the waver in his voice. He was scared, and she couldn't blame him.

"Dad," Bo grumbled, but Wayne put up his hand to stop him.

"It's okay, Bo. Your family deserves to know the truth." Wayne took a deep breath and continued. "Andy's mother was an Angel," he paused, letting it sink in, and continued. "Andy is an angel. That creature must have caught Andy's scent somewhere along the way, and it led the demon to our last location."

"So, this is *your* fault!" Ace had been listening from the car. He jumped out and took off into the woods. Thankfully, Lindy was strapped in her seat and staying put.

"Ace!" Andy yelled after him, forcing herself to get to her feet. Wayne tried protesting, but she pushed his arms away. "He's right, Dad! This is my fault. I need to go after him. I'm not letting him get killed because of me, too." Andy turned and ran into the woods, following Ace's path. She could hear Bo running along behind her.

"Bo! Come back here!" His mother shrieked, but they were both beyond the tree line and running hard to catch up with Ace.

"Ace!" Andy yelled. "Please, let me explain!" She heard sobs coming from her left, and she stopped short. Bo ran into her and knocked them both to the ground.

"Oomph, sorry," Bo mumbled, jumping up and brushing himself off. Still weak from her episode, Bo had to help Andy to her feet. Following the sound of the sobs, Andy found Ace with his face buried in his hands behind a fallen tree. She sat beside him, and he turned away.

"I am so sorry, Ace," Andy began. "You are right, this is my fault, but I had no idea the creature was tracking me. If I had known, I would have never come to your family's house. If I could change it all…"

"But you can't!" Ace yelled, cutting her off. "You can't change anything! My whole family is dead now because of you!" Andy closed her eyes and took Ace's hand. He tried to pull it out of her grip, but she held on.

"Listen to me, Ace. This isn't about me anymore. I'm not asking you to forgive me, or to even talk to me, but we need to leave. That demon knows by now I'm not at your house, and he's angry and probably not far behind us. Lindy is waiting for you back in the car, and she needs you," as Andy said this, Ace peered at her with hostility in his eyes, but she knew he understood what she said to be true. He stood and started stalking back the way they came.

"You did good, Andy," Bo remarked, following Ace.

"Don't praise me right now, Bo." Tears ran down Andy's face again. Bo grabbed her hand and pulled her along beside him. She let him lead her back to the car.

"Like you said, we have to go. We can talk later." He held Andy's hand until they made it out of the woods. She knew he was the only reason she even made it out, because the exhaustion from her episode was overtaking her and she struggled to keep her eyes open. They all piled back into the car, and Andy fell asleep the second they pulled away from the side of the road.

∞

While Andy slept, the car filled with the sound of quiet bickering. Phillip and Eleanor were trying to figure out what exactly was going on, while Wayne tried to explain he had no idea what was happening, but it was not Andy's fault they had demons chasing them.

Bo sat gazing out his window, watching the pine trees slide by. He tried to focus on a few, but it made him dizzy. There wasn't much to do to pass the time but listen to the silly arguments being tossed around.

"What does it matter now, we can't go back and change anything. Even if we could, would you guys have chosen to stay alone out in the wilderness? We would have never made our way to Patrick and Stella's without Wayne and Andy," Bo slipped into the argument. Wayne gave him a thankful look, glad to have a break, even for a second.

"That's not the point Bo, and you know it. They should have told us from the beginning she was an angel so we could make an educated decision. Whether it would've changed our course, we can't know, but at least they would've been *honest,*" Eleanor hissed out the last word. Bo rolled his eyes. It didn't bother him that Andy had waited to tell him she was an angel. It wasn't something he imagined angels went around doing, since he had never even known they existed before the war.

He let the parents go back to their own talks and returned to gazing out the window. Among the trees ahead he thought he saw a figure, but by the time they passed the spot, whatever it was, had gone. A trick of the light probably, or sleep deprivation. Bo yawned and closed his eyes, leaning his head against the window.

7

The Camp

Andy's dreams were filled with horrors. Demons flitted in front of her eyes, their pets drooling beside them, anxious to tear out her throat. She woke screaming with Lindy tugging on her sleeve.

"It's okay, it's not real, you're awake now." Lindy was no longer crying, but she still had tear streaks on her cheeks.

"I'm sorry." Andy glanced out the window and realized they were no longer surrounded by trees. They were in the middle of a town. A comic book store slid past her window, followed by a coffee shop. Glancing at the clock on the radio, Andy saw she had been asleep for nearly three hours. They must be getting close to the angel camp. When they had been studying the map, they figured it would have taken a week to walk, but it should have only taken a few hours to drive. Wondering if she could connect with the angels as that demon had connected with her earlier, Andy closed her eyes. She tried to focus on finding the camp. *Please, please, please...*

"What are you doing?" Lindy asked, giggling. "You look funny." Andy opened her eyes.

"I'm trying to figure out which way the safe place is. Do you want to help me?" Bo's parents and Ace glared at Andy with hostility, but she ignored them. "Hold my hands." Andy put her hands out and Lindy grabbed them. "Okay, now close your eyes." Lindy did as Andy said. "Now picture a safe place in your mind." Andy tried to picture a camp with angels milling about, chatting, and laughing, and focused all her energy on finding that place in her mind. Voices came into her head, and she could hear actual words. *There's a horde of demons to the east. We need to send a guard to take care of them... I can feel someone coming...they are finally getting close...we need to send someone out; I can sense them coming in range.* Andy opened her eyes and silently cheered. The angels were coming to save them!

"I saw my house," Lindy said as she opened her eyes and smiled. "I pictured a safe place, and I saw my house," she repeated. Andy squeezed Lindy's hands and let them drop back onto her lap.

"Good job, Lindy. You helped me find the angel camp. Help is coming for us," Andy said, and Ace rolled his eyes. "I sensed the angels near here and I think they are going to send someone out to find us," Andy told Wayne. He glanced at her in the rearview mirror and slowed the car a fraction. They drove through the town for another ten minutes before Andy noticed a light off to her right in the distance.

"Wait!" She yelled, pressing her hands to the window, and staring at the light. It was bright enough to cut through the town, even in the middle of the day. She tried focusing her eyes again and found herself in front of a group of three men walking towards them. They all had sharp, but strong features. Andy noticed they all had gold in their eyes, which were illuminated by a ball of light hovering about a foot in front of them. *Come to us.* Andy heard inside her head. "That's them, Dad!"

"What do you mean? That could be anything out there," Phillip protested.

"No, they're angels. I saw them and heard them," Andy became exasperated. "Stop the car, or I am jumping out!" She opened her door to show her dad she was serious, and he stopped the car. Andy jumped out and started running towards the light.

"Andy! Wait a second!" Wayne yelled after her, but Andy kept running. A smile spread across her face. They had found it. Somewhere they could feel safe again and finally take their part in the war that had claimed all their loved ones.

Andy neared the three men and finally slowed down, trying to catch her breath. That was where she was meant to be. She had no fear of these individuals standing before her.

"Hello!" She called out to them. One of them cracked a

smile, but the other two remained stoic. Finally, she came face to face with them and the one who smiled at her gave a slight bow.

"Welcome, I am Ephram," the man in the middle introduced himself.

"I'm..." Andy started but he cut her off.

"Andromeda. We know." He finally cracked a glimmer of a smile. "This is Malachi, and this is Septimus." Malachi stood out with his blonde hair, rather than the other two who had jet-black hair. Septimus had wavy hair that stopped at the nape of his neck. He was taller than Andy by about four inches, with a muscular build. Andy had begun to realize all angels were well built and attractive. He seemed like he could not be older than twenty or twenty-one.

Ephram had the same frame as Septimus, though his hair wasn't as curly, and he had it cropped shorter. Andy could tell they were related. Though they didn't appear far apart in age, Ephram had a much older and wiser aura around him.

The others had caught up to Andy and seemed wary as they sized up the three men. Andy viewed Malachi, who was Andy's height, and again, well built. His muscles were a little bigger and more pronounced than the other two. He also gave off a vibe that he had been around quite some time.

"This is my dad Wayne, my friend Bo, his parents; Phillip and Eleanor, and..." Andy gestured to each of them as she introduced them, "this is Lindy and Ace."

"They are all humans?" Ephram asked, his eyebrows raised, and Andy nodded. "Very well. Follow us." The three men turned and walked back towards the trees that outlined the town.

"Um, excuse me, sir, but how do we know we can trust you?" Phillip asked, not moving to follow Ephram as the rest of the group had. Ephram turned back to face him.

"You do not know. You simply need to have some faith," is all he said, and he began to lead the way into the woods again. Phillip sighed but spoke no more and followed along with the rest of the group.

After walking for about ten minutes, a doorway of light appeared out of nowhere in front of them. It glowed amidst the shadows on the trees. Ephram opened the door, letting the light seep out into the night. They all filtered through the doorway, Ephram bringing up the rear, and closing the door behind him. They were still in the woods, but they could see tents everywhere and people. It was as if a veil had been lifted to reveal a campsite behind it. There were not as many people as Andy had imagined, but still quite a few.

"Welcome to the camp of Jeremiah." Ephram gave a flourish with his hand. "Septimus will show you to your tents, then you can all eat and settle in. We will talk more in depth in the morning." Ephram and Malachi went off in another direction, while Septimus began leading Andy and her group towards the tents. She watched as he ran his fingers through his curls and noticed a gold ring glint on his middle finger.

"This is where I sleep, if you need anything." He gestured to a tent off to the right. "If you have any questions, save them for the morning, we will have plenty of time to discuss everything then. But for now, you all appear as if you could use some food and some sleep." He stopped abruptly and turned back to the group. Andy ran headlong into his chest, which was as solid as a rock.

"Oomph," she puffed, stumbling a little, but Septimus steadied her. "Sorry," she mumbled. Septimus laughed and focused his gaze on the others.

"Here is our first tent for you. We only have two to spare, and they sleep four people max," he explained, waiting for them to determine who would sleep with whom.

"Well, I want to stay with Andy." Lindy grabbed Andy's hand. "And Ace," Lindy added.

"I'll join them too, then." Bo squeezed past his parents and joined Andy and Lindy at the front.

"Bo, you should stay with us." Eleanor reached for his hand, and he let her take it.

"It's okay, Mom. You bunk with Dad and Wayne; we'll be right here if you miss me too much," he joked, and she tried to smile, but it was forced. She still had a scowl every time she glanced Andy's way. Andy knew it was deserved. She had put Eleanor's family in danger.

"Good. So, children can sleep in this tent, the adults right next door." Septimus gestured to the tent right beside Andy's and Wayne's shoulders sagged in relief. He could still be close enough to protect her if she needed it.

"We're not exactly children but thank you for your help," Andy said.

"Yeah, we're not kids!" Lindy piped up and everyone laughed at that.

"The dining tent is right over there." Septimus pointed to a tent a few yards away. "I will see you in the morning." He gave a little wave and moved off in the direction of where Ephram and Malachi had disappeared to. The rest of them went into their tents to get settled in with their few belongings. There were four cots in the first tent. Lindy and Ace took the two on the right side of the tent and Bo and Andy took the two on the left.

They checked out the dining tent, which was about four times the size of the sleeping tents. There were two rows of four picnic tables each, with people sitting at all of them eating. After they grabbed some food, they went back to their tents. Even though it was still early, they all climbed onto their cots. After a few minutes, Andy could hear Ace snoring and Lindy's breathing became a steady rhythm, telling Andy they were both asleep.

"Bo," she whispered. "Are you awake?"

"Yeah..." he mumbled, yawning. "I am now."

"What do you think?" she asked, wondering if he was in awe, as she was, of the camp.

"I think we're finally safe again, and I want to get some sleep." He yawned again and Andy let him fall back asleep, but she could not stop her mind from racing. *I wonder how long this place has been here. Who is Jeremiah? Did my mom know any of these angels?* After getting lost in her thoughts for a while, she finally closed her eyes and drifted off.

When she opened her eyes, darkness had fallen. Snores filled the space all around her and she knew she was the only one awake. Swinging her legs over the side of her cot, she stood and crept to the entrance flap of the tent. She saw no one outside their tent, so she stepped outside into the fresh air. She took a deep breath and let it out slowly. It was weird being in the woods at night and not fearing for her life. A sense of freedom came over her.

A step around the tent allowed her to see back towards where they had entered the camp. A few people stood around a fire talking about the horde of demons they had eliminated earlier. As she watched them, something grazed against the back of her upper arm. She nearly jumped out of her skin and a scream built in her throat. Realizing it was Septimus, she let out a huff of air instead.

"What are you doing out here?" he asked, concern in his eyes.

"I couldn't sleep. I needed some fresh air," Andy explained, though even fresh air could not help her go back to sleep. She was too excited to learn more about the place, and she knew these people could help teach her more about herself. Septimus let go of her arm and his features softened.

"Come on, we can go for a walk." He started walking

in the opposite direction from the people standing around the fire. Andy paused, glancing back at them. "Are you coming?" Septimus glanced at her over his shoulder, and she fell in step beside him. They walked in silence for a little while.

"How did Ephram know my name?" Andy asked. Septimus did not say anything for a few seconds, and he took a deep breath.

"Everyone here knows your name, Andromeda," he said, as if that was enough explanation.

"Call me Andy," she insisted. It was weird to hear her full name when she was not being scolded or beckoned by her parents. "But *why* does everyone know my name?"

"I don't see why you wouldn't want to be called by your full name," he diverted. Andy was aware that getting answers was going to be harder than she thought. "It's quite beautiful, and the story behind it doesn't hurt either."

"It is more interesting than other names I guess…" she blushed, impressed he knew the story of Andromeda, but then again, angels probably knew *all* the stories. "What about Septimus? Where does that come from?"

"It's Latin; it means the seventh son and I do in fact have six brothers." Andy gaped at him, and he laughed. "What about you? Do you have any siblings?" All the blood rushed out of her face and the weight of grief threatened her psyche. Septimus did not seem to notice, and she recomposed herself and answered.

"No, it's just me," she lied, not wanting to talk about

her brother and what had happened to him.

"How did the children come to be with your group?" Septimus asked, wondering about Ace and Lindy.

"We were staying with their family in a house not too far from here, but my dad and I always planned on coming here, and we knew we had to keep moving. We left, and a demon arrived later that day and killed Ace and Lindy's whole family," Andy explained, leaving out the part about it being her fault.

"Demons are cruel," Septimus growled. "But they don't usually attack whole households without being provoked." There was a question in his eyes, he knew Andy was hiding something. "The demon was there for you, wasn't he?" he guessed, and Andy let out a long sigh. She was beginning to think they knew a lot more about her here than just her name.

"I didn't know I had one of those creatures tracking me…" She looked away, ashamed of what had happened.

"They're hellhounds," Septimus explained. "They are under complete control of the demons and have no free will of their own. Once they have your scent…"

"They never give up. I know." Andy had not let herself feel scared until now. Before, she had a purpose, they had to get to the camp, and so she was able to push aside her fear. But now, out in the open woods, fear crept up her spine threatening to overtake her whole body.

"They can be killed, too. This is not a death sentence,

Andromeda." Septimus stopped and Andy turned to gaze up at him. "You are hidden from them here; we will keep you safe."

"Thank you," was all she could think to say. A shadow flitted in the corner of her vision, but when she turned, there was nothing there. Bo burst out behind Andy and Septimus and they both whipped around to face him.

"Andy! Come quick…" he panted. "It's Lindy." Without hesitating, Andy started running back towards the camp and their tent. Bo and Septimus were right behind her. Inside the tent, Ace was trying to calm Lindy down, but she kept saying Andy's name over and over. Andy burst in through the tent flaps and raced to Lindy's side. Running her hand over Lindy's hair, Andy smoothed the curls that had started poking out in all directions.

"What is it, Lindy? I'm here." Andy continued stroking her hair. When Andy was little and had nightmares, her mom would do the same for her, it helped calm her down. Andy hoped it would help Lindy now. Wayne entered the tent and stood back, beside Bo and Septimus.

"I dreamed…" Lindy started and gazed past Andy towards the group of people huddled near the tent entrance. "I dreamed…" She tried again, but Andy could tell she was uncomfortable with all these people watching her. Andy turned to them.

"Everyone out," she demanded. They all turned and stepped out of the tent, except for Ace who stayed crouched next to Lindy holding her hand, and Septimus who continued to watch Lindy with great interest. "Okay, Lindy, now tell me, what did you dream?"

"The bad things… they were there. They were talking. They were talking about you, but they called you by your other name…" her brow furrowed, and she clutched Andy's hand tighter.

"Andromeda?" Andy offered and Lindy bobbed her head, continuing.

"They were saying they lost you. They were mad, and I saw the scary monster there too, that pushed me down." The terror the dream had caused her was written on her face. "There was one really bad man, he was yelling, and they called him Ger-eg-or." She sounded it out. "He said he wants you, but he can't get you. He said the others are going to come for you. They really want you, Andy." She started crying. "T-they're going to t-take you away like M-Mommy and D-Daddy," she sputtered as she dissolved into sobs.

"Shh…" Andy pulled her into an embrace and stroked her hair. "It's okay, I'm here. No one is taking me away," Andy tried to reassure her, though she was beginning to worry as well. Lindy's nightmare seemed to have been far too vivid to have been a dream. Andy wondered if the demons had somehow found a way inside Lindy's head when they had attacked the house. "We're safe here. Shh." She noticed Septimus leave as she turned to lay beside Lindy on the cot. Andy laid there while Ace sat against the cot, until Lindy fell back asleep. Ace finally stood and went back to his cot. Careful not to wake Lindy, Andy stood and left the tent. Everyone else still hovered around the entrance. Wayne approached Andy first.

"Are you okay?" he asked, searching her face. Andy paused, imagining herself giving over to her emotions, and letting her dad comfort her. Breaking down and letting out all the built-up tears and frustrations, she knew what a release it could be. But, instead, she bit back her fear, guilt, and grief and said nothing. Wayne stepped forward and embraced her, lending a small amount of comfort. Andy hugged him back, relishing in it, before turning to face Bo and Septimus.

"Are you sure you're okay?" Bo eyed Andy warily. She forced a smile. He took her hand and squeezed it. Andy needed to hold herself together for Lindy and her dad's sake. She knew how much it hurt him to see her hurting, and she did not want to cause him anymore pain or grief.

"Yes, I'm okay," Andy said.

"I'm going back to bed, don't stray too far, just in case." Bo blew Andy a kiss and disappeared back into the tent. She couldn't help but laugh a little, which helped lift her spirits back up the tiniest bit.

"Thanks, Bo," she said loud enough for him to hear.

"I think we need to talk about that child." Septimus was standing with his arms crossed, presenting a serious demeanor. Andy furrowed her eyebrows.

"It was only a dream. Wasn't it?" Andy glanced at

Wayne and back to Septimus, but they both had on hard to read, steely expressions. "What's going on?" she asked, a hint of panic in her voice.

"Come into the dining tent with me, both of you." Septimus led them to the dining tent, and they took a seat at one of the tables inside. They were the only ones there. "There is only one way the child can see and hear the demons," Septimus laid out for them, and Andy had a bad feeling about where he was going. "She is part demon." Andy shook her head in disbelief.

"No. It's not possible. She is a *child*, and she is more of an angel than I have ever been," Andy protested. Lindy was innocent, and pure. There was no way she had an ounce of demon blood within her.

"You have to understand, she doesn't have to be a full-blooded demon, or even half-demon to be able to connect with them. She could be a quarter, or an eighth. It doesn't matter. Eventually, the demon part takes over and she will be claimed by them." Septimus shone with pity. "I know you care for her, but you cannot change what she is."

"She doesn't need to change! You saw her in there, she's afraid of them. She could never be one of them. Dad, back me up here!" She turned to Wayne who sat beside her.

"I'm sorry, Andy. Septimus is right. He knows more about this than we do, and we have to trust he and the other angels will make the right decisions here." Gaping at him, Andy shook her head in disbelief. How could he possibly believe any of this?

"No. This is crazy." She stood and walked out. Back in her tent, she moved her cot closer to Lindy and Ace. She sat on her cot with no intention of sleeping, but of keeping watch. Andy didn't know these people and what they were capable of, but she knew they would not touch a single hair on Lindy's head without going through her first. No one came in after her, though, and eventually she drifted off into a fitful sleep.

8

The Trainee

When Andy woke in the morning, she was alone. In a panic, she jumped off the cot and slipped on her sneakers. Running out of the tent, she scanned the area around her. Voices filtered out from the dining tent, so she headed in that direction. Searching the tables, Andy found them. Ace, Lindy and Bo all sat together. with plates full of pancakes and bacon in front of them.

"Good morning, sleepy head," Bo greeted Andy cheerfully. She inspected Ace and Lindy, but they seemed unscathed and in good spirits. Andy settled onto the bench beside Bo. "You seemed so peaceful; we didn't want to wake you. Here." He slid his plate of pancakes in front of her and handed her a fork. "Our parents already ate, you just missed them."

"Thanks," Andy mumbled and devoured the pancakes. Septimus sat with Ephram and Malachi two tables down from them. They leaned close to one another. *Talking about Lindy probably*. Andy rolled her eyes. They all stood at once, and Andy turned away before they would notice her staring. She finished her pancakes as a familiar hand came to rest on her shoulder.

"It's time for us all to talk," said Septimus. "You too, Bo. Ace, keep an eye on your sister, we will fill you in later." Bo and Andy stood and followed Septimus out of the dining tent and back towards where they had come in through the door the night before. Near the entrance was another tent that Wayne, Eleanor, and Phillip were entering. Bo, Andy, and Septimus walked in behind them.

"Thank you all for coming." Ephram was already there, sitting in a chair at the head of a long table. They all took seats around it, with Malachi and Septimus sitting on either side of Ephram. "We have much to discuss. But first, tell me, how did you come to be here, together?" Wayne took the wheel and told the angels their story. He began with the demon breaking into Wayne and Andy's house.

"We had to leave my wife behind...and she didn't make it." He cleared his throat and Andy saw the flush in his cheeks as he mentioned her mom. Ephram's eyes widened, and his shoulders slumped. Andy was taken aback at his response. Surely, he was used to people dying at that point, why care so much about her mom?

"Angeline is...dead?" Ephram's voice came out strained. Andy gasped as he said her mom's name. *How did he know her?* Wayne faltered as well.

"Y-yes. How...?" he stuttered.

"Forgive me," Ephram said, dipping his head. "She and my Amelia were close before Angeline left Rhode Island and though you and I never met, I saw plenty of pictures of your family. Angeline would send them from time to time. I'm sorry to hear she didn't make it." Ephram cleared his throat and clasped his hands in front of him on the table. "Now, what happened next?" Wayne recollected himself and started again, picking back up at the garage where they met Eleanor and Phillip and finished with yesterday when they were running from the demon.

"I see," Ephram said, leaning on his elbows and steepling his hands. "Well, as you know this is a camp for angels who are fighting in the war. We only have so much room here for our people and I'm afraid we will not be able to accommodate all of you for long." Eleanor gasped.

"But where will we go?" Phillip asked, anger and disbelief in his voice. Andy sympathized with him; they had worked so hard to get here, and the angels were throwing them out.

"We have a camp nearby for humans, similar to ours, and there are a few of our people there to help keep everyone safe. I promise you; it is practically the same as living here, but with your own kind." Ephram clasped his hands in front of him and managed a pity smile. Andy scowled. "It will be more comfortable for you there, anyway. It used to be a small trailer park, so you'll be living indoors." Eleanor seemed to perk up a little at that.

"So, when do we have to leave?" Andy asked, trying to hurry them along. There was no point putting off the inevitable.

"Oh, *you* won't be leaving. You have angel blood in you. You are welcome here as long as you want," Ephram said that as if it would be a welcome revelation.

"So, my friends and family are being forced to leave, and I get to stay here alone? How kind of you." Andy grimaced and crossed her arms. "I'd rather stay with my family than with you lot."

"We can teach you how to use your gifts," Septimus finally spoke up. "There is a lot you do not know about being an angel." Andy remained staring at the ground. If they thought that was enough to make her want to stay here without her dad, they were mistaken.

"If you would like, you can choose one person to stay with you," Ephram offered.

"What about Ace and Lindy? They're kids, you can't throw them out." Andy began to wonder if angels were as different from demons as she had once believed. They clearly did not care what happened to them.

"Oh, we aren't throwing them out. The children will be

staying. The girl could be of great use to us if she can learn to control her visions," Malachi chimed in.

"She's not an experiment! She's a little girl! You can't use her like that!" Andy burst out, jumping out of her chair. She couldn't believe what she was hearing.

"Would you rather we release her out into the world where the demons can claim her as one of their own?" Malachi became defensive. "There is a lot more going on outside of your little world, Andromeda. It is time to start thinking of more than the people in your immediate vicinity."

"NO," she said forcefully. "You. Will. Not. Use. Her." She tried to make it as clear as possible for them.

"Now, let us decide." Ephram ignored her protests and continued the conversation. Andy sat back down, grumbling under her breath. "Who is it that you wish to stay with you? Your father I assume?" Ephram gazed expectantly at Wayne who stared down at his hands.

"No." Andy was surprised to hear her dad's voice, since he had been silent for so long and even more surprised by his response. He glanced over at Phillip and Eleanor who appeared terrified and clasped each other's hands.

"No?" Ephram was as surprised as Andy. Obviously, she was going to choose Wayne, if last night proved anything, it was that she still needed her dad.

"No. She won't be choosing me. Bo will stay here with her." Andy understood immediately what her dad was doing when she saw a wave of relief come over Eleanor and Phillip's faces. Wayne was thinking as a parent and knew they would give anything to have their child safe, as he would.

"This is all crazy talk!" Andy yelled. "You can't separate us! Either we all stay, or we all go, and that includes Ace and Lindy."

"As I have said before, we cannot accommodate anymore people. We are already at capacity, and with you, Bo, Ace, and Lindy, that fills even our guest tent." Ephram remained calm, as if he knew that, in the end, he would get his way.

"Fine. Then we all go," Andy snapped, folding her arms over her chest with finality.

"Andy, I need you and Bo to stay here. I need to know you're safe," her dad pleaded with her, and she knew it would not take long for her to cave. It was no use arguing with him, he would not back down from his decision.

"I can't lose you, Dad." She grabbed his hands across the table. He smiled and squeezed her hands in his.

"You can visit them at the other camp any time you like," Septimus added. That did not ease Andy's anxiety at the thought of being separated from her dad for the first time since they lost her mom and Jason.

"So, it's settled. Those who are staying, you may go on about your day. Those who are leaving, we will set off in ten minutes. Any other questions?" Ephram added, though Andy could tell he did not want any questions. They were all too shocked by the new turn of events to speak, and so Ephram took that as a 'no.' He stood and strode out of the tent with Malachi and Septimus on his heels.

"Thank you so much, Wayne. It means everything to us to know our son will be safe." Phillip and Eleanor left the tent with Bo to go pack their things and say their goodbyes.

"This isn't right." Andy pouted like she used to when she was a child. "They can't separate us like this. You told me we stick together, no matter what. Damn everyone else, even angels." Anger welled inside of her.

"Don't you understand, Andy? It *has* to be this way. This is what we have been working so hard for: getting you here. You need to learn everything you can about being an angel, and I can't teach you that." His eyes filled with tears, which in turn brought tears to Andy's eyes. "If your mother were still here…" He wiped a tear off his cheek.

"I know. You don't have to say anymore." Andy stood to leave, but he caught her wrist. She turned back. "There's something else I wanted to tell you." She sat back down across from him. But he didn't have time to say more because Septimus stepped back into the tent.

"It's time to gather your things, Wayne." Septimus motioned towards the exit, and Wayne stood up, glancing back at Andy, and giving her a reassuring smile.

"Yes, right." He squeezed her hand one last time, leaned over, kissed her forehead, and left.

"We can start your training now, if you'd like," Septimus offered once he and Andy were alone. She scoffed and wiped the tears from her eyes, standing to face him.

"The *last* thing I want to do right now is train. I would like to say goodbye to my dad before he is forced to leave me for the first time since my mom died." She went to walk past him, and paused, adding, "and you think demons are cruel." He flinched and Andy felt a small amount of satisfaction as she turned towards the exit. His hand gently landed on her arm, but she shook it off and stormed out. She hurried to Wayne's tent, wanting to know what he had been about to tell her before they'd been interrupted.

When she arrived, Wayne and Bo's parents were leaving their tent with their packs. Andy hurried towards them, throwing her arms around her dad. He hugged her tightly and kissed the top of her head.

"Stay safe," he whispered to her before pulling away and leaving with the others. Andy watched them leave before returning to her own tent and noticed Bo lying on his cot.

"They just left," she told him.

"So, what now?" he asked as she laid beside him. They barely fit on the cot side-by-side.

"I have no idea. Septimus offered to start training me," Andy said, searching Bo's face for his reaction.

"Well, what are you waiting for? You can finally figure out what angels really do!" Bo was excited enough about the whole idea for the both of them. "And he's so gorgeous, I mean come on. You can't *not* want to spend some alone time with him." He grinned and Andy nudged his arm.

"Not in a million years. He's standing by as they force our parents to leave, and they plan on using Lindy like a one-way walkie talkie," she huffed and rolled over so she could see Bo. "I'm worried about what they're going to do to her. She is part demon, after all."

"They wouldn't hurt her. She's only a kid," Bo reassured her. Andy didn't fully believe the angels wouldn't hesitate to dispose of a demon, no matter their age. They were in the middle of a war, after all. "Hi, Septimus," Bo said, turning his focus towards the tent entrance.

"Ha ha, funny." Andy stuck her tongue out at him. "I told you, I don't..." But she stopped because she realized from the look on Bo's face that Septimus was truly standing at the entrance to their tent. She flipped around, sitting up on the edge of the cot.

"Sorry, am I interrupting something?" Septimus asked, flicking his eyes from Andy to Bo. Bo laughed and sat up as well.

"Don't worry, bud. She's all yours." Bo walked out of the tent, giving Andy a thumbs up as he passed behind Septimus. Her cheeks burned, and she knew they were bright red.

"Look, I really am sorry your father had to leave, but I think it's important for you to start training right away. Lindy's dream proved you are in more danger than we first thought, and you need to be able to protect yourself," Septimus argued.

"Alright," Andy agreed, already having been swayed by Bo. "Let's do this, then." He appeared surprised she had caved so easily, but she knew he and Bo were right. She needed to train and find out as much as possible about being an angel. Then, she would be able to protect herself and she could be reunited with her dad.

"Okay. Let's take a walk." They went out to the path they had taken the night before. "To start, do you have any experience with any of your gifts?"

"Well, I think I have super vision, and I've started to figure out how to use the walkie talkie in my head." Andy knew she was much more inexperienced than he expected.

"Super vision and walkie talkie. Got it." He laughed. "The inner communication system is how angels stay in touch within a couple mile radius because we have not always had cell phones. You seem to have the enhanced vision figured out, though, from what I remember that first day we met. You used it to make sure we weren't demons." Andy nodded. "But there are more gifts we have." He walked over to a fallen tree and with some effort, but still inhuman strength, lifted one end off the ground. Andy gaped at him.

"Well, I don't think I have that gift," she joked. "I could barely lift my backpack when I was in high school." Septimus laughed and shook his head. His black curls bounced lightly around his face, and one fell across his eyes. He swept it aside and the sun glinted off his ring.

"The gifts come with practice, and most of them come

to you as you come of age, which is why you never noticed anything off before. For this task, you must concentrate on lifting the object, like how you have to concentrate to use your sight, or communication system. Come here and give it a try." He motioned for Andy to stand beside him. She bent down and placed her hands on the bottom of the tree trunk. "Okay, now focus on everything it would take to lift this tree. Think about the strength flowing out of you and into the tree." Andy narrowed her eyes and pursed her lips, wary, but she sighed and closed her eyes. She eased her way out of her squatting position, and when she opened her eyes, she realized she had done it.

"I did it!" she cheered, her face beaming with excitement. "I am Superwoman!" Overcome with the weight of the tree, she dropped it and jumped back, bumping into Septimus. He laughed as he steadied her.

"Good for your first try. We will work on holding it longer another day." He moved away from the tree and continued walking on the path. Andy jogged to catch up to him.

"That felt amazing," she admitted. "I have never felt so...alive." She couldn't stop herself from smiling. Her whole body was exhilarated from using her new-found strength, leaving her feeling invincible.

"Just wait, there's more," as he said this, Malachi came jogging up to them. He was not out of breath like Andy would have been and she wondered if that was one of the gifts she did not know about yet.

"Ephram is requesting a meeting," Malachi announced. Septimus bowed to him, and they both started walking back towards the camp.

"What about me?" Andy called after them, but neither of them turned back.

"Remember, it is not all about you, child," Malachi called back. Andy rolled her eyes. He was set on the idea she was a selfish brat. Andy started following them back to the camp and veered off into her tent. Bo laid inside flipping through a comic book on his cot. As soon as he saw her, he threw the comic book down and the questions began.

"How was it? Can you fly? Shoot lightning? Did Septimus fall madly in love yet? What about you?" He wiggled his eyebrows and Andy side eyed him, laughing, before collapsing onto her cot.

"It was pretty amazing. But no on all counts."

Bo's face fell, and he let out a dramatic sigh making them both laugh even harder.

"I have to live through you, I know no one else here." Bo came and sat on the edge of her cot.

"You're right. We need to find some friends." Andy had to imagine there were some angels who wouldn't mind being friends with them.

"How are we going to do that?" Bo asked.

"I guess we have to actually talk to people…" Andy groaned and Bo grinned. "Come on." She sat up and grabbed his hand, pulling him out of the tent. A group of angels who appeared younger hung out near the dining tent. Walking over to them, with Bo at her side, Andy cleared her throat to get their attention.

"Hi everyone," she said sheepishly. They all turned to stare but didn't seem annoyed, even though she had interrupted their conversation. "I'm Andy and this is Bo." Bo waved and turned bright red.

"I'm Micah." A blonde Adonis who appeared to be their age introduced himself. "This is Seraphina, Nathaniel, and Gabrielle; or Sera, Nathan, and Gabby." He smiled and created a space in their circle for Bo and Andy to join. The others seemed a little wary. They were all so attractive it intimidated Andy. She knew that she also had those traits from being an angel, but she had never been surrounded by so many perfectly sculpted people before. They all had the signature shimmering golden eyes. Sera and Nathan both had ebony skin that looked as smooth as silk. While Sera had shiny ink black hair that she had pulled back into a ponytail, Nathan had courser, matte black hair, that seemed to fit his more muted style.

"So, you're the famous Andromeda." Gabby scrutinized Andy, as if sizing her up. Gabby had similar hair to Andy, a white blonde, but hers was shoulder length and pin straight.

"Well, Andy, but yeah, I guess I am." Andy glanced at the others hoping to get some kind of explanation, but no one offered anything.

"Huh...so anyway, like I was saying, they are forming a guard to head out this afternoon to take out a group of demons that have moved into a farmhouse along the outskirts of Jamesville. I'm going to request to be a part of it," Gabby said, her expression one of excitement. Andy wondered why going up against a group of demons would be exciting.

"I'm already going," Sera mentioned. She grinned when the others reacted with jealousy.

"You're lucky, they haven't let me out in over a week," Nathan sighed. Andy wondered how many fights they had each been in, and how many demons they had killed. "They'll probably never let you leave, Andy," Nathan commented, and Andy was surprised to hear her name, thinking they had forgotten she was even there.

"Why? They said I could visit my dad at the other camp anytime I want," Andy replied, as if that would make them realize she was not some prisoner. They all exchanged glances that made her doubt her statement.

"So, Bo, what's it like?" Micah turned to Bo.

"What's *what* like?" Bo asked, appearing puzzled and embarrassed to be the center of attention.

"Being human," Micah said as if, *duh*, what else would he be talking about.

"I mean...it's okay, I guess. I've never been anything but human, so I've nothing to compare it to." He looked to Andy for help.

"I was raised as a human, so I have some experience with it too," Andy mentioned, drawing the attention away from Bo. They all observed her with puzzled expressions. "You know, my mom was an angel, and my dad is a human,"

"Andromeda!" She turned to see Septimus striding towards them. Sera, Gabby, and Micah blushed and swooned as he came closer. Jealousy rolled off them in waves as Septimus took Andy's arm and led her away from the others. "We should continue your training," he announced and walked back towards the path as he let go of her arm. He had a much harder, more serious air about him now. Andy followed along like a lost puppy, until they came to the spot where they had left off. He turned and glared at her. "Lift the tree again."

"I thought we were going to work on that another time?" Andy was still a little sore from the first try when she had lost focus and the weight took over.

"Lift the tree again," he repeated, and she walked over to the tree. She bent down and closed her eyes. Imagining her strength building in her arms and flowing outward into the tree itself, she was able to lift the tree again by remaining calm and focused.

When she opened her eyes, she lost her grip and the tree crashed down again with a force that knocked her off balance and had her lying on her back in the muck. Sitting up, she saw Septimus still watching her from where he stood, waiting for her to lift the tree again. So, she stood, brushed herself off, and bent down again, closing her eyes, and focusing.

This time she only held the tree aloft for a few seconds before it crashed down again, almost landing on her foot, which she whipped back just in time, causing her to slip and send herself back down into the muck, landing on her butt. Septimus let out an exasperated sigh. Andy whipped her head around to face him.

"I'm sorry, is my failure inconveniencing you?" she snapped. He softened a little and walked over to her, helping her up.

"You have to *really* focus. Push everything else out of your mind. Don't let anything distract you," he instructed. Andy rolled her eyes, like she had *not* been trying to do that the first two times. She bent down and tried one more time. She pushed every other thought from her mind and held the tree aloft for a full minute before lowering it back to the ground where it settled back into the mud with a squelch. "Very good. We can conclude our training for the day." Septimus turned on his heel and headed back towards camp. Andy huffed and trudged along behind him.

9

The Family Tree

Bo watched Andy walk away with Septimus. He noticed everyone else also watched her leave with him.

"She must be more important than I thought if she's being trained by Septimus," Sera commented. Bo thought he could hear a hint of jealousy, but her face was unreadable. Septimus was exceptionally attractive, but so far, *all* the angels Bo had met were crazy beautiful. He assumed it was another perk of being an angel.

"What do you mean, he doesn't normally train angels?" Bo asked, and Sera turned back to him.

"We all were trained by our parents or our guardians." Sera swept her hand around, indicating herself and all the others standing in their little circle.

"Andy didn't know she was an angel until after the war began. She hasn't had any time to train," Bo explained. "Who *is* Septimus exactly?"

"He's Ephram's only remaining son. His six brothers all died when the war first started," Sera began, the others seemed bored, like they had heard the story a million times already. "Ephram is our ruler here."

"But this camp is the camp of Jeremiah, who's that?" Bo asked, trying to get as much information as he could about the place he was to call home.

"He is of the dominions order, which is who Ephram reports to in heaven. All our instructions come from Jeremiah, but Ephram is the one who makes the final calls since he's here on Earth and knows what's happening in real time. Jeremiah is usually preoccupied with more important issues." Sera seemed to love giving Bo the history lesson, and he was equally curious about it all.

"Huh. What about Malachi?" He prompted her.

"Ephram's right-hand man. Not sure how he got that role, it's always been that way."

"Is there anything else you can tell me about Septimus?" he asked for Andy's sake. He wanted to make sure he had nothing to worry about with her going off alone with him. Septimus may be an angel, but Bo was sure even angels had skeletons in their closets.

"He's reckless." Nathan spoke up, and the others all shook their heads. "It's true and you know it. You're all too wrapped up in his allure to care," he snapped. Interested in what Nathan had to say, Bo nodded for him to go on. "He likes to take risks. He will go off by himself when we are out on missions, or he will take the more dangerous route when we are hunting for demons. Don't get me wrong, he follows Ephram's orders, and he always gets the job done, but he takes too many risks for my liking."

"Not to mention that one time," Micah chimed in. "Septimus and his brothers were all out on a mission. We don't know the whole story, but Septimus went off on his own and when his brothers went to find him, they fell right into a demon trap. That was how his first brother, Mathias, died." A grave look came over his face, and his eyes turned to the ground. He obviously knew Mathias, and still mourned for the loss of him.

"No more of this sad, sappy crap," Gabby chirped. "I'm going to go find out more about the guard that's going out later." She skipped away, with Nathan and Sera following closely behind her. Their heads dipped together as if they were discussing something.

"I guess it's just the two of us now." Micah smirked at Bo, and Bo sighed. "What, you don't want to watch me do some sweet tricks?" Micah joked, playfully pushing Bo's shoulder, making Bo grin.

"Alright, let's see some of these *sweet tricks* and I'll let you down gently when they turn out to be lame." Bo crossed his arms over his chest, puffing it out a bit, and gave Micah a challenging look. Micah closed his eyes and clasped his hands together. Bo noted how angelic he seemed as he did this.

Micah slowly moved his hands apart, and between them a spark of light appeared as he opened his eyes. The light grew until it was the size of a basketball. Bo gaped for a moment and applauded for him. "Impressive." Bo went to touch the ball of light and Micah clapped his hands together, dispersing the light.

"You don't want to touch that. It would probably burn you. You know, human and all," Micah explained, shaking his hands out as if he was shaking water off them.

"Gotcha. Thanks for the heads up. You have any other tricks up your sleeve?" Bo asked, genuinely curious.

"I gotta keep you guessing." Micah winked. "Find me tomorrow and I might show you another trick." He gave Bo a slight bow and walked off towards the meeting tent where the others had disappeared to.

Bo stood rooted to the spot where Micah had left him. He was unsure whether Micah had been flirting with him or being nice. Either way, his spirits lifted. He was feeling a bit down after having to say goodbye to his parents that morning and was still worried about them. They hadn't been apart from each other since the war began, but at least he knew they were all safe, even if they weren't together. He swayed back to his tent in a happy daze.

∞

Andy made her way back to her tent and found Bo already there. "How did it go with our new friends?" she asked, collapsing onto her cot. Training had taken its toll on her and she was exhausted. Bo folded his hands behind his head.

"Pretty good." His face lit up, beaming. Andy turned onto her side and propped her head up with her arm.

"You look like it went better than *pretty good*. Come on, spill." Andy was not so tired that she wasn't curious what had caused such a change in Bo's mood. She was happy to see his spirits had lifted.

"Well, I did have a good chat with them about Septimus." He smirked and Andy rolled her eyes.

"I'm telling you, I. Do. Not. Like. Him." She stood off her cot and walked over to sit on the edge of Bo's. "But I am curious because he was acting weird earlier. It was like he didn't even want to be training me, like he had better things to do." She thought about his standoffish stance, and how he kept sighing like he was bored. It was a complete change from their earlier training session.

Bo relayed all the information he had learned from the others to Andy. She nodded to let him know she was still listening, but otherwise she remained silent as he talked.

"I knew he had six brothers, but I didn't know they…died," she gulped. It was unimaginable, losing so many siblings. She could barely deal with the loss of one. "And it makes sense Ephram is his father. They look so much alike, and when Ephram summoned him earlier, he went without question or hesitation. I would do the same if my dad wanted to see me." She laid her head beside Bo's, and he turned to face her.

"I think there's something else they're not telling us," Bo started. "The way the group looked at you when you said you could visit your dad anytime you wanted, and they said you would probably never be able to leave..." He shuddered and Andy understood, she had been wondering about the same thing. "Maybe we need to start asking more questions around here."

"I noticed that too." Andy sighed. "I'm not sure what is going on here, but I'll find out. Right now, though, I need sleep." As she closed her eyes, Bo pulled the blanket over her, and she dozed off. When she woke, Lindy crouched inches from her face. Andy couldn't help but let out a short scream.

"Lindy!" She gasped, clutching at her chest. "What is it?" Bo stirred behind Andy and sat up to see what was going on. He chuckled. There were footsteps outside of the tent, and Septimus burst in.

"What's happening? I heard you scream." He took in the sight of Lindy crouched in front of Bo and Andy laying on the cot and Andy saw a flash of what appeared to be confusion.

"I'm sorry. I wanted to talk to Andy, but I was waiting for her to wake up," Lindy said, her lower lip quivering, and Andy sat up. Ace snickered in the corner, amused by the events happening in front of him. Lindy climbed onto Andy's lap and laid her head against Andy's shoulder.

"Well. Everything seems to be okay here, so I- uh, I'll go." Septimus spun around and left the tent. Andy watched as the tent flap rustled behind him and turned her attention back to Lindy.

"What did you want to talk to me about Lindy?" Andy asked, searching her eyes and gasped. She had not noticed it before, but Lindy's eyes seemed to be darker than when they had met the week before. Andy stroked Lindy's hair, more for her own comfort than Lindy's now.

"The nice man talked to me today. Eph-er-am." Lindy smiled and clenched the front of her shirt in her hands. It caused a pang in Andy's chest. "He told me I can help! I can help the angels! I don't have to be scared of the bad people anymore!" Lindy sounded so excited and happy. Andy couldn't find it within herself to rain on her parade, though she was wary of Ephram's motives.

"That's awesome, Lindy." She hugged her and Lindy stood up. "I'm sure you're going to do a great job!" Andy faked a smile then glanced over at Ace, who scowled. He had his CD player clutched in his hands, but his headphones hung around his neck. "Ace, did they talk to you about this too?" Andy asked him, hoping he at least might help her fight to protect Lindy from whatever plan the angels had for her.

"Yeah. I was there." He didn't look at Andy but turned his head and spit into the grass. "It's all good now, right?

Lindy's a demon…"

"Ace!" Andy snapped, cutting him off before he said anything else. Lindy studied him, concerned. "Lindy, can you get me a glass of water, please?" Andy asked her, and she bobbed her head, running out of the tent. Andy walked over to Ace's cot and sat on the edge of it.

"Do I get a lecture now, Mommy?" Ace said in a mocking tone.

"Look, I am *not* your mother, and I never meant to act like it. Lindy looks up to me because I am the only female figure in her life right now, and you are her main male figure. You need to help her. You cannot let them use her like this," Andy tried to get through to him. "Please, work with me here. I know you hate me, and I accept that, and fine. Hate me. But do not turn on your sister because you learned she has demon blood in her. It changes nothing." Ace's head whipped up from staring at his CD player and he glared at her. She could almost feel his anger piercing into her through his eyes.

"It changes *everything*," he choked out. Andy did not realize it before, but he had tears welling in his eyes and his face flushed with anger. "How is it that she's a demon, and I'm not? Didn't you wonder about that? Maybe I *am* a demon! Maybe I'm just as damned as she is." He shuddered. "There is something I never told anyone." He paused, dipping his head towards his chest as he clenched his fists.

"What is it, Ace? You can tell me." Andy tried to sound as reassuring as possible, but she was a little worried about what he had been hiding.

"My parents...it didn't happen exactly like my grandparents thought," he admitted. "I *did* go back in for my CD player, and my parents came in after me. I ran upstairs and when I came back down, my parents were in the kitchen with demons all around them," he paused and let out a sigh. "The demons weren't there to kill us. They were there to recruit my parents. I didn't understand what was going on at the time, but my Uncle Tim came running in and when he saw what was happening in the kitchen, he pulled me out of the house. My parents were still alive when we left, and they may still be," he finished, sniffling.

"I don't understand why your Uncle Tim let you all leave without them, surely they would have turned down the demons." Andy tried to understand everything Ace had told her, but it didn't add up.

"I wondered that, too. I was so confused, I never mentioned it to anyone. Uncle Tim told Grandpa they were dead, so we left and that was it. But when we arrived at my grandparents' house, Uncle Tim pulled me aside and told me everything. He and my mom's parents were demons. Uncle Tim was a demon, but he wanted nothing to do with them. He always wore colored contacts so no one would know." Ace took a deep breath before continuing.

"Mom, I guess, had always kept in touch with other demons and had been saying she wanted to join the fight. Uncle Tim knew when he saw the group of demons in the house, she had called them there, and he knew dad would never let my mom go without him, so he took me away before they could get us too." Ace took a deep breath and laid his hands on his knees.

"I am so sorry, Ace. But, if your Uncle Tim was a demon, why did he not want to fight with them?" Andy still had so many questions.

"He didn't believe in the war, and he didn't want to be a part of it," Ace said. "If Lindy is a demon, and I'm not, that means we've been lied to all our lives. That means my parents may not have been *my* parents. All this time, I've been thinking I could become a demon at any moment. I was so terrified I would *change* into a monster, and hurt someone, or worse now...I don't even know." Tears broke free and spilled over his cheeks. Knowing he would never accept a hug from her, Andy put her hand on his arm instead to try to comfort him.

"You know who your parents are, Ace. The people who raised you, and loved you, are your parents. It's Lindy whose life is changed. You're not a demon, Ace. That much I know," she reassured him.

"Lindy is still your sister, no matter who your birth parents were. *Your* parents raised you both, and that's all that matters. Lindy's not a demon because of her blood, just like I'm not an angel because of my blood. I'm trying. I really am, but… the point is, we are who we were raised to be. We have our parents to thank for that, not the blood running through our veins." Andy finished, and heard Bo clapping from his cot, trying to lighten the mood. She couldn't help but laugh a little. "Thanks, Bo." She gave him a grateful smile. Just having him there was comforting.

"I don't hate you, Andy," Ace said it so quietly, Andy almost missed it. "It's not your fault that the demon came to our house. It may have been looking for you, but it probably sensed Uncle Tim and Lindy there too. I heard they can sense their own kind, kind of like how you knew when we were close to the angels. That's probably the *real* reason the demon let us leave the house alive." Ace wiped away his tears and finally looked up at Andy. "I don't hate you," he repeated. "I'm sorry I blamed you before."

"It's okay. Want to go get some food? I'm starving." Ace finally smiled, a real smile. Lindy reappeared with a water for Andy, still in her usual cheerful state.

"Thank you, Lindy." Andy took the water from her. "It's time to go eat, come on." They all headed towards the dining tent, leaving their worries behind for the moment.

10

The Clearing

That night, Andy dreamt of Hell.

Andy stood Inside a cage, surrounded by hellhounds. Flames licked around the edges of the room that had no doors. She screamed until her throat was raw and she could barely breathe. Grabbing the bars of the cage, she reeled backwards as they burned her hands. Gazing down at her hands, she saw the burn marks. Outside the one window in the room stood a figure, glaring at her. She couldn't see their face, but she could hear their voice, and their laughter. She was being drawn to it but couldn't leave the cage.

"Andromeda, darling." The voice was deep and harsh. "We're waiting for you." A cackle set Andy on edge, and she recoiled back against the wall. The figure appeared directly in front of her, *and she caught a glimpse of their face before they disappeared into the darkness. It was no one she had ever seen before.*

The cage that had been separating her from the hellhounds dissipated, and a whistle sounded outside the window. The hellhounds began to creep towards Andy as one, and they lunged.

Andy woke screaming and realized Bo was shaking her shoulder.

"Andy..." He kneeled next to her cot. "Andy, move over." He climbed in beside her and hugged her close to him. "It's okay, Andy. You're okay. It's okay." He stroked her hair as Andy had done for Lindy when she'd had her nightmare. "Go back to sleep, I'll be here if you need me," he murmured. Andy relaxed in his arms and drifted back into her dreams.

She was in the woods behind the camp where she had trained with Septimus. Now she was alone, though. She turned around, searching for someone.

"Looking for me?" The figure she had seen before stepped out from behind a tree, but his face was hidden by his hood. He took another step towards her. "Andromeda...come to me." His voice came out a bit more desperate than before. He stretched his arms out towards her and she shrank away from them. He whistled and hellhounds surrounded them. Andy turned away from him, and came face to face with long, sharp fangs gnashing at her, and she let out a scream.

This time she woke herself up, the scream dying in her throat. Lindy and Ace were moving about on the other side of the tent. She had woken them too. Bo still had his arms around her, which she was grateful for.

"I'm still here," he grumbled, half asleep.

"Us too," Ace whispered from his side of the tent. Andy smiled into Bo's shoulder.

"Thanks guys." It came out muffled against Bo's shirt. She heard the tent flap rustling, and saw a figure appear at the entrance. All she could think about was the figure from her nightmares, and her heart started pounding. The figure came closer to her cot, and she crushed herself as close to Bo as possible. As the figure kneeled beside the cot, she could make out Septimus' features and she let out a long breath. Her whole body relaxed. Sitting up, she untangled herself from Bo's arms.

"Do you need to take a walk?" Septimus whispered, so as not to disturb the others, who were already falling back asleep. He held his hand out to help her off the cot.

"Yes." Taking his hand, she carefully stepped over Bo and let Septimus lead her out of the tent into the open air. The sun rose over the horizon and relief washed over Andy. She took a deep breath in and let it out slowly, feeling completely awake. "Thank you."

"You've been screaming off and on all night." Septimus pointed out, and she blushed. Everyone probably thought she was crazy and hated her for keeping them awake all night.

"Sorry…" Andy muttered, running her hand along the leaves of a bush they walked past. The dew came off on her palm and dripped back to the Earth. She watched it, thinking about her nightmares.

"If you don't mind me asking, what were you dreaming about?" Septimus observed her, clearly wondering what he was dealing with when it came to her and her troubles.

"I'm not sure…" she lied. There were some things she wasn't ready to share yet. "I don't remember." He seemed to accept that and didn't press the issue.

"Well, you're lucky to have Bo with you. You two seem close." He walked with his hands clasped behind his back, and Andy noticed the ring on his middle finger again. He saw her studying it and started twisting it around on his finger.

"Bo's the only friend I have," she admitted. "We became close fast because we had no one else. I mean, I have my dad, and Bo has his parents, but there's certain things you can't talk about with them." She sat on the fallen tree she had worked so hard to lift the day before and Septimus took a seat beside her.

"I understand." He crossed his ankles in front of him and leaned his head back to glimpse the sky, which lit up as the sun continued to rise.

"I feel as if I've always known him, now. It's weird, but he makes me feel safe, even though I'm the one who's supposed to be keeping *him* safe." Andy rubbed her hands together. She hadn't realized how chilly it was, but the sun creeped up and her body ached to absorb some of its warmth.

"I'm glad you've found each other, then. Everyone deserves to find happiness in another person." He played with his ring again, and Andy found herself moving to touch it. He froze as she placed her hand over his.

"Where did you get that ring?" she asked, staring into his eyes to see if they would give anything away.

"It was my brother Anthony's ring. He was wearing it when... when he died." Septimus let out a puff of air and Andy could see how much it hurt him to remember that moment. "It was given to him by the love of his life, the woman who he died defending." A spark lit where her hand covered his, and she jerked back, nearly falling off the log. She cradled her hand to her chest. The spark didn't hurt, but she saw a welt forming on her palm where it had touched his ring. Septimus seemed surprised and glanced at his own hands.

"What was that?" Andy asked, still staring at her hand.

"I think I know what we need to focus on for our next training session. You need to learn how to control your spark. But, let me look at your hand." He took her hand with both of his and examined her welt. "Not too bad, you'll survive," he joked and placed her hand back into her lap.

"I'm sorry about your brothers," Andy said, knowing she was diving into a deep pit she may not be able to climb back out of. "I lied before when I said I had no siblings. I lost a brother, too." Her breath hitched as she said this, and she felt like she might choke. Septimus turned to her, and she saw her grief reflected in his eyes. She'd kept it squashed down and packed away; until now.

"I'm sorry, Andromeda." He used her full name, like he always did, but she didn't mind anymore.

"His name was Jason. He was my best friend." Tears came into her eyes, but she held them back. "The demons, they took him from me." Barely able to get the words out, she began hyperventilating. It took all her strength to keep her grief at bay.

At first Septimus stared, unsure how to react, and then his hand was on hers again. "I never even got to say goodbye…" she said, leaning into Septimus as his arm came up around her shoulders. She cried for the brother she had lost, and for all the brothers Septimus had lost. Knowing the pain of losing someone so important, she knew she never would have survived had she lost as many brothers as Septimus. It was a marvel he was still functioning. Andy pulled away from him and wiped her eyes.

"I'm sorry, I shouldn't have let myself go down that road." Reeling her grief back in, she pushed it back into its tightly sealed compartment.

"Don't be sorry…" Septimus began, but he was interrupted by someone clearing their throat and Andy noticed Malachi on the path.

"Septimus. You are needed. Come with me." His voice was thick with disapproval. Septimus stood and followed

Malachi back to the camp, leaving Andy alone with her memories.

Andy made her way to the dining tent and found Bo sitting with their new group of acquaintances. She veered towards them, glad they had a place within the camp, and Bo had someone else to hang out with when she wasn't around.

"Good morning!" Bo greeted. Everyone else seemed to be in a better mood today as well. Andy tried to fake a smile, but she was too drained already, and the day had just begun.

"Try to keep it down tonight, will ya?" Sera joked and gave her a teasing grin. "I kept waking up thinking we were under attack."

"Sorry about that." Andy yawned. "Nightmares." They all nodded as if they knew the feeling, which they probably did with all the nightmare fuel Andy imagined fighting demons provided. She shuddered at the thought of having to fight anyone, let alone a demon.

"So anyway, the whole attack lasted maybe twenty minutes. We caught the demons unaware, and we were able to take them out lickity-split." Sera recounted the fight she had been a part the day before. Everyone hung on her every word. Andy assumed the rest of them had been left behind.

"Well, that is cause for a celebration! Sera's mission: success!" Gabby appeared to be genuinely proud of her friend. "And of course," she paused and glanced towards Micah. "We can't forget, Micah's birthday!" He rolled his eyes at her and let out a long sigh.

"Yes, finally an adult. Time to put on your big boy pants," Nathan joked, punching his arm playfully. "The big one-eight."

"Angels have birthdays?" Bo asked. Everyone turned and gave him a look that said *duh*, and he blushed. "Right. Of course you do." He glanced down at his plate and pushed his food around with his fork.

"We stop aging once we reach our peak, around twenty-eight or so, it's not exact, but we still like to have some fun." Sera winked and pulled a flask out from underneath the table. "And we have a higher tolerance than humans, so we better get started now." Micah laughed and grabbed the flask from her.

"Hey, I'm the birthday boy." He took a big swig and passed the flask back to her.

"Come on guys." Nathan scanned the tent, ensuring no one watched them. "We have to be alert in case we get chosen for a guard." He grabbed the flask from Sera who gave him a sour look and stuck her tongue out at him. "I'll return this tonight, when the actual party starts." He shoved the flask into his jacket pocket.

"I feel like I'm gonna like hanging out with angels," Bo commented, making everyone laugh.

"I guess we'll be seeing you tonight then." Micah nudged Bo's shoulder, and Andy noticed Bo blushing again. Micah and the others all stood and left the tent together.

"Our first angel party." Andy couldn't believe she was

saying those words. She would have never expected that angels had...well, fun. She had thought of them as constantly vigilant and protecting. But maybe that was when they had finished their training and had stopped aging. Maybe that was what marked you as an adult when you are an angel. "This should be interesting."

Bo and Andy headed back to their tent. Bo planned on spending the day with Ace and Lindy while Andy trained. Instead of Septimus training Andy today, Malachi showed up outside of her tent. She cringed a little at the thought of spending an extended amount of time with him.

"Where's Septimus?" she asked him, looking around as if he was going to walk into view at any second.

"He has other duties that take priority over you, child. Remember..." Andy cut him off there because she already knew what he was going to say.

"It's not all about me," she recited as if they were in school. Malachi turned away from her and, instead of heading towards the pathway into the woods where Septimus had been training her, he led her to another tent. The tent was empty except for two chairs that stood facing each other.

"Please. Sit." He gestured to one of the chairs, and Andy sat, while he remained standing. "Today we will work on your control over your spark."

"My spark?" she questioned, not understanding, but remembering the spark that had burned her earlier when she had touched Septimus' ring. In response Malachi closed his eyes and clasped his hands. He took a few deep breaths and opened his hands and his eyes. A spark lit between his palms and solidified into a ball of light that grew as he moved his hands further apart.

"Now, I want you to close your eyes, and put your hands together," he instructed, and Andy did as she was told. "Imagine in your mind there is a light flowing through your whole body. Focus on pushing that light to your heart, and out into your arms, and through your hands. Imagine it taking shape in your hands and slowly pull your hands apart." She did as he said and as she started to pull her hands apart, they grew warmer. It didn't hurt, and it wasn't burning her like it had earlier. When she opened her eyes, she saw a golf ball sized orb of light had formed between her palms. She tried to focus and make it bigger, but it faded to nothing.

"Do you want me to try again?" A part of her wanted to keep trying, but another part of her was exhausted from her sleepless night, and her outpouring of emotion earlier.

"Yes. Again." Malachi paced the room as she closed her eyes and began again.

It took her another twenty tries before she could create a ball of light the size of a basketball that lasted more than thirty seconds. After that, Malachi decided they should take a break for lunch. Bo found Andy in the dining tent, and he brought Lindy and Ace along with him.

"How's training going?" Bo asked between bites.

"Well, for starters, Malachi is training me today." Bo

scrunched his nose. "I know. It's definitely different. He doesn't talk much, just kind of waits for me to make a ball of light, and then says 'again.'"

"Micah's good at that trick," Bo mentioned, and Andy cocked an eyebrow at him.

"Micah? When did he show you that?" She hadn't expected Bo to be hanging out by himself all day in the tent, but she was also a tiny bit jealous he was spending time with their friend group without her.

"Yesterday, when you were training with Septimus." Bo ran his fingers through his hair.

"What else did Micah show you?" Andy was curious about what else she might be learning.

"Nothing yet." Bo smirked. "But maybe he'll show me something new tonight." Andy recognized that look of hope and new beginnings in his eyes and it dawned on her.

"Oh. My. Gosh. You like him, don't you?" She giggled and could feel Bo's excitement as if it were her own.

"Maybe." He feigned nonchalance, but she saw through that.

"As long as no one is bringing anyone back to our tent…" Ace grumbled. "There are children present." He motioned to Lindy who was engrossed in building a fort out of her mashed potatoes and corn. Andy snorted.

"We'll behave ourselves, won't we Andy?" Bo eyed her, and she knew who he was thinking about.

"I will have no problem with that, seeing as I have no

prospects, and I don't plan on having any anytime soon." Andy took one last bite from her plate and stood from the table. "I have to get back to training." Lindy gave her a quick wave and went back to building her mashed potato fort.

After training, Andy made her way back to the tent in a daze. The tent was empty, so she went straight to her cot and flopped onto it. She passed out within moments of her head hitting the pillow. Andy woke to find Bo vigorously shaking her shoulder.

"Ahh…" she grumbled. "Yeesh." Andy sat up and stretched her arms over her head.

"Come on, we have to get ready for the party!" Bo almost jumped up and down with excitement.

"What do you mean, 'get ready?'"

"We haven't bathed since we were at Ace and Lindy's house. It's been a couple days, and I didn't want to say anything… but you're starting to smell. And I can't help but smell myself either. I think it's time we restore ourselves to our former glory." Andy couldn't help laughing as he laid it all out for her, but she knew he was right.

"Okay, fine. But where exactly do you intend for us to get clean?" Standing up, she followed him out of the tent.

"There's a shower tent here. They leave soap and full buckets of water in there. Someone has the chore of refilling them every day. Oh, and sponges. Don't worry, those get cleaned and replaced too. Sera told me all about it. She even gave me some of her clothes for you, so you have a change of clothes now. You should have the clothes you're wearing cleaned, too." He wrinkled his nose as he scanned her outfit. Andy gave his shoulder a small shove and he stuck his tongue out at her. "Sorry, just speaking the truth."

Bo led Andy to the shower tent and inside there were four stalls sectioned off by curtains, along with buckets of water, like Bo had said. He handed her the clothes from Sera he had been carrying and Andy took them gratefully. They grabbed a bucket, some soap, a sponge, and each chose their own stall.

After Andy finished her sorry excuse for a shower, she put on the clothes Sera had given her. Black pants, a blue tank top and a black leather jacket, perfectly matched with a pair of black boots Sera had given her, since Andy's sneakers were falling apart. With a little effort, Andy brushed her hair with her fingers and pulled it into a high ponytail to keep it out of her face. Bo came out of his stall and Andy realized how dirty they had been before. He looked like a whole new man.

"Oh, swoon." Andy pretended to fan herself with her hand and fluttered her eyes at him. "You were right about our needing showers."

"Indeed." He whistled. "You look like the beautiful Andromeda from the myth now, except the sexy demon hunter version." They both laughed and strutted out of the tent. As they walked, Andy noticed most people were heading to bed.

"Andromeda." She heard Septimus' voice and turned

to see him walking towards them.

"I'll wait by our tent," Bo said, giving Andy a nudge as he walked past.

"Hi," she said as she fiddled idly with the zipper on her jacket.

"I hope all went well with training today," Septimus said, and she nodded. "Good. You look..." He paused, and Andy could tell he wasn't sure how to word it without being rude, or forward.

"Clean?" She filled in the blank for him and laughed. A blush crept across his cheeks.

"Refreshed, I guess. Anyway, I was headed to get some food. Have a nice night." He went to walk past her, and she started walking as well, heading in the same direction. They walked in an awkward silence until he veered off into the dining tent.

"Good night!" Andy called out and fast walked the rest of the way to where Bo waited for her. "Don't ask," she said as she continued walking past him and he laughed, catching up with her. They made their way to the path that led into the woods and out to a clearing where the birthday party for Micah was being held. The clearing was within the camp's concealed boundaries.

Everyone else was already there when they arrived. Music played, but not too loud, so they didn't draw any unwanted attention. The only people, besides Bo and Andy, were Micah, Sera, Gabby, and Nathan. Andy had not expected anyone else, since there were not too many younger angels at the camp. A small fire crackled in a little pit they all gathered around.

"How nice of you to join us." Micah grinned at them and handed Bo the flask Sera had carried earlier. Bo took a swig from it and offered it to Andy. She took a sip. It was way stronger than she had expected, and she ended up in a small coughing fit, which caused everyone to break out laughing.

"Don't worry, we have more." Micah pulled a whole bottle of the liquor, which turned out to be vodka, from behind the stump Sera sat on. "This one's for me, though." He smirked and grabbed another bottle.

"I'll take that one." Sera grabbed it and unscrewed the top, starting it off, then passed it to Nathan.

"Did any of you go out with a guard today?" Andy asked, taking a sip from the bottle as it was passed to her. This time she choked it down without coughing, but it still burned all the way to her stomach.

"No, there seems to be lower demon activity this week," Sera answered.

"Well, that's a good thing, right?" Andy asked, hopeful the tide was starting to turn in the war, but the look on Sera's face told her she was wrong.

"Not necessarily. It could mean bigger, worse things to come, or that they're in other areas right now," Sera explained.

"What areas does this camp defend?" Andy asked.

"Pretty much anywhere within a three-hundred-mile

radius of here. So, most of New England." Andy wondered how they could cover such a large area, but she stopped asking questions.

"So, how about a game of never have I ever?" Sera wiggled her eyebrows. "Birthday boy, you start."

"Fine. Never have I ever...kissed a girl." Micah laughed, and Andy noticed him glance over at Bo. Nathan and Sera each took a drink.

"If we're playing that way, never have I ever kissed a guy," Nathan said as he shoved the bottle into Micah's hands. Micah took a giant gulp and gave a little bow after. Bo seized the bottle from Micah, followed by everyone except Nathan.

"So, now that's out of the way, never have I ever left the country," Gabby said. Sera and Micah were the only two to drink.

"Never have I ever fought a demon," Bo chimed in and everyone except for him and Andy drank. "Your turn Andy."

"Alright. Never have I ever...had a crush on an angel." She smirked, glancing over at Bo who blushed but took a drink and said, "If I drink for this one, so do you. Septimus is an angel." Bo handed Andy the bottle and she protested.

"I do not have a crush on him." She passed the bottle around and everyone else drank, but Bo would not let her off the hook that easy.

"Andy, come on, you have to drink. There's nothing to be ashamed of." He pressed the bottle back into her hands.

"It's physically impossible not to be attracted to him,"

Sera said. Andy let a smile creep onto her face and took a long swig from the bottle. She could feel all the alcohol rushing to her head at once and couldn't help but giggle. Everyone else started laughing with her.

"Well, this one is too easy. Never have I ever had a crush on Septimus." Nathan clasped his hands behind his head and leaned back. "Drink up!" He laughed as everyone took a drink except for him.

"You're cruel, Nathaniel," Gabby joked. "I think we need a break." She held up the two bottles to show they were already empty. Andy stood to stretch her cramping legs and the whole world seemed to move with her. She almost toppled over onto Bo, but he stuck out his arms to steady her.

"Woah there," he laughed.

"Sorry," she mumbled.

"Let's take a walk." Bo stood and looped his arm through Andy's, leading her back towards the woods. "How are you feeling?" he asked when they were out of earshot of the others.

"Great, actually. It's like I can see every little detail and hear every little noise." She gawked in wonder at the woods surrounding them and saw them in a whole new light. It made her feel encompassed, safe, and carefree.

"You do realize you are putting all of your body weight onto my arm, right?" Bo laughed and Andy tried to move away from him to relieve him of her weight but fell back into him.

"You know, maybe I am a little drunk," she admitted, making them both laugh. "How are you fine?"

"Oh, I'm not. I used you as an excuse to get away before I did something stupid." He laughed. Andy felt better knowing she was not the only one being affected by all the alcohol they were drinking. The others had seemed to be, if not still sober, then only buzzed. Andy had tried to take small sips, so she knew the other angels had drunk most of the alcohol. "I'm sorry I forced you to admit you have a crush on Septimus." Bo averted his gaze, dipping his head down.

"Don't be, I forced you to admit you have a crush on Micah, and he was actually there. We're even." Andy rested her head on his shoulder as they walked.

"We should get back to the others. They probably think we've been eaten by a bear or something," he joked, though, in her mind Andy thought they would be more likely to encounter a demon than a bear out there, but she kept that to herself.

Back at the fire, the rest of the group all laughed at a joke Gabby told.

"Mind if I steal your date?" Micah asked Andy as soon as they rejoined the group.

"By all means, take him." Andy released her grip on Bo, practically shoving him into Micah's arms, and sat back next to the fire. She watched as Bo and Micah walked back in the direction of the woods. Andy glanced back to the rest of the group, and they all gazed at her with concern in their eyes.

"We love Micah," Sera started, "but make sure Bo's careful. Micah tends to fall easily but leaves just as easy. I've known him since before the war, and that boy is a heartbreaker," she warned.

"I think Bo can handle himself, but I'll make sure to give him a heads up. Thanks." Andy truly appreciated that these angels were already looking out for her and Bo even though they had only recently joined their group.

"As for Septimus..." Gabby spoke up. "You should be careful too. I've seen many angels try to break through his armor, and they all come away a little worse off for it." Andy could see in her eyes she spoke from experience.

"Oh, I never planned on trying to be with him or anything." Andy shook her head a little too quickly and a wave of dizziness came over her, but it faded. "I have much more important things to worry about."

"Well, I'm glad to hear it." The concern left Gabby's face and she turned to Nathan and Sera. "I'm ready for bed." She stood and Nathan mimicked her movements. "Goodnight, ladies," she said cheerily and headed off towards the woods with Nathan on her heels.

"Can I ask you something?" Andy turned to Sera who picked at her nails.

"Sure." Sera leaned back onto her hands.

"How did you all know who I was when I first came here?" Andy couldn't keep her curiosity at bay with the alcohol in her system.

"I'm probably not supposed to tell you…" Sera hesitated before shrugging and continuing. "Jeremiah sent a message to Ephram a couple days before you showed up. The message was for everyone in the camp. It said something along the lines of… *there's a girl named Andromeda who is coming to the camp. Protect her at all costs.* And that was it." Sera feigned a yawn and stood up. "I'm going to bed. I'll tell the boys if I come across them, which I kind of hope I don't." She swayed off towards the woods, but Andy remained by the fire, alone.

After what seemed like an hour, Andy decided Bo wasn't coming back. The fire was pretty much dead, so she figured it was safe enough to leave it. As she started towards the woods, she noticed a figure standing among the trees. It caused her to stop dead in her tracks and the figure slipped behind a tree. Andy's breath caught in her throat, and her heart began to pound. She kept trying to tell herself it was Bo or Micah, or maybe even Septimus.

Andy took a few steps forward and the figure appeared again. It emerged from the trees and Andy realized it wore a hood like the man from her nightmare. She searched the area around her, praying there was something she could use as a weapon, a branch, a rock, something…but there was nothing.

Andromeda. A voice broke through the panic seizing her mind. The voice was different than the one from her nightmares, though. *Trust me, Andy.* Andy squeezed her head, trying to keep the voice out. The figure grew closer, and Andy couldn't bring herself to move. Her limbs felt like jelly and when she tried to take a step, nothing happened. She wasn't sure if that was because of the alcohol or the terror that was taking over.

"Who are you?" She tried to sound confident and strong, but her voice came out sounding mouse-like and scared. She noticed another figure appear at the tree line. She assumed he was a friend of the first hooded figure, and they were both coming to capture her, or kill her.

The new figure approached at a rapid pace, and when the other one, who was only about twenty feet away from her, realized they were no longer alone, he vanished. Andy's knees buckled and she fell forward. Kneeling on the ground, she put her head in her hands as it started to throb. Another figure was still coming for her, and she stayed on the ground, waiting for the end. A scream escaped her as two hands gripped her arms, pulling her to her feet.

"Are you okay?" Andy opened her eyes and saw Septimus staring back at her. She almost fainted in relief that she was not dying that night. She managed to nod, unable to find any words to speak. "Why are you out here alone?" He yelled, or maybe it seemed like he was yelling because Andy's head still throbbed. *Next time, Andromeda.* The words formed inside her head, and she lost consciousness.

11

The Blade

When Andy woke up, she was lying on a cot in a tent much smaller than the one she was used to. As she jolted up, her head started to spin. She put her head in her hands and groaned.

"You're awake." Andy turned to see Septimus standing in the entrance to the tent.

"My head…" Andy's throat was dry, and her voice sounded rough and scratchy.

"Yeah, too much alcohol will do that to you." Septimus sounded stern, and Andy assumed he was upset with her, not that he had any right to be. "Here, I got you some water." He handed her a paper cup filled with water, and she took it gratefully, chugging it all at once.

"Thank you." She tried to stand up, but her legs betrayed her and wouldn't hold her weight. She ended up right back on her butt on the cot.

"You should rest." Septimus remained at the entrance, with his hands clasped behind his back and his lips pursed. Andy could feel the disapproval coming off him in waves.

"Why weren't you training me yesterday?" Andy still had some liquid courage running through her veins and she was not letting it go to waste.

"I have other responsibilities," was his answer, which made Andy scoff. Why did they all have to be so cryptic around here?

"What kind of responsibilities?" He didn't respond to her, and she noticed his jaw clenching. "Why are you here if you're clearly annoyed with me?" Andy stood successfully, though she stumbled a bit.

"You need to rest." Septimus motioned for her to lie back onto the cot, but she shook her head and made to walk past him out of the tent. He moved further into her path and blocked her from leaving. "Please, I need you to rest so you'll be ready for training today."

"I will rest on my own cot." Andy shouldered him out of her way, and he let her pass him, but he caught her arm before she left.

"You need to be more careful, Andromeda." Instead of sounding as if he was still scolding her, she heard concern in his voice, and her annoyance towards him faltered.

"I-I will. Goodnight." He took his hand off her arm and she left the tent. Stumbling a little as she walked, she continued walking without looking back. It dawned on her that she had been in Septimus' tent.

It was still dark outside, so Andy figured it was probably around three in the morning, but when she returned to her tent Bo was lying awake on his cot.

"Where have you been, young lady?" He sat up and spoke in a whisper so as not to wake Ace or Lindy.

"Somehow I ended up in Septimus' tent." Andy sat on the edge of Bo's cot and noticed the shock on his face, and then the grin that spread across it.

"Damn, you work fast girl! And a few hours ago, you were saying you didn't even like the guy!" he exclaimed. She shook her head, trying not to laugh.

"No. It's not like that. Everyone else had left, but I stayed by the fire in the clearing. But then, I wasn't alone. Someone else was in the woods, watching me…" A shudder ran through her as she recalled the hooded figure. "He started to come for me, but Septimus showed up and the figure disappeared into thin air." Bo gaped at her and fear filled his eyes.

"I'm so glad I sent him out there for you!" Bo said.

Andy gaped at him and smacked his arm. "What do you mean you sent him there for me?" Mortification washed over her, causing heat to creep up her neck and her shoulders to sag as she ran her hand over her hair.

"Sera found Micah and I and told us everyone was going to bed, but you were still out by the fire. So, when Micah and I headed back to the camp, I may have come across Septimus, totally on accident, and told him you were all alone out in the clearing," Bo explained, looking like a child who had admitted to breaking a vase. "You should have seen how worried he seemed, and he hurried off without saying anything. I might have winked too...but I can't remember." He gave Andy puppy dog eyes.

"Omigosh. He probably hates me now." She buried her face into her arms as she collapsed back onto the cot. So, he *did* have a good reason to be upset with her after all.

"If I had known you were in danger, I would have *never* left you alone, Andy." She could hear the apology coming, and she stopped him.

"Sera told me tonight that the angels here were given a command to keep me safe at all costs," she said, "and I chose to stay out there alone instead of going back to camp with her. *I* knew I was in danger, and I stayed out there. It's my own fault."

"Yeah, it is, why do you keep trying to blame me?" Bo joked, lightening the mood.

"So, how did things go with Micah?" Andy changed the subject, tired of talking about her and her stupidity.

"I mean we didn't end up getting as far as you did with Septimus, winding up in his bed and all." Bo winked and

Andy punched his arm lightly. "Kidding. But really, we talked a little and he kissed me goodnight."

"I should tell you, the others wanted me to give you a warning that he's a heartbreaker." Andy relayed the message. Bo thought about that for a moment.

He sighed. "I'd rather have the chance to be in a position to have my heart broken than go on alone forever," he responded, shrugging off her warning.

"I guess I would too." Andy also thought of the warning Gabby had given her about Septimus. "Just, be careful. I'm here if you need me, but I have no experience in repairing hearts." She held his hand and they both drifted off to sleep.

∞

Bo woke in the morning before anyone else. He had only slept for a few hours, but he felt wide awake. He maneuvered over Andy, so as not to wake her, and left for the dining tent. Still a little fuzzy from the night before, he figured food would be his priority.

After he finished eating, he walked off into the woods behind the camp to have some alone time. A fallen tree marked where the path diverged, and he took a seat there. It was still tolerable outside, but the sun was climbing higher in the sky and the heat of it began to penetrate the trees. The slightly cooler, refreshing air beneath the shade of the giant maple above him, helped to clear his senses. The summer had been fairly mild so far, but it had only just begun.

It was hard to know what day it was without any kind of calendar. Bo lost track a few days after he had to leave his home, figuring he had more important things to worry about.

As he continued to enjoy the morning, Bo couldn't help but think about the night before and what Andy had warned him about Micah. Micah was the exact image of an angel if Bo had ever thought about one. He had the golden eyes that matched his near golden blonde hair. He was tall, not unlike Bo, and had the same muscular build. Though, Micah had more definition, because he needed to workout often to keep in shape to fight demons. He had a glow about him too, like an aura. It was more visible when he was happy, which Bo noticed last night during their walk together.

Bo told Andy he was fine being with Micah even if it meant he might get his heart broken, but he was still worried. He was beginning to have real feelings for Micah, but he didn't want to get too close if Micah was going to leave him broken. With what little experience Bo had with relationships he wasn't sure what to think of Micah's attention towards him. He knew, though, he would keep himself guarded. So, if the time came when Micah was done with him, he could pick himself up and walk away unscathed. If that was even possible.

Twigs and leaves crunched as someone walked down the path towards Bo. He couldn't help but think of the figure

Andy had told him about from the night before, and guilt filled him. He'd left her out there all alone and vulnerable to any demons. From then on, he made a promise to himself he wouldn't leave Andy alone again. She needed him right now. That was more important than anything else, even whatever may happen between him and Micah.

"Hello, Bo." Septimus appeared from between the trees, walking towards him. Bo gave him a small wave. "What are you doing out here?" Septimus scanned the area, as if expecting Andy to be with him.

"This is a nice place to come and think," Bo said as he noticed the strain that pulled at Septimus' features. "Is that why you came out here?"

"Kind of." Septimus crossed his arms and gazed up towards the sky, letting the sun warm his face. He had a glow about him, as Bo had noticed with Micah, but Septimus' glow seemed to be a bit dull at the moment. "Malachi has taken over Andy's training, so now I have some free time on my hands. Also, the demons are keeping unusually quiet."

"Why aren't you training Andy anymore?" Bo wondered if that was something that had been Septimus' doing, or if the others had made the decision for him.

"I follow my orders. Ephram and Malachi have their reasons." That was all he offered as an explanation. Bo stretched his arms out in front of him and noticed how tan he had gotten since the summer began. There was a time when he would have loved to be that tan, but it reminded him of the time his family had spent on the road, trying to stay safe and alive. Bo pushed these thoughts aside and turned back to face Septimus.

"Well, I know Andy would rather have you training her. She's not as... comfortable with the other angels," Bo tried to explain without giving away anything Andy would disapprove of.

"Malachi is one of the best trainers we have. She will learn more from him than I could teach her." Septimus ran his hand through his hair.

"Thank you for saving her last night. I would have never left her alone if I had known she was in danger." Bo believed he owed Septimus for saving his best friend, especially since it was his fault she'd been alone to begin with, no matter what she said.

"I took an oath to protect her at all costs. I was simply upholding that oath." Septimus betrayed no emotions, which annoyed Bo. Bo was usually good at reading people, but Septimus was particularly challenging. Bo eyed him for a moment, deciding whether to push him on the topic of Andy, but he figured Septimus would not give him anything anyway, and Andy would be pissed. So, he dropped it.

"Well, thank you." Bo stood off the fallen tree, ready to head back into the camp. He stretched one last time, letting the sun warm his limbs.

"Try to keep a closer eye on her, please," Septimus said it almost too quiet for Bo to hear, but he caught it as he walked by and smiled to himself.

∞

Andy was awoken when Malachi's voice erupted into her dreams.

"You're still asleep? Clearly training is not as important to you as it should be." He had his usual disapproving tone. Andy squinted, glancing around, and realized everyone else was already gone. She stood up, noticing she no longer had the jacket Sera had given her. She must have lost it somewhere between the clearing and the camp. Of course, she didn't *need* the jacket, it was already hot outside, but it acted as a security blanket for her. She pulled her boots on and followed Malachi out of the tent. He led her back to the same place they had trained the day before. There were no chairs to sit in, but a rack full of weapons was placed in the corner of the tent. "Today we are going to practice your fighting skills. Have you ever used a sword before?"

"No... I've used a gun, does that count for anything here?" Andy tried to joke with Malachi, but he remained as serious as ever. She fought the urge to roll her eyes at him, he already hated her enough.

"We'll start with the easiest sword then." He plucked a broadsword from the weapons rack that was about as long as Andy's arm and handed it to her. "How does that feel?" she pretended to know what he was talking about and examined the sword.

"It's...surprisingly light," Andy noted. Malachi grabbed a similar sword for himself.

"All of these weapons have been blessed with holy water, and so they are capable of killing a demon. Any other ordinary weapon, including your guns, will not kill a demon, only wound them temporarily. Just as an angel cannot be killed with any weapon unless it has been forged in hellfire," Malachi explained. "Now, follow my lead." He shifted one foot in front of the other, widening his stance, and keeping the arm without the sword positioned to be able to block any blows coming at his heart.

"Like this?" Andy copied his movements exactly. It felt natural for her to be wielding the sword.

"Yes, good. All angels have an instinctual knowledge of basic fighting techniques, let's see if you inherited them even as a half angel." They began their practice. Malachi kept his movements slow, so Andy had a chance at figuring out how to wield her sword effectively enough to cause potential harm to her enemy without hurting herself in the process. It seemed as if she did inherit at least some of those natural fighting abilities, because she was able to keep up with Malachi after a short while of training. By the end of their training session, Andy's arm ached, and it felt like jelly when she put the sword down.

Broken Angel

"You did well today, go get some food and some rest." Malachi started to leave the tent, but Andy stopped him.

"Wait, I want to visit my dad today." Andy needed to talk to Wayne about the dreams she'd been having and that figure she had seen in the woods. Not to mention the fact she had a hole that grew in her chest everyday she didn't see him.

"I'm sorry, but that is not possible," Malachi said, and he was gone. Anger welled inside of Andy. They had promised her she could see her dad anytime she wanted to, and they had changed their mind. She was not going to let it go. But first, she needed food. When she arrived in the dining tent, no one she knew was there, so she sat alone.

Andy's mind wandered to the previous night, and that figure in the woods, it had to have been a demon. She shuddered thinking that they could have taken her had Septimus not come along. The woods behind the camp and the clearing were supposed to be warded against demons and yet that demon last night seemed to have no trouble being there. So, was she even safe in the camp at all?

12

The Invasion

Over the next few days, Malachi trained Andy on sword fighting, strength training, and communicating using the angel network; the method angels used to speak to each other in their minds. Every session left Andy exhausted. She saw little of Septimus, except for one night, when she had her usual nightmare. He appeared in her tent and took her for a walk in the woods again. Neither of them spoke about the night of Micah's birthday.

Septimus seemed to be MIA during the daytime, and Andy was usually so busy with training anyway, she didn't seek him out at all. Bo and Andy became closer with Sera, Micah, Gabby, and Nathan. They ate each meal with them, and hung out whenever Andy wasn't training, or the others weren't out with a guard. It brought Andy a sense of normalcy, having people to talk to about things other than the war. Sometimes she could forget that they were angels and pretend that such supernatural beings did not exist.

Andy kept asking Malachi if she could visit her dad, but he kept turning her down without so much as an explanation as to why not. So, after her fifth attempt, she decided it was time to take matters into her own hands.

After another exhausting sword fighting session with Malachi, and his refusal of her request to visit her dad, Andy ate her lunch and then went off to find reinforcements. Andy found Bo lounging on his cot, chatting with Ace and Lindy.

"Want to help me with something outside, Bo?" Andy asked casually so as not to alert the others to anything. Bo stood and followed her out of the tent. "I need your help on a little mission." She gave him a mischievous look.

"What kind of mission?" Bo seemed wary, and Andy figured rightfully so.

"I want to go visit our parents," she announced. Bo didn't look shocked, which she took as a good sign. He missed his parents as much as she missed her dad.

"Alright, let's do it," he agreed, but they both soon realized they had no idea where the human camp was; they needed to bring someone who did into their circle. Bo's first instinct was to recruit Micah, but Andy thought maybe Sera would be more willing to help them sneak out of the camp. They found Sera leaving the shower tent.

"I needed something to keep my mind off the attack in Baltimore," Sera admitted.

"Wait, there was an attack?" Andy had wondered why the camp seemed a little emptier than usual.

"Yeah, the demons attacked our Baltimore camp. Nathan left with a group of ten others this morning to help fight them off," Sera explained. "Anyway, do you want to do this or not?"

"Yeah, let's go," Andy said.

"We have to go through the front entrance; the clearing is as far as you can go the other way before triggering an alarm. This way we can get out without anyone knowing, if no one notices us," Sera said, Bo and Andy nodded in agreement. They made their way towards the entrance along the backside of the tents, to be less noticeable, when they came across Micah and Gabby arguing about something behind the dining tent. Micah saw their group before they could avoid him and Gabby. He strolled over with Gabby trailing behind him.

"What are you guys doing?" Micah crossed his arms over his chest, puffing it out a little.

"We're on a top-secret mission, care to join?" Sera replied, making Bo and Andy lock eyes, regretting their decision to trust Sera to get them out of there unnoticed. More people in their group was a sure way to draw more attention to themselves.

"Sure." Micah winked at Bo.

"Yeah, I need something to distract me from worrying about Nathan," Gabby agreed. They both fell in step behind Bo and Andy as they continued making their way towards the entrance to the camp.

Sera led them beside the meeting tent and motioned for them to wait. She made sure the coast was clear, before waving them on to go through the doorway that had appeared.

Once they were all through the doorway, Sera had them running through the woods towards the town where Bo and Andy had first met the angels. Sera veered off to the left and, after about a minute, she stopped to let them all catch their breath.

"We're not that far. It will take twenty minutes to walk there," Sera said. Bo and Andy were the only ones still breathing heavily, everyone else seemed to have already recovered. "You two need to work on your cardio," Sera joked as she started walking again.

"We'll get right on that." Bo nudged Andy and mouthed *not*. She stifled a laugh, and they followed the others as they continued at a slower pace.

Micah fell back to walk beside them. "So, what exactly is this secret mission we're on?"

"I need to see my dad, and Malachi kept refusing my requests, hence the formation of the secret mission group." Apprehension flashed across Micah's face.

"You know, if Malachi finds out about this…" He trailed off, and Andy figured what he was about to say had something to do with them being in serious trouble of some sort. Seeing her dad was more important than whatever was going to happen to her when they returned.

"Don't worry, we'll go into the human camp alone, and we'll go back into the angel camp separately. Then, if anything goes wrong, you can all claim you were doing something else and Bo and I got into this mess all on our own," Andy reassured him. The plan was risky, and she didn't want anyone else getting in trouble because of her.

"And what's in it for you, Bo?" Micah turned to Bo.

"My parents are at the camp, too, but I go where Andy goes, no matter the consequences." He gave Andy's hand a squeeze, and shame filled her heart. She knew Bo was making up for leaving her alone the night of Micah's birthday. If they were caught, she needed to make sure Bo was not held responsible for any part of her plan.

"Well, she's one lucky lady, that's for sure." Micah gave Bo a heart melting smile. Andy looked away, feeling like she was intruding on a private moment. She fell back so Bo and Micah could walk together for a little while. Andy peered around at the surrounding woods and thought she saw a shadow moving between the trees parallel to her. She shook her head, blinking a few times, figuring she was imagining things. When she did a double take, the shadow was gone.

The rest of the way was uneventful, and Sera stopped them before they came into view of the camp.

"Okay, this is where we will wait for you. You have twenty minutes, and then we have to get back, or else they will definitely notice we're missing." Sera scanned the area to make sure no one roamed the woods between them and the camp. "There's a side entrance to the right, use that and you'll be less likely to be seen. There usually aren't any guards posted there during the day. Good luck."

Bo and Andy made their way to the side entrance. A tall, wooden fence surrounded the camp. It stood about twelve feet high. There was a gate straight ahead. Bo gripped Andy's hand as they crossed the threshold into the camp, but no alarm sounded, and no angels jumped out at them. They made it into the camp without being spotted.

Once inside, they made their way between the trailers, peeking inside the windows, trying to find either of their parents. After a few minutes, Andy was about to give up when she noticed Bo's parents sitting at a picnic table outside of what she assumed was their dining tent.

"Mom! Dad!" Bo ran to them, and they stood to embrace him.

"What are you doing here?" Eleanor asked, with a mix of concern and happiness on her face. Phillip's expression matched hers.

"We came to see you," Bo said, and they relaxed a little, glad to hear nothing was wrong. "Where is Wayne?"

"He's in our trailer. Come on, we'll bring you there." Eleanor hugged Bo one more time and led them to Wayne. They had been right, and he laid on the couch inside.

"Andy!" Wayne jumped up when they walked in and ran to hug Andy. "What are you doing here, it's not safe!" he exclaimed. She continued hugging him.

"I needed to see you and talk to you." She took a step back and noticed how haggard he appeared. "Are they taking care of you here?" He laughed, taking in the irony of her treating him as if he was the child. His laugh made her smile, she had not heard it in so long.

"Yes, yes. Everything is fine. What was it you needed to talk to me about?" He searched her face, inspecting for signs of any distress or mistreatment.

"I wanted to ask you what it was you were going to tell me before Septimus interrupted you, right before you left." It had been eating at her ever since.

"That's not important. It's better for now that you don't know anyway. But I did want to tell you something else…" Wayne paused flicking his eyes to Bo's family still standing in the entryway. "You and Bo need to stick together. Do not trust *anyone* else. The angels may mean well, but they also may hide things from you. I need you to make sure you keep looking out for yourself. Trust your instincts and if something feels wrong, it probably is. You're an angel which means you have a gift that allows you to know if someone is telling you the truth or not. Use that gift and trust your gut."

His eyes bored into Andy's, trying to convey how important that was.

"We'll stick together, but I also wanted to talk to you about my nightmares..." Andy began, but her dad cut her off.

"I'm sorry, kiddo, but you both need to go before someone finds you here. I'm sensing you came of your own accord and it's in all our best interests to keep you out of trouble." He kissed her on the forehead. "Stay safe, kiddo."

"But we just got here, can't we stay a few more minutes?" Andy pleaded, not ready to leave him yet. He shook his head. His eyes filled with sadness, and Andy knew he wished it could be different.

Bo and Andy said their goodbyes and hurried out of the trailer. Before they could get any farther, the nightmare inducing howl of a hellhound stopped them in their tracks. On instinct, Andy drew her sword from its sheath that she kept by her side since she'd started training.

"Go back in the trailer, Bo," Andy commanded.

"What do you mean? As if it's any safer in there," Bo argued.

"Fine. Just get behind me." She scanned every direction. People were coming out of all the trailers to see what the noise was. No one appeared nearly as scared as they should be. A hand came down on her shoulder, and she turned her head to see her dad. Bo's parents stood beside her as well.

"You need to get back to the angel camp," Wayne

spoke low and calm. Andy shook her head.

"I'm not leaving you here," Andy protested. A large crash rippled through the air as the front gate of the camp collapsed inward. Andy heard screams and people started running towards them as figures streamed in from the new hole in the fence.

∞

Ephram sat leaning back in his chair with his hands steepled in front of him and his eyes closed. He had sent Septimus to retrieve Lindy. He needed her to try and connect with the demons to find out their plans. They had attacked the Baltimore camp, but they had been otherwise dormant. Lindy would give them a chance to see inside the demons' minds.

Ephram opened his eyes as he heard the scuffling of feet and the rustle of the tent flap opening. Septimus approached with Lindy clinging to his hand. She appeared to be terrified, and Ephram empathized with her.

"Bring her here." Ephram waved them forward. He held out his hand to Lindy. After she took his hand, he gestured for her to sit in the chair across from him. She did as he wanted and glanced back at Septimus.

"She wanted Andromeda to be here with her, but I couldn't find her anywhere, Sir," Septimus said. Ephram cocked an eyebrow at him but did not respond. Ephram knew Andromeda was headstrong and he worried she would do something to get herself into trouble, but he couldn't think about that now.

"Is this going to hurt?" Fear was apparent in Lindy's voice, but Ephram could see she was trying to be strong. He felt a twinge of guilt, but knew he was doing what was best for his people.

"No, no. It won't hurt at all," he reassured her, and she seemed to relax a little. "Now close your eyes for me...good. I need you to think about the demon you saw when leaving your old home." Lindy shuddered, but she didn't open her eyes. "Focus on that image and think about connecting with him. You want to talk with him." Lindy started to shake.

"I... can see him." She sounded so vulnerable and scared; but Ephram powered on. "He's watching someone. Someone in a place like this. He's moving now...I-I see..." She stopped and her eyes flew open in terror "I can't watch anymore. Please don't make me watch anymore." She started crying. Ephram put his hands on her shoulders.

"You were very strong, Lindy. Thank you for your help. Septimus is going to bring you back to your brother now. Everything is going to be fine." Ephram knew it was wrong to promise her this, when in fact he was not sure if anything *would* be fine. He knew she needed the reassurance, though. Septimus walked to Lindy, and she took his hand again. Lindy looked at him, cocking her head to the side. She stopped crying.

"They're not happy with you at all." She spoke in a frighteningly calm voice, and in that moment, Ephram noticed her irises had turned black with no hint of her former bright blue innocence within. Lindy stood from her chair, no longer crying, or upset. Septimus and Ephram shared a look of apprehension before Septimus led Lindy out of the tent.

∞

Septimus brought Lindy back to her tent where her brother laid on his cot, headphones blaring. He barely acknowledged their arrival and turned away towards the side of the tent. Lindy bounced over to her cot and plopped onto it.

"Where's Andy?" she asked, still smiling.

"I don't know…" Septimus had hoped Andy would be back in her tent by now. Lindy laughed and threw her head back.

"Oh, don't you want to know?" Lindy's black eyes gleamed in the darkening tent. "Even if I tell you, you'll be too late." Lindy twirled her hair around a finger.

"What do you mean, you know where she is? Lindy, please, tell me." Septimus knew Lindy was not really herself at that moment. She was still connected with the demons. Her eyes held a blank gaze. He knew she was not going to be giving him any other information. He did know at least one group who would know where Andromeda was. He reached out in his mind towards Sera, Micah, and Gabby. He would reach out to Andromeda directly, but he knew she was still inexperienced with communicating on the angel network. He sensed their minds close by, but not as close as they should be.

He knew exactly where they were. *Of course.* He thought.

Sera, Micah, Gabby. Get back here now. He called out to them in his mind, and knew they could hear him, but did not get an immediate response. He decided to try to reach out to Andromeda.

Andromeda. He sensed her, but she did not respond either.

Septimus! Send help. Sera finally responded and Septimus jumped into action. First, he annoyed Ace by telling him to keep a close eye on Lindy. Once he left the tent, he realized everyone else was already on the move. Someone else must have reached out. Septimus followed the line of angels leaving the camp to protect the humans. All he could think about was Lindy's warning though, *you'll be too late...*

13

The Casualties

Andy and Sera stood side by side fighting a pair of demons. Andy could tell the demons aimed to harm, not kill, which confused her, but she couldn't let her guard down. Sera ran through the demon in front of her with her sword and he fell to the ground, dead. Andy gaped for a moment, leaving herself unguarded, and experienced a searing pain in her left arm as her attacker gained the advantage. Sera disarmed him in one swift motion, and he retreated towards the throng of people fighting.

"We have to get you out of here," Sera gasped. "They're here for you."

Andy squeezed her eyes shut, wiping the sweat from her brow. She had brought the demons straight to the camp. A hellhound had been tracking her, but she hadn't been thinking about that when they left the angel camp. Shame burned inside deep in her gut.

"I'm going to get the others. Help is coming, but we need to get you back to the other camp. Stay put, I'll be right back." Sera sprinted towards where they had seen Micah and Gabby disappear. Someone bumped into Andy from behind and she stumbled forward. She spun around with her sword held high, bracing herself for an attack. The first feature she saw was his black hair tied back into a bun, but when the demon lifted his head, she gasped.

"Cory." His name left her lips before her brain had time to catch up. She did not recognize him at first. When she knew him, he wore his hair shaved, but now it was shaggier, and he had more muscle than before. He gave her a devilish grin and it sent an unsettling chill down her spine.

"What a small world, Gorgeous." He took a step forward, but Bo ran up behind Andy, grabbing her arm.

"Time to go," he yelled over the commotion going on around them and pulled her along behind him. Andy glanced back once at Cory, but he was still right where she left him, staring after her with that same grin plastered on his face.

The others waited for Andy and Bo on the hill where they had originally parted what seemed like hours ago now. They all started to run as soon as Andy and Bo reached them.

Andy couldn't shake the feeling they were being watched as they ran. Every time she looked around, though, there was no one to be seen. A shiver ran up her spine, and she knew she was being paranoid, but she paused for a moment anyway. Everyone else kept on running, not noticing her fall behind.

"Hello?" Her voice came out as a whisper. She noticed the same shadow she saw earlier disappear behind a tree. "I know you're there. You may as well come out." She kept her voice calm and put some annoyance into it, so whoever was watching her didn't think she was afraid.

"Well, look what we have here...interesting to find you so far away from home, and so *alone*." Andy whipped around as a chilling voice spoke behind her. She figured he must be the demon who had killed Ace and Lindy's family.

A wicked grin spread across his face as he gazed at her, but the grin disappeared, and a scowl replaced it. He shook his head as if trying to clear it and gripped it between his hands. "Get. Out. Kaden," the man growled through gritted teeth. Before he could recover his senses, Andy made a run for it. After a few seconds she allowed herself to look back and saw the demon still struggling to free himself from whatever, or *whoever*, gripped his mind.

Gasping for air, Andy caught up to the others as they came into view of the camp. Bo turned to Andy and gave her a concerned look.

"You alright? I guess I didn't think we were going that fast..." He was referring to her panting.

"All good." She gave him a thumbs up, deciding not to

worry him any further by telling him about the strange encounter she'd had. They followed the others into the camp and noticed how empty it was. Everyone who had not gone to Baltimore, had gone to help defend the humans.

Andy clung to Bo as they stood in the middle of the deserted camp. "Did you see either of our parents before you left?" she asked him weakly.

"I was with them until help came and they sent me to find you and get out. Septimus told me he would bring us to them once it's safe," Bo told her, though he sounded a little off. Andy assumed it was because he was worried about their parents.

"So, what now?" Andy looked around at the rest of the group who seemed as if they were itching to get back to the action.

"We stay here and keep you safe," Sera said, though she sounded a bit disgruntled by the thought. "Ephram will want to see us as well." At that, the group seemed to deflate. They all knew they were in for a scolding. Andy hoped Ephram would not be too hard on the others since the whole scheme had been her idea.

"You're right, Sera. I do wish to speak with all of you." Ephram seemed to appear from the shadows, and they all jumped at his voice. "Please, come with me." They all remained silent as they followed him to his tent, and he gestured for them to sit in the chairs strewn about. Andy assumed they had been knocked over in the haste to get to the human camp once the attack had been revealed.

"Now, I know you're all thinking I'm upset with you for your thoughtless actions. However, this attack was inevitable. Lucifer wants Andy, so he would have sent his lackeys to attack eventually." Ephram laid it out for them. A tension in the air seemed to dissipate as everyone relaxed.

"*Lucifer* wants me?" Andy gasped. "But why? I thought it was just the demons who wanted me."

"I am unclear as to his motivations or intentions, but yes. That is why it is imperative you remain safely within our camp's boundaries." He didn't appear to be confident she was safe there.

"I'm sorry," Andy mumbled. "I should have never left."

"There is no need for apologies, Miss Andromeda. We cannot change what has already transpired. I do wish you all will make better choices moving forward, though, and that's all I can ask of you. That and picking up two extra days of chores each this week." His eyes glinted, and a smirk danced at his lips.

"I knew there would be a punishment in there somewhere," Micah groaned.

"Don't think of it as a punishment; think of it as helping out your fellow angels while they recover from their battles." Ephram folded his hands in his lap.

"Yes, Sir. Thank you, Sir." Sera seemed relieved. Andy knew Sera's reputation here meant a great deal to her. Guilt gnawed at Andy for dragging Sera, and the others, into her mess. The group of them stood to leave.

"Andy, if you'd stay a moment, please," Ephram beckoned her to his side while the others left. "There is something else you should know. I brought Lindy in to see if she could help us by connecting with the demons. She did well, at first. But now, she has me worried." Andy's blood began to boil.

"You…Is that why you didn't come down hard on us?" She threw her hands in the air. "You knew you had done something horrible too! How dare you *use* Lindy like a pawn!"

"Do not think I made the decision to use her connection with the demons lightly. I am going to ask that you keep hold of your temper with me, Miss Andromeda, for I have a bit more experience with leadership and life." Ephram kept his tone neutral, but Andy could tell he was upset by the darkening of his eyes.

Andy bit her tongue, but she couldn't stop the anger from swelling inside of her. She turned on her heel and fled from the tent.

Andy made her way back to her tent. Lindy was fast asleep on her cot while Ace listened to his music. He took his headphones off when he saw Andy come in.

"Is she alright?" Andy whispered. He nodded, stood from his cot, and beckoned for her to follow him out of the tent.

"I'm sorry, I should have gone with her when

Septimus told me what they were doing." The guilt was plainly written on his face. "She was definitely acting strange when she came back, but she's been sleeping ever since."

"It probably wore her out, connecting with them. We'll have to keep a close eye on her," Andy said. "Why don't you take a break, go get some food. I'll watch her for a little while. And, if you see Bo wandering around, let him know what's going on with Lindy." Andy hadn't seen Bo after she left Ephram's tent and she wondered where he had disappeared to. Probably somewhere with Micah.

∞

Bo sat with his head in his hands on the log in the woods. His breath came in ragged gasps. Every time he closed his eyes, he could see them... his parents.

After Andy had run off to help Sera, Bo and their parents were approached by a demon that appeared less human than the others. He hunched over as he walked, and he had lost most of his hair, though he still didn't look older than twenty-five. His eyes were pale and more of a faded gray color.

Wayne stepped forward with his pistol, but the demon cackled. It was a horrible sound, like nails on a chalkboard. Two more demons stepped out from behind a nearby tent and seized Wayne, causing him to drop his weapon. They hauled him away.

Bo noticed a few angels coming toward them and

figured these must be the reinforcements. He breathed a sigh of relief. He took a step back and as he did, the demon still standing before them, lunged forward with a sword he had pulled out of nowhere and slammed it through Phillip's chest. Eleanor screamed. The angels started to run towards them, but the demon was fast, and he lunged for Bo next. Eleanor threw herself in front of him. Bo closed his eyes, but he heard the thump of the sword striking home in his mother. It was followed by another thump, and Bo opened his eyes to see the demon's head rolling past Septimus.

Bo doubled over and threw up. He could not believe what had happened. It didn't seem real; it couldn't be real. His parents lay lifeless on the ground beside him, surrounded in pools of their own blood. Still Bo thought they *must* be alive, they *had* to be okay. Septimus dropped down beside them and checked each of their pulses. His father was dead, his mother hanging on by a thread. Bo threw himself to the ground to hold her hand as she opened her eyes enough to see her pupils.

"We love you," she rasped as her eyes closed again, and she let out her last breath.

"Bo, I am so sorry," Septimus said, but a roaring echoed in Bo's ears. How could he go on? How could he survive without them? "Bo, listen to me." Septimus had been talking the whole time, but Bo had not heard a word he'd said. "Bo, I will take care of them. I promise you. I will bury them in a nice place and bring you to them when it's safe. Right now, I need you to find Andy and get her out of here. Can you do that?" He gripped Bo's shoulders, holding him upright, otherwise Bo thought he might fall into oblivion. Bo nodded his head in a daze. Septimus helped him to his feet.

"You can do this," he reassured Bo, who felt nauseous, and let go of him. For a moment, Bo felt like he was floating, as if he could drift away, but he heard shouting and swords clanging. It brought him back down to Earth, and he knew what he needed to do.

Bo wiped his mother's blood from his hands and ran to find Andy. When he found her, she stood stock still, as if she had seen a ghost. Before her was an attractive young man, Bo assumed a demon, but neither of them made a move towards the other. Bo didn't hesitate as he grabbed Andy's arm and led her away. If either of them had said anything, Bo didn't remember, he had been working on autopilot.

In the woods behind the angel camp, Bo relived the horror of watching his parents die. He had lied to Andy and told her they were fine. He didn't want her to hear that her dad had been taken and go running back to endanger herself to save him. And Bo hadn't been able to tell her about his parents. He was still processing it all himself.

"Bo?" Bo stiffened as he heard Micah's voice. He didn't want anyone to see him like this, and he didn't want to explain what was going on.

"I can't," Bo managed to get out, and even that was shaky.

"Okay. Is it alright if I sit here?" Micah asked, and Bo nodded. Micah sat beside him, and Bo peeked over to see him staring up at the sky. It made his heart twinge a little, lightening his mood ever so slightly.

They sat there together in silence for a long time. Bo let himself grieve while Micah waited until Bo was ready to talk, or not talk.

Memories of his childhood swirled around in his head: his parents were always there for every football game, or concert when he had to play clarinet in the middle school band. They had accepted him and loved him when he had come out as gay. They never faltered. He could never have made it this far without them. Now, they were gone. He would never see either of them again; never have the pleasure of introducing them to a boyfriend or be able to tell them about his day. There would never come a day he wouldn't want to talk to them, as he wanted to reach out to them in that moment for comfort.

After about an hour, Bo finally lifted his head, his legs numb from sitting in the same position for far too long. They could hear people moving around in the camp. The attack must have ended once Andy left, since that's who the demons were after.

"I know you can communicate with the others in your mind." Bo's voice was hoarse and came out much softer than he had expected. "Are they talking about how the attack ended?" He wanted to know how the rest of the humans fared.

"Yes." Micah seemed to be gauging how Bo would react to whatever he was about to tell him. There was nothing worse Micah could tell him than what he already knew and what he'd already seen. "It was bad. Many of the humans were killed before reinforcements arrived. They were unprepared. But, of the thirty who were living there, thirteen survived and will be joining our camp until transportation arrives to take them to a safer place." *Thirteen. Thirteen... More than half slaughtered by those...monsters.*

"How many of *them* were killed?" Bo asked. Micah gave him a questioning look. "The demons," he clarified with a grimace.

"Oh, well once reinforcements showed up and Andy disappeared, they scattered. About 10 were killed before that though," Micah explained, and Bo scowled. He had been hoping there would have been at least as many demons killed as humans. It wouldn't have changed anything, but it would have made him feel a little better.

"My parents..." Bo tried but the word's died in his throat. Micah took his hand.

"I know," he said, and Bo was thankful he didn't have to say anymore.

"I need to tell Andy." Bo gulped, he knew it was going to be difficult, she would be upset he had lied to her.

"I can tell her for you, if you want," Micah offered but Bo shook his head.

"No, I should. Thank you." Bo stood from the log, his legs shaking, and turned back to Micah. "I don't think I can do this," he blurted out. Micah was quick to stand and wrap Bo in his arms.

"You don't have to; I can tell her," Micah offered again.

"No, not that," Bo blubbered. He sniffled and tried to contain himself. "I d-don't think I c-can live without my p-parents." He forced the words out, unsure whether Micah could even understand him through his sobs.

"You can, and you will. Andy, Sera, Gabby, Nathan, and I will be here for you every day, and eventually it will hurt a little less. Don't be afraid to ask for help." Micah pulled away. He wiped the tears from Bo's cheeks. Bo calmed down a little, and his breathing started to return to normal.

∞

Andy sat on her cot for a while trying to clear her mind. There were so many questions she needed to figure out, but her thoughts were all too jumbled to make heads or tails of anything. What on Earth was Cory doing in that camp? How was she going to keep Lindy safe? Why did the demons want her?

All these questions kept nagging at Andy, but she pushed them away. She preferred to pretend she was back at home, safe with both of her parents and her brother. Angels and demons didn't exist. But that only lasted a moment before Lindy woke up.

"Ace?" Lindy's voice was still groggy from sleep. Andy hurried to her side.

"He went to get some food, but I'm here, Lindy." Andy tried to put a smile on for Lindy, but it was hard. Ace walked into the tent and stopped when he noticed Lindy was awake, grinning broadly.

"The demons are talking to me. They know me now. They let me see because they wanted the others to know," she said, still smiling.

"What do you mean?" Andy asked as Ace knelt beside her in front of Lindy's cot. He took Lindy's hands in his own and squeezed them, but Lindy stared at Andy.

"They want *us*, Andy. We belong with them. That's why they're here." Andy could tell Lindy believed it to be true, which scared her.

"They're messing with your head, Lindy. Don't listen to them. Close your mind to them," Andy pleaded with her. "Don't let them take you from us."

"It's too late. They're already on their way." Lindy looked a little sad as she turned to Ace. "You can't come, Ace." She laid down and rolled away from them to face the side of the tent. She fell asleep again within moments. The whole ordeal today had left her exhausted. Andy remembered how drained *she* had been after she first connected with the angels.

"You can't let them take her, Andy." Ace was panic-stricken.

"I know. I have to talk to Septimus. He might know

what to do. He's one of the people who caused all of this, and he owes her. Keep a close eye on her until I get back." Andy stood and hurried out of the tent, leaving Ace to watch over his sister. Andy stopped as she saw Bo coming towards her. She ran to him and hugged him.

"Thank goodness you're here," Andy mumbled against his shoulder. "Lindy is all out of whack, and I need you." She pulled away to see a stony expression on Bo's face. Bags had formed under his eyes and for the first time in a long time, no smile graced his face when his eyes met hers. "What's wrong?"

"I have to tell you something. I lied to you earlier," Bo began, and his face crumbled. Tears welled in his eyes. "Our parents, they're not okay. I lied to keep you here, to keep you safe."

"W-what do you mean? My dad?" A knot the size of a cantaloupe formed in Andy's stomach, pushing all her organs aside, making room for a space to shove more grief deep down into to lock away.

"He's alive, but he was taken by the demons. But my parents..." Bo could not finish. He broke down and sobbed against Andy's shoulder. She held him while he cried and led him into the tent. Ace didn't say anything, opting to respect their privacy. Bo and Andy sat on Bo's cot.

"I'm so sorry, Bo. I led the demons there," Andy admitted, knowing he would probably never forgive her for the part she played in his parents' deaths.

"*We* led them there, Andy." He sniffled, and she could tell he was trying to pull himself together. "You're not the only one to blame. We all went with you willingly." He pulled away from her, tears streaked his face, but he had a look of determination. "I won't let you blame yourself. We never could have known this was going to happen."

"You are more of an angel than I will ever be." Andy wiped the tears from his face. "I will never forgive myself for what happened…but there is something else I need to tell you." She could tell he was still being torn apart on the inside, but he needed to know more about Lindy. Andy glanced over at Lindy, still sleeping on her cot, and lowered her voice. "They made Lindy connect with the demons…and it changed her."

"What do you mean, changed her?" Bo matched her volume. Andy could hear the uneasiness in his voice, under the lingering sorrow.

"The demons were able to get inside her head and she isn't the same now. I can't protect her anymore." A lump caused Andy's throat to ache, but it was not the time to cry, she had to stay strong for Bo and Lindy. "I'm scared she's going to choose to go with the demons and we won't be able to keep her from them." Andy hoped Ace could not hear them through his headphones.

"We won't let them take her too." Bo shook his head, but doubt flitted across his face.

"They want me, too, Bo. They have my dad now, and

they'll want to make a trade," Andy added.

"Well, that won't be happening," Bo said.

"I can't let them kill my dad." Andy tried to reason with Bo.

"If you give yourself up, my parents will have died for nothing. If you give yourself up, that's something I will never forgive you for." Bo was serious, and Andy knew he was right.

"I have to go find Septimus and talk to him about Lindy. Are you alright?" As soon as the words left her mouth, Andy realized how stupid of a question it was. But he nodded and gave her his best smile despite the pain it most likely caused him. Andy wouldn't have even considered leaving him if it wasn't important.

"I'll be okay. Just, don't be hard on him." Bo nudged Andy and she cocked an eyebrow at him, not sure what he was talking about. "Septimus, I mean. Don't give him a hard time about Lindy. It was his father's decision to use her against the demons." Bo gave Andy a knowing look.

"I'll do my best," Andy lied. She knew she had a quick temper and Septimus was about to receive the brunt of it.

Andy left Bo behind and noticed most everyone was in the dining tent. She assumed they were replenishing their energy from the fight earlier. Watching them all eating made her realize how hungry she was. As she gazed longingly at the food, she sensed someone watching her. She turned and saw Septimus coming towards her.

"What have you done…" he said, pulling her to the

side, into his tent.

"I was coming to ask you the same thing." A fire burned in Andy's veins as the anger surged through her. Anger about Lindy, but also anger over losing her father and Bo's parents.

"You *knew* you had a hellhound following you. You told me about it the first night you were here. Yet, you endangered an entire camp filled with helpless humans." Septimus wasn't yelling at her, but Andy could feel heat coming off him in waves. He used the same calm tone that Ephram had used with her earlier. *Like father, like son,* she thought, internally rolling her eyes.

"I had to see my dad," she stated. Her heart raced as she imagined what was happening to her dad at that moment. The guilt of putting all those people in danger began to set in and weigh her down. She had heard someone mention only thirteen people had survived out of thirty. That was seventeen deaths on her hands. It was almost too much to bear. A crushing feeling built up in Andy's chest.

"You doomed an entire camp full of people for your own selfish needs," Septimus spat out. "Our illusions did nothing to stop the demons from tearing that camp apart. The attack in Baltimore was a distraction so our forces would be weakened. The angels who were posted at the human camp...the demons killed all of them." Hurt clouded his eyes, and Andy knew some of those angels had been his friends. The knife of guilt twisted a little deeper into her gut. "The demons took your dad as a bargaining chip. They want to make a trade."

"They want me." Andy already knew this. "So, bring me to them. I won't let anyone else die because of me. I made a mistake, and I can't undo it. Let me make up for it by giving myself up," she pleaded with him, but he scoffed.

"We can't give them what they want." Septimus talked to her as if she was a child, which reignited her anger.

"Lindy told me the demons are coming for us. For her, and for me. Letting her connect with them was the worst possible thing you could have done to her, short of throwing her to the demons. It changed her." It was Andy's turn to be the bearer of bad news. She needed to push off some of her guilt and anger on someone, and Septimus had the misfortune of being the only one around. "That is *your* fault. You and Ephram, you took away whatever shred of goodness was left inside of her." She shoved him backwards, and he stumbled, though only slightly, but it was the burn marks she left on his shirt that shocked them both. Andy blinked and stared down at her hands, which seemed to be *glowing*.

"It's the heavenly fire..." Septimus murmured. "You need to calm down."

Andy scoffed. "You expect me to calm down? Everything is falling apart! And whatever you had Lindy do has *broken* her!" Andy clenched her fists at her sides to try to contain the fire burning there.

"We realize that now. We should have never let her

connect with them. She is too young to have been able to make sure they weren't looking back in, they took advantage of her youth and messed with her psyche." Andy could tell he was feeling regret, but it did nothing to calm her anger now.

"It's your responsibility to keep her safe now," Andy snapped. She went to walk out of the tent, but Septimus blocked her.

"You can't give them what they want. I won't let you." He crossed his arms to make himself appear more impenetrable, Andy assumed, making her laugh.

"You won't *let* me? Is that because you actually care about my wellbeing, or because it would make Daddy mad?" She matched his stance, not budging either. Septimus didn't answer right away, so she kept going. "I've already lost everyone else I love; I won't let them take my dad away from me too." Septimus looked a little guilty, which did not make Andy feel any better.

"I'm sorry, Andy." He finally came down from his high horse. "I arrived a moment too late…I could have saved him and Bo's parents." Andy realized he was holding almost as much guilt as she was inside. "I'm sorry I yelled at you. Malachi told me you asked him if you could see your father. I should have known you would go anyway, and he should have told you why you couldn't. Maybe you would have seen why it was so important for you to remain here." Andy was surprised he was trying to take some of the responsibility away from her, not that it made her feel any better.

"I went to see my dad because I hoped he could help me understand why the demons want me. But all he told me was to trust my instincts and to stay safe." She left out the part about not trusting anyone, because she knew that *anyone* included Septimus.

"I don't know why the demons want you, but I will do everything I can to make sure they never take you." Concern filled his eyes, which surprised Andy because she was beginning to think she was just another responsibility for him. He reached under his cot. "Here, you left this the other night." He held out Andy's jacket and she took it. She had forgotten all about it, assuming it was lost in the woods somewhere.

"Thanks," she managed to say. "I don't think I ever thanked you for saving me that night, so, thank you for that too." A blush creeped up her neck.

"It was nothing," he replied, playing with his ring.

"The demons would have taken me if it weren't for you, so it isn't nothing to me. I'm sorry I make your job so hard...keeping me alive and all." Andy tried for a smirk, but it felt more like a grimace.

"Don't worry about it, really. If you ever need me and I'm not around, give a shout." He pointed to his head, indicating the angel network, making Andy smile. She left and bumped into Gabby on her way back to the dining tent.

"Everything good?" Gabby asked. Andy assumed her expression was one of exhaustion and defeat.

"For now," Andy said. "I need some food."

Gabby laughed. "Come on." She took Andy by the hand and led her to a table where Micah, Sera, and Bo already sat. Bo looked as if he was still in the thick of his grief, but the fact that he was out and about made Andy proud of him.

"We received an update on the Baltimore attack. They were able to defeat the demons with only one casualty on our side. The fight was over when our guard arrived, so they're on their way back now." Gabby informed Andy.

People in the camp were starting to relax since they knew the demons had not entirely won the day. Though the loss had been great, most of the angels had no attachments to the people in the human camp as Bo and Andy did.

"Why didn't you go with the guard?" Andy asked Gabby.

"Nathan and I aren't allowed on the same guards," she said matter-of-factly. Andy furrowed her brows.

"Why not?"

"It would be a liability," Sera said, speaking for Gabby as Gabby had just taken a bite of her steak. "If one got hurt, then the other would be distracted."

"Seems silly," Andy muttered but dropped the subject.

After dinner, everyone dispersed. Bo headed back to the tent to rest, and Andy walked towards the path to the woods. She paused, thinking about how she had felt so safe there before, but now it seemed eerie and filled with monsters. She thought she saw a shadow moving among the trees. Her mind flashed back to the demon who had approached her in the woods. What if he was out there…watching?

14

The Origin Story

Ephram sat alone at his desk. A stabbing pain pulsed between his eyes. Everything that had happened today could have been avoided. If only Malachi had informed Ephram of Andromeda's queries about visiting her father, Ephram could have talked her out of it. Or, Malachi could have explained why it was out of the question. The hellhounds would find her too easily; and they had.

Now, Ephram had added to the misfortunes of the day by convincing Lindy to communicate with the demons. He knew the risk of them sensing her and using her as their own tool. He thought the risk had been worth gaining useful information, but he had been wrong. It was all too little too late. The demons had already infiltrated the human camp and

Lindy had to watch as they made their first kill, because *he* had made the call to use her. What would Amelia think of him now?

He couldn't think like that. If he did, he would spiral down into a pit of self-loathing. Ephram had been down that road many times before in his long stay on Earth. It was not an easy place to claw himself back out of, but he had done it, time and time again.

Ephram had more pressing issues. First and foremost was the guard he had sent to Baltimore. He was waiting on Septimus to report to him about the mission. Ephram stayed off the angel network as much as possible to be sure that no one, not even his own people, could see any of his thoughts. When communicating on the network, it was easy to let one's walls down and let others see more than should be revealed. Ephram had others report to him what was being said on the network.

Another pressing issue was that of Septimus and his interest with Andromeda. Ephram had seen it in his eyes the moment she appeared that first day. She was something special, unlike any angel Septimus had ever known, much like her mother. Ephram understood why Septimus was so taken with her from that moment. However, Ephram worried Septimus would lose his focus, and become vulnerable. Ephram could not, and would not, lose his last living son.

As for Jeremiah's order to keep Andromeda from Lucifer's clutches at all costs, Ephram was beginning to wonder what he may have to risk in keeping her safe. The demons were trying their damned hardest to get their hands on her, and he wasn't sure how much longer they could hold out. The demons seemed to be able to get to her even inside the camp. They had taken her father as a bargaining chip, and Ephram worried she may give herself up to them. Would the dominions blame him if she *chose* to leave? He certainly would not *force* her to stay.

"Father..." Septimus said, and Ephram was startled to find his son standing before him. Ephram had been so wrapped up in his thoughts he hadn't seen him enter the tent.

"Yes?" Ephram glanced up.

"I talked with Andromeda, and she has decided not to give herself up to the demons," Septimus told him, and Ephram sighed in relief. One less problem to worry about.

"And what of Lindy?"

"She's sleeping now. I will check on her again in the morning," Septimus said. Ephram could see Septimus was upset; his eyes were much darker than usual.

"Tell me what's bothering you." Ephram knew it could be one of so many things, but he wanted to try to help his son with whatever was eating at him.

"It's Andromeda, and Bo, and everything..." Septimus trailed off. Ephram thought about Bo's parents in that camp. He had sent them away from here, not allowing them to stay with their son, and they ended up being slaughtered by the demons. Ephram closed his eyes and took a deep breath. He could not let it get to him. Many other humans in that camp had also lost their lives, and he could not have predicted the demons' plans.

"You feel the guilt as well." Ephram placed his hand over his son's. "It will fade. You will soon find not everyone can be saved, and you cannot be everywhere at once."

"The word is spreading that the guard that went to the Baltimore camp fared well and are on their way back. The demons fled, and there were limited casualties." Septimus changed the subject.

"Good. That is good. Thank you, Septimus." The pounding in Ephram's head grew. "Now, I need some time alone, if you do not mind." Septimus nodded and left the tent. Ephram closed his eyes and rubbed his temples trying to ease the strain pulsing there. It was not common for angels to suffer human afflictions such as headaches, but it was the dominions way of keeping rulers in check. By subjecting the rulers to these afflictions, it reminded them of their main purpose on Earth: to try to ease the suffering of humans. Ephram did not resent headaches; they did their job. His trivial concerns in the moment would pass, as his headache would.

He could hear people walking around outside his tent, no one daring to enter. If he opened the flap of the tent, it signaled he was taking visitors. He decided to wait until his headache subsided. There was some chatter outside, but he ignored it all. Instead, he went to his cot at the back, hidden from view by a room divider. Lying down, he dozed off as soon as his head hit the pillow.

As usual, Amelia filled his dreams, weaving in and out, leaving an impression on each one. Her smile, her laugh, the light shining in her eyes, and her hair whipping in the wind all stuck with him.

"It will all work out in the end, Ephram. Do not worry." Her voice was the last thing he remembered before he woke and was forced back into the turmoil of the camp.

∞

The day after the attacks, Malachi approached Andy expecting her to train as she left the dining tent with a plate of food for Bo.

"I don't feel up for training today..." she told him, hoping to spend the day with Bo. She knew Malachi wouldn't like her answer, but she figured it was better to be honest, rather than be unfocused during training.

"If you don't want to be trained to be able to defend yourself against the demons practically beating down our doors to get to you, that is your choice. You will either train when I want you to train, or we will not train at all." Andy wondered what had happened in Malachi's life to turn him so cold. She thought maybe he had some demon blood in him, but his eyes were too golden to be demon eyes, and she didn't even know if someone could be both angel *and* demon.

"Fine, I won't train with you then." She was too stubborn to allow him to control her life, even if it meant giving up her training sessions. Malachi scoffed at her response and turned on his heel, walking back the way he had come. She could hear him mumbling something about her selfishness. Andy ignored him and continued back to her tent to bring Bo his food. After she dropped it off, she decided to give him some time alone, and took a walk out into the woods. The fallen log was as welcoming as ever as she approached it and took a seat. She stretched out her legs and leaned back to let the sun filtering through the trees warm her face.

"How is Bo doing?" Andy opened her eyes to find Septimus leaning against a nearby tree. She wondered if he had been there the whole time and she hadn't noticed.

"Not great, but that's to be expected." Andy sighed. "I wish I could do more to help him."

"Give it some time. This is not something he's going to bounce back from easily." Andy remembered Septimus had also lost his mother, as she had.

"I know. It still hurts to this day," she said, gulping past the lump in her throat.

"How are *you* doing?" he asked, and Andy tried to give him a small smile.

"Holding in there. Of course, I lost my privileges when it comes to training with Malachi." She feigned disappointment. "Why does he hate me so much?"

"He doesn't hate you, and I'm sure he will train you again," Septimus said with little confidence.

"How am I supposed to defend myself if another

demon approaches me? I can't light-ball them away." Andy laughed, and Septimus joined her.

"I can help you. Meet me in the clearing tomorrow, I will train you until Malachi decides to give you a second chance," he offered.

"Really? That would be great." Andy stood off the log and took a step towards Septimus. He stared into the trees and cleared his throat.

"I should be going. My father needs my help reorganizing the guards." He side-stepped out of Andy's path and headed back into camp.

After another day of regrouping and grieving, things seemed to return to normal and the demons went back to wherever they had been hiding out before the attacks. Andy knew better than to think the demons would leave them alone for a little while. They would be back, and soon. They still wanted her and Lindy, and they would be furious when they found out they were getting neither of them.

Bo and Andy sat alone at breakfast. The day was hot, but not unbearable. It was the first time Bo had left the tent in two days. Neither of them wanted to talk to anyone, so when they saw their friends, they walked to the other side of the tent to take a seat. Nobody bothered them, understanding their need to be separate.

Andy and Bo knew everyone else would be talking about the attack on the camp in Baltimore, and neither of them had the resolve to listen and pretend to care about that considering what had happened during the *other* attack. Andy was shocked Bo was even functioning today. She knew if the situation were reversed, she would still be sulking in bed for at least another week. But, somehow, he was in better spirits. They didn't talk, preferring the silence over pointless words. The chatter around them sounded like white noise.

"I have to go train with Septimus." Andy told Bo once they finished eating.

"Oh really?" He cocked an eyebrow at her, smirking. "Training for what exactly?"

"Oh stop." Andy laughed. "He's helping me because Malachi is a jerk who refuses to."

"Well, have fun and I want to hear all about it when you get back!" Bo winked at her as she stood to leave. Andy waved as she left the tent and made her way to the clearing. It was nice to be training outside again, rather than in that stuffy tent with Malachi. Septimus was waiting for Andy when she arrived at the clearing. He gave her a small wave that she returned with a smile.

"I talked with Malachi, and he caught me up on what you two were working on together. I think today I'm going to go over all the abilities you have, and what we are up against when it comes to the demons. It is important for you to know both sides." Septimus paused, and Andy made eye contact with him to let him know she was paying attention.

"Malachi told me he informed you about the weapons

we use, being blessed with holy water," Septimus started.

"And it takes a weapon forged in hellfire to kill an angel," Andy finished for him.

"We also have the heavenly fire that can be used against demons. Using it is a similar process to when you create your ball of light. We will practice that later. Demons can use hellfire against us, and as we can create light, they can destroy it by absorbing it. You will notice that demons can move a little faster than us, but that is because we are a little more weighed down." He caught her eye and smirked. "I don't suppose you've seen any of the other angels flying yet?" Andy gaped at him and shook her head. For some reason she had not even thought about whether angels would have wings or not.

"That would explain a lot. I was wondering how they got to Baltimore and back so quickly, but I was too distracted to think about asking." Andy searched his back as he continued talking, thinking she might be able to see where his wings would be... but there was nothing.

"God wanted us to be able to blend in with humans, so our wings are concealed by a kind of... magic, I guess is a good way to put it. It's like our illusion that hides our camp, our wings are hidden from sight by the same magic," he explained. Andy was still trying to see his wings, though. He walked further away, out into the clearing. He took a deep breath and arched his back a little, and out of nowhere, wings unfurled from beneath his shoulder blades. They spanned about five feet across, and stretched about three feet above his head, and down to just above the ground. They were white, feathery, and glorious. The edges of his wings appeared to be dipped in gold.

"Amazing," Andy murmured, admiring them, and fighting back the urge to reach out and touch them. "But, how...I feel like you shouldn't be wearing a shirt." She blushed and rushed to explain herself. "I mean, it seems like your wings would rip through any clothing."

"It's all a part of the magic. We can't have angels running around half naked all the time, it might give us away." He joked with her, and she blushed again, thinking about him half naked.

"How have I not known about this?" Andy turned her head to try to glimpse her own back, thinking if she had wings, she would know it by now.

"It is possible that because your father is human, you may not get wings," Septimus said.

"Oh..." Andy tried to keep the disappointment out of her voice, but she had been so excited to *fly*.

"Angels do not usually receive their wings until their sixteenth or seventeenth year, so it is possible you are a little behind," Septimus said. Andy appreciated his attempt to try to make her feel better.

"I'm turning nineteen soon, I think. I honestly have no idea what today is." If he was right, she could be getting her wings any day now. She wondered what it would be like, if she did receive her wings, and whether it would hurt.

"Yeah, you're not too far behind. I received mine when I was fifteen, so I was a little ahead of the curve." *Of course he was*, Andy thought.

"How old are you now?" Andy took advantage of the perfect opportunity to find out something about him.

"I just turned twenty-one actually. I don't celebrate birthdays, though. Enough about me, we need to focus." He began to pull in his wings, and they folded back in on themselves until they were no longer visible. "Do you have any more questions about the wings?"

"Not about wings, but I do have a question. How did this war even start?" Andy was ready to start pulling her weight, fighting alongside the angels, but she needed to know what it was she was fighting for.

"Depending on who you ask, the answer will be different, but the common thread that ties them all together is that the demons became greedy," Septimus said. "In the beginning, angels were the only ones who walked the Earth alongside humans. We were sent here to protect humans from themselves, but we can only do so much. A suggestion, or a finger pointing you in the right direction. We were not even allowed to be in a relationship with a human." Andy narrowed her eyes at that but said nothing as Septimus continued.

"What humans choose to do with the information we give them is out of our hands. They have free will. As time went on, though, some of the angels began to question their purpose. They wanted to know why humans were so important that we needed to protect them. They were jealous, they wanted to find love and happiness for themselves, and they did not want to be guides anymore. Those angels fell from grace. They were not the first, though." At that, Andy knew what was coming next.

"You know of Lucifer, I'm sure." Andy nodded. *Who doesn't*, she thought, but remained an avid listener and Septimus went on. "Well, he heard of these angels falling from grace and he decided to recruit them for his own purposes. They could come and go from Hell freely, living among the humans as they had before, but with no rules, and no consequences, as long as they did something for him in return. He needed them to collect souls for him. He couldn't leave hell himself, having been imprisoned there after he was cast out of heaven. The fallen angels agreed and began their work. They were the first demons." Septimus paused to take a breath and Andy pursed her lips as she thought about the monster that had been created.

"Now, angels had a new task. They not only had to try to keep humans from harming each other, but they also had to protect them from the demons trying to collect their souls. So, truthfully the war began then, however, it was kept at bay for many centuries. The demons were able to collect enough souls, even with the angels trying to stop them, to keep Lucifer appeased, and they were happy to be living human-like lives on the side."

"But why does Lucifer need to collect people's souls?" Andy interrupted.

"Well, when they were first created, all humans went to heaven. Hell was only meant to be a prison for Lucifer and the other angels who fell with him. However, once people began turning away from God and committing sins, they started being sent to Hell. Lucifer was the one who was supposed to be a kind of warden to make sure justice was served to those who had joined him in his prison. In return for doing this service, God had agreed to set Lucifer free for one day every hundred years. It probably doesn't seem like a lot to you, but for an immortal like Lucifer, trapped for eternity in Hell, it was everything." He was right, it didn't seem like a lot to her, but even she could agree that one day of freedom every hundred years was better than nothing.

"Lucifer had held up his end of the deal, but after spending so much time torturing other people, you can imagine the effects it had on his psyche. After Lucifer's first day of freedom, God revoked his privileges."

"What did he do that was so horrible?" Andy asked, curious how he could have lost his privileges after one day.

"Well, that was the day he learned he could control people if they signed over their souls to him. So, he used people to torture other people. As you can imagine, this did not go over well with God. He sent Lucifer right back to his prison and he's been there ever since." Septimus paused, and

Andy took the opportunity to cut in again.

"So, Lucifer doesn't serve justice to those in Hell anymore?" she asked.

"Oh, no, he still does that, but just for fun now. He is always wanting for more souls, though, so he has more people to torture. It's as I said, greed led to this war we are fighting now."

"The angels had started to take over more territory, covering more areas and saving more souls. Lucifer became angry and started demanding even *more* souls. This way he could have more recruits to help him win back some of the territory the angels had taken. More souls, to build more armies, to recruit more souls... and on and on. We underestimated the number of humans who were suffering so greatly they were willing to turn themselves and their souls over to the devil. Suddenly, we were outnumbered, and so the war began."

"Wow." Andy let out a huff of air. It was a lot to take in all at once. "So, to be clear, demons are fallen angels who wanted to be cut a little slack; to have more freedom of their own and live more like humans?" It was hard to believe such a small desire could have such dire consequences.

"It's not that simple." Septimus shook his head. "Most demons, now, are people who have given themselves, body and soul, over to Lucifer. There are many who remain from the initial fall, and some who are born demons, which I will explain. But also, not all fallen angels choose to become demons." Septimus seemed a little defensive now.

"But the original demons, they still have their souls?" Andy thought about whether it made a difference if demons had their souls or not, they were all still doing despicable things.

"Again, it's not that simple. You could technically say all demons still have their souls; Lucifer simply owns most of them. Those who have given their souls to him must do *everything* he asks of them," Septimus explained, but Andy remained slightly confused, her face pinched as she tried to consider Septimus' explanation.

"If demons still have their souls, shouldn't they seem less...soulless?" she asked.

"The people who demons target for their souls already have a darkness inside of them, some greater than others. Lucifer pulls out their darkest desires and magnifies them, turning them out onto the world to commit atrocities and find him more darkened souls," Septimus explained, and Andy nodded as if she was understanding all of this.

"If someone is born a demon, though, like Lindy..." Her heart hurt thinking about Lindy.

"It is uncommon for someone to be *born* a demon, or an angel really. All angels and demons can procreate with humans; however, their offspring will be born human. They tend to develop special gifts as they grow up. These people would be known to you as mediums, psychics, empaths, and the like. As with any human, though, none of them are inherently good or bad." Andy gaped at Septimus. It made so much sense.

"Would Lindy be put into that category?" Andy asked.

"No. Lindy was born a demon. You see, God gifted our principalities, or rulers, who are the higher ups of the angels who live on the Earth, the ability to bear children that would become angels. This was to ensure that angels were never outnumbered by the demons." Andy realized her mom must have been a ruler to have had her and Jason with their dad.

Septimus continued. "It is a lot harder for demons to bear a child who is born demon. The only demons who can do this are demons who were either once rulers, or the children of rulers, who fell from grace and chose to side with Lucifer. It happens *very* infrequently," Septimus tried to explain. "That was how Lindy was born, though. Her mother was once a ruler, and she fell from grace. We have not had a lot of experience dealing with people who are *born* demons, because it is uncommon. So, we were unsure how connecting with the demons would affect Lindy. Clearly, we misjudged the situation, and it cost us dearly."

"You didn't know." Andy held no anger anymore for the part Septimus played in Lindy being taken over by the demons. They all could have done better for her. "Why hasn't Jeremiah or whoever else is up there, stepped in to help us?"

"Angels and Guardian Angels are the only ones of our kind who can walk among humans on Earth. There are different orders of celestial beings. At the top are the seraphim, the cherubim, and the thrones, then there are the dominions, powers and virtues. Jeremiah is among the dominions. They are the ones who send down the orders to the different rulers, like my father. The rulers guide and protect the rest of us angels. We are like the foot soldiers, carrying out our orders and keeping the inhabitants of the Earth safe. The Guardian Angels are the ones who protect specific individuals, but that's a whole other topic. You only need to worry about the basic angel side of things for now," Septimus finished and took a deep breath. "I think we should take a break for the day; this is all a lot to digest," he declared. "Tonight, I want you to practice creating your light on your own, and tomorrow we will work on you using the heavenly fire."

15

The Bracelet

On her way back to her tent, Andy ran into Bo, who was returning from hanging out with Micah. Andy wanted to ask him how that went, but she wanted to check on Lindy first.

They had left her sleeping in the tent that morning. Ace had moved his cot closer to hers so he could sleep but would still be woken if she climbed out of bed. She had slept through everything that had occurred after the attack and had been in and out of consciousness since. Connecting with that demon had taken a toll on her. Bo and Andy had brought some breakfast back to Ace before they ate that morning, and she had been still asleep then.

Now, as they walked into the tent, Lindy was awake,

sharing some of Ace's lunch he must have fetched for her. She looked like her old self, except her eyes were still black. Andy wondered if Lindy knew of the change, or if she had yet to see her own reflection. Andy gulped back her fear as Lindy gazed up at her.

"Hi guys." Ace greeted them as they walked in. He had a smile on his face, which Andy took as a good sign. "Lindy's feeling a little better today."

"Glad to hear it!" Andy walked over to Lindy and sat beside her on her cot. She gave Andy her usual smile, without the eeriness it had held a few days earlier. "Do you remember what happened the other day?" Andy needed to know if the normalcy was real, or if it was another manipulation of the demons.

"I remember being with Eph-er-am," Lindy said, her little brow furrowing. "But I fell asleep." She smiled again, and Andy sighed with relief. It *seemed* like the demons had lost their grip on her, for now.

"Well, I'm glad you're feeling better." Andy stood off the cot. "She seems okay now," she murmured to Bo. "I'll let Septimus know when I see him." She heard someone clear their throat outside the tent. "Come in!" she hollered. Sera entered holding a pile of clothes.

"I thought you might need more than one set of clothes. They're the same as the ones you're wearing, but at least these are clean. You can leave the dirty ones on the end of your cot, and I'll take them later to be cleaned." Sera handed

Andy the change of clothes. Laundry must have been the extra chore Sera had picked up as her punishment from Ephram.

"Thanks, Sera. I appreciate everything you've done for me." Andy hugged Sera, grateful to have gained her as a friend.

"No problem." Sera waved as she left the tent.

"I'm going to shower and put on these clean clothes." Andy clutched the clothes in her arms and started out of the tent.

"I'll stay here with Ace and Lindy. I'll come get you if anything changes." Andy turned and gave Bo a smile to let him know she had heard him and continued to the showers.

When she finished scrubbing the layer of dirt off herself, she put on her new set of clothes. Sera was right, they were the same as the other clothes she had given her. Andy pulled on her jacket and left the tent feeling refreshed.

Septimus was walking by as Andy came out of the shower tent and he paused to talk to her.

"How is Lindy today?" he asked.

"She seems better, actually. I wanted you to talk to her, though, and see if you think anything is...off. I tried, and she seems okay, but I feel like you might have a little more experience with this kind of thing," Andy told him. She needed Lindy to be okay. Septimus agreed and followed Andy back to the tent. Septimus approached Lindy warily even though she wore a bright smile. Andy cocked her head at that but said nothing.

"Are you still feeling better?" Septimus asked her. She bobbed her head and did a little twirl as if to emphasize her answer. Her innocence caused Andy's heart to ache, knowing Lindy had to deal with demons invading her mind because of *their* mistakes.

"Septimus wanted to give you a quick check-up, is that okay?" Andy asked. Lindy seemed a little more serious, and a bit wary, but she agreed. Ace stood close by, still not willing to leave his sister's side.

"Take a seat, Lindy." Septimus crouched in front of her as she sat on the cot, crossing her legs. He searched her eyes first and took her wrist to check her pulse. Andy wondered if maybe she should have checked that the other day, so they would be able to compare it to when Lindy had been...possessed. That was the only word Andy could think of to describe how Lindy had been acting. "Did you dream last night, Lindy?" Septimus asked and she shook her head.

"I don't think so." Her eyes widened. "Is that okay?"

"That's okay. What did you eat for breakfast?" Andy cocked her eyebrow at Septimus. What did that have to do with anything?

"Toast, and eggs," Lindy answered. "Ace shared with me."

"Good. He's a good brother. Who gave you this?" He pointed to the bracelet that dangled from her wrist. It was too big for her, and it kept threatening to slip off. She furrowed her brow as she inspected it.

"She wasn't wearing that yesterday," Ace spoke up. Fear clouded his eyes now, and Andy started to feel it too.

"That...that isn't mine." Lindy shook her wrist, the charms on the bracelet jingled and caused light to bounce around the tent.

"It's pretty. Can I look at it?" Septimus reached for her wrist, but she pulled it back. She turned to Andy with her brows pinched together and her mouth parted slightly, just as confused as the rest of them.

"It's okay, Lindy. He just wants to look at it," Andy reassured her. Lindy still seemed wary but stuck her arm out so Septimus could inspect the bracelet. When he touched it, though, he yanked his hand back as if it had burned him. His reaction scared Lindy and she curled up, reaching out for Ace who came to her side and wrapped her in his arms.

"I'll look at it," Ace offered, taking Lindy's wrist in his hand, examining the bracelet. "It's just a normal charm bracelet. It looks like the one mom had." He grabbed one of the charms and his face paled. "This *is* the one mom had. I gave her this..." He revealed the charm that had caught his attention. It had a heart with *A+L* engraved on it. "Lindy where did you get this?" His voice was forceful, and it made Lindy's lip quiver as if she was about to cry.

"I s-said. I d-don't know," she whimpered, squeezing her eyes shut.

"Stay here with her," Septimus told Ace as he stood up. "Andy, come with me." He strode out of the tent and Andy followed, glancing back at Lindy once more before leaving. They made their way towards the dining tent, so Lindy and Ace wouldn't overhear them talking.

"Ace has been with Lindy constantly since she connected with the demons." Andy ran her hands through her hair nervously.

"He slept, though, didn't he?" Septimus pointed out. They had *all* slept, thinking they would hear Lindy if she left her bed, since she would have had to either crawl over Ace, or...crawl under the side of the tent. It dawned on Andy. That is probably *exactly* what had happened.

"She could have crawled under the tent." Andy filled Septimus in on her theory. "It wouldn't have been hard, she's so little."

"But why would they have not taken her then?" He seemed to be asking it rhetorically, not actually expecting Andy to answer, but she did anyway.

"They want her to bring me with her. They don't want her as badly as they want me." Andy knew what she was saying was the truth, and it scared her.

"Why not take her as a hostage, though? They know you care about her." Septimus waited for a real answer, letting Andy help him work it all out.

"They already tried that with my dad. They can't be sure I will respond to her being taken as a hostage. They probably think they have a better chance if they still have eyes on the inside." As she said this, she wondered if they knew she had already decided not to give herself up, and whether they had already killed her dad. She couldn't even think about it. It hurt too much. She *had* to believe her dad was still alive.

"We can't keep her here anymore. It's too dangerous," Septimus said.

"What are you suggesting we do, then?" Andy began to worry the angels were about to abandon Lindy when she needed them the most.

"She needs to be moved to a more secure location." Septimus paced and it was making Andy more nervous.

"If by secure, you're talking about some kind of prison, then absolutely not," Andy protested.

"That is not what I meant. There are other camps that are more substantial and heavily guarded that she could go to, along with her brother. I'll go talk with Ephram now, and we can probably have her out of here within the hour." Andy's heart dropped. She had not imagined Lindy would be leaving so soon, and she wasn't sure she was ready to let her go yet. Septimus seemed to see this, and he placed his hand on her shoulder in sympathy. "It's better this way; she will be safer away from here and away from..." He stopped but Andy knew what he was going to say.

"Away from me," she finished for him. "I'll go say goodbye then." They went their separate ways, Septimus to talk with Ephram and Andy to say goodbye to the kids who had become her family over the last two weeks.

When Andy returned to the tent, Ace was alone. Her

heart tightened as panic took over. "Where is she?" Andy searched around the tent thinking maybe she had overlooked Lindy. It was in that moment that she noticed the complete devastation on Ace's face. He was shaking his head.

"Sh-she had to go to the bathroom. I waited...she was there, and I looked away, and when I turned back, she was...gone." His voice was hollow. She was the last family member he had left.

"Did you look for her?" Andy asked, not meaning for it to come out so harsh, but it caused Ace to cringe.

"Of course! That's what I was doing here now. I thought maybe she came back here," he snapped. Andy gave him an apologetic look, and she ran out of the tent, straight to the meeting tent. She burst in through the entrance without announcing herself. Ephram and Septimus both gawked at her in bewilderment.

"She's gone," Andy huffed. "We need to find her." She turned back around, ducking out of the tent, and became frantic, searching between and inside every other tent. She received some glares, and baffled reactions. Ace did the same on the other end of the camp. Someone grabbed Andy's arm and she whirled to face them. It was Bo.

"Andy, what's going on?" His calm demeanor helped to ease the crushing grip that had taken a hold in her chest. She took a deep breath.

"It's Lindy, she's missing," Andy said, and even though they both know it was futile, he helped her continue searching for Lindy. Septimus caught up to them.

"I've sent out a message to everyone in the camp to look for her. So far, no one has seen her." Andy could see he did not believe Lindy was there, but he was still trying to help, for Andy's sake, she assumed.

"I thought they weren't going to take her, because they wanted to use her to bring me to them," Andy yelled for no real reason as she began spiraling out of control.

"It's possible they knew we were planning on sending her away, and so they decided they couldn't leave her here anymore," Septimus reasoned.

"I should have never let you..." Andy knew she should not be blaming anyone but herself here, Lindy was her responsibility, but any sort of logic and reasoning had left her. "I need to find her." She spun around looking back towards the woods. She ran towards them with Bo and Septimus following closely behind. She continued until she reached the fallen log that marked where the path split and led either to the clearing, or deeper into the woods. She took the path to the clearing since that was where she had seen the hooded figure who she assumed was a demon.

"Lindy!" she called out, praying Lindy would pop out from behind a tree, as if they were playing hide and seek. "Lindy, where are you?" Andy hurried out into the clearing and saw nothing. Lindy was gone. "No. I should have never left her." Andy fisted her hands in her hair in frustration. "I knew she was in danger, but Ace was with her... I only left them alone for a few minutes," Andy spoke aloud to herself.

"Andromeda..." Septimus was at her side. "I'm sorry." Suddenly, the clearing in front of Andy disappeared and a narrowing black hole took its place. Her whole body became warm, and her heart raced. Her breaths came out short and labored. Voices seemed to echo through her head, though no one was around other than Septimus.

"Andromeda. We are waiting for you." She fell to her knees and the clearing appeared before her eyes once more. She placed her hands on the ground in front of her, trying to push herself up, but all her strength had left her body.

"Do you need my help?" Septimus still stood beside her. She shook her head and sat back on her heels, taking deep breaths.

"I need a minute." She was tired of being taken care of. She needed to continue her training so she could start defending herself. Septimus sat beside Andy and pulled his knees to his chest. He showed no signs of realizing she had seen anything out of the ordinary, and she wasn't about to divulge anything to him. "I was supposed to be protecting her. I failed her," Andy choked out.

"We all failed her, not just you." Andy glanced over at Septimus and noticed how young he seemed sitting beside her. He was always so serious and composed, it was strange seeing him that way.

"I need you to train me in combat," Andy said.

"I am training you. These things take time," he told

her, but she shook her head.

"I need to learn how to fight as soon as possible. I need to get Lindy back." Andy gritted her teeth in anger. The demons had taken yet another person she loved.

"Alright. We'll start training with swords tomorrow," Septimus conceded.

It was quiet for a minute, until Andy asked the real question she had been wondering about. "Why did you stop training me before?"

"My father thought it best for Malachi to take over," he stated.

"Buy why?" she pressed.

"It's difficult to explain." His jaw clenched.

"My dad told me angels have the ability to sense when someone is telling the truth." Andy left the statement hanging for him to think about. He was not being entirely honest, but Andy was tired of always having to pry information from him.

"That's right," he sighed. "The reason Malachi took over your training is because he and my father are worried about me becoming too close to you, and you potentially becoming a weakness for me. My father has already lost too many sons, he wants to make sure I am as strong as possible, so I don't end up like them." He stared at the ground the whole time he said this, and Andy wondered if he worried about becoming too close to her as well. She waited a moment and spoke again.

"I get it. Gabby mentioned to me before, about how she

and Nathan are not allowed on the same guards because it would be a liability, and I get it, I do. But I also think they would make a great team. They know each other better than anyone else and they would be able to communicate more efficiently, knowing how the other thinks. I believe they should be given the choice to fight together, and God forbid something happens to either of them, it's their right to be there and decide how to react; risk their life for the other or play it safe." Andy examined Septimus for his reaction. His face gave away nothing.

"Maybe you're right, but no one else seems to see it that way, or at least no one else has challenged the current rule." Andy was surprised Septimus might actually *agree* with her argument.

"Well, if you're supposed to be distancing yourself from me, you're doing a poor job." She nudged him with her elbow.

"I'll admit, keeping you safe from a distance was nearly impossible." He joked back.

"I'm sorry about that. I'll try to stay closer to camp from now on," she promised.

"I would appreciate the extra effort. Though, I do enjoy our walks in the woods," he admitted, making Andy wonder if he might like her.

"Me too." She smiled.

"We should be getting back. Do you think you'll be able to manage now?" He stood and stretched.

"I think so," Andy said. Septimus held his hand out to her and helped her to her feet. She wobbled at first, but after a few seconds, she regained her balance.

They came across Ace also heading back to the camp. His eyes were filled with grief, and Andy knew he'd found no sign of Lindy either. She shared in his grief more than anyone, having cared for Lindy, while the others had used her to spy on the demons.

"Ace..." Andy walked over to him and gathered him into her arms. He let her hug him, but he didn't hug her back.

"She's gone, Andy. She's really gone." It seemed that him saying the words aloud made it final.

"We'll get her back. I promise I will do everything I can to bring her back to you." It was probably impossible to bring Lindy back, but Andy had to say it. She had to hang on to at least the tiny shred of hope they might be able to do it. Lindy was the last family Ace had left.

"I wish it had been me..." Ace mumbled, and Andy could see the guilt written on his face. She sympathized with him. "Lindy...she's too young. She didn't know how to protect herself. I could have. Why did it have to be her?" His eyes were pleading, and Andy didn't know how to respond. They all walked back to the camp in silence.

16

The Heavenly Fire

Bo stopped following Andy when she veered off to the clearing. Septimus was with her, and Bo knew he was much more capable of keeping her safe anyway. Instead, Bo turned and walked back to camp. When he reached his tent, he noticed Micah coming towards him. Bo gave him a halfhearted smile.

"Did you guys find her?" Micah asked, and Bo shook his head, feeling dejected. He knew Andy was going to take it hard, since she had felt responsible for Lindy. "Damn...I actually came to find you for another reason, though." Micah ruffled his hair nervously.

"Sure, what's up?"

"I was wondering, we haven't hung out much since my

birthday, and well...do you want to take a walk with me?" Bo was surprised to see Micah so nervous around him. He was supposed to be the 'heartbreaker,' after all. It sent butterflies fluttering through Bo's stomach.

"Yeah, sure. Come on." He took Micah's hand and they walked back the way Bo had come from. They didn't talk for a few minutes, simply enjoying each other's company. Micah broke the silence first.

"I can't believe the demons were able to get Lindy inside of the camp." Micah seemed a little worried, and Bo sympathized with him. It was hard to believe the demons were able to get past the angels' defenses without being detected. "They're not supposed to be able to get in here. The dominions placed a barrier around the camp that was supposed to alert Ephram of any demonic activity. I'm surprised Lindy didn't set it off when you first came here, since she's a demon."

"Well, she's only half-demon, I think. When we first came here, she had never connected with them before, and I think that part of her was kind of...dormant, I guess. I'm not sure how it all works, though. You probably know more about it than I do." Bo blushed, remembering Micah was an *angel* and had way more experience dealing with demons than Bo ever thought of having.

"No, I think you're right. I may fight demons, but I'm not an expert on all things demon related," Micah said, which made Bo feel a little better.

"You should have seen Lindy after she connected with them...it was scary. I wouldn't be surprised if she left without the help of any demon. I think she was drawn to them. They wouldn't have even needed to get past any defenses." Bo knew that was the most likely scenario, but it didn't make him feel any better about it. It was hard to think about Lindy walking out, all alone. She was so young, he tried not to imagine what it was like for her, being with the demons.

"There's nothing we can do about it now, except prepare ourselves better for the next attack." Micah stopped walking and turned to face Bo. "If you ever need anything, or someone to talk to, I'm here. I have a lot of experience dealing with loss and... just know I'm here if you need me." Bo was grateful for Micah, but he didn't want to talk about his parents now. He thought about them every other second of the day, he needed a break.

Instead, he said, "Thanks, Micah. I'll remember that." Micah squeezed his hand a little tighter, and they continued walking.

∞

That night, Andy sat on her cot across from Bo and Ace, practicing creating her light. They oohed and ahhed in support. Ace and Bo had vowed to help her train in any way they could, and they also wanted some combat training themselves, to make sure they stood a chance at getting Lindy back.

Andy barely needed to focus anymore to create the light. She could think about it for a few seconds and the spark would appear, and the light grew easily between her palms.

"I think that's enough for tonight," she announced. Ace leaned back and let out a sigh of relief.

"Oh, thank God. I'll be honest, it became boring after about five minutes." They all laughed. It was nice to feel lighthearted, rather than worried and depressed. "Can we get food now? I'm starving." Bo and Andy nodded eagerly, feeling hungry themselves.

At dinner, Ace joined Andy and Bo's group at their usual table. He had been feeling Lindy's absence in everything he had done that day. They had been pretty much inseparable since they had arrived, and Ace seemed lost without her. Andy felt a little lost too, but the motivation to get Lindy back drove her forward.

"So, there's a guard going out tonight," Sera began. "Gabby and I are on it. Some of the demons are getting restless and were spotted over the border into Vermont, headed for Shaftsbury to harass the people there."

"There're still actual towns filled with people out there?" Bo appeared hopeful.

"Yeah. There are quite a few, but they are so spread out, you don't come across them often," Gabby explained.

"What will the demons do to the town?" Andy worried about the people there, being preyed on by demons.

"Well, all the existing towns have angel guards there to

help protect them, along with their human armies. We're going in case they need backup. But the demons aim to collect more souls to strengthen their ranks. That's pretty much their sole purpose now. Besides killing any angels who cross their path, and sometimes humans." Gabby glanced at Bo but said nothing more.

"Oh. Well, if they keep trying doesn't that mean sometimes they succeed?" Andy pointed out.

"Yeah, but at least we can minimize the damage and souls lost," Gabby said.

"Well, I guess that's something." The war seemed to be going in circles, in Andy's opinion. It was too evenly matched, and no one was willing to back down. She was beginning to wonder if it was ever going to end.

Micah plopped on the end of the bench next to Bo. "Ready for your training tomorrow?" He flashed a wicked grin, and Bo paled a little.

"*You're* not training me, are you?" Andy knew Bo worried about embarrassing himself in front of Micah.

"You may call me Master." Micah gave him a wink and laughed. "Since I turned eighteen, they thought it best that I start doing some training. You and Ace are only being trained in basic combat, so they thought this would be a good place for me to start."

"Oh, great." Bo still seemed worried, so Andy gave his shoulder a squeeze.

"You'll do great, Bo," she said low enough only he

could hear her. He gave her a grateful smile and relaxed.

"I'll be helping train you guys, too," Nathan spoke up. "Since Gabby and Sera will either still be out with the guard, or on their way back."

"Oh, good. I was worried I was going to be a third wheel," Ace joked. Bo glared at him, but Micah smiled.

∞

"Andy..." Andy's eyelids fluttered as Bo hovered over her. "Andy, wake up. Time for breakfast." He walked out without waiting to see if she was following him. She caught up with him at the dining tent. Bo sat beside Micah and Andy took the seat next to Bo.

Today everyone seemed to be in good spirits. The chatter was light. Bo listened to everyone else talking while he ate. It was kind of nice and it calmed his worries for a little while, which he needed after the fretful day yesterday. His heart was still hurting for the loss of Lindy, but he was staying positive they would get her back. He kept reminding himself Lindy was not lost to them forever.

Once they finished breakfast, Micah and Nathan took Bo and Ace to a large empty tent to train. Bo was still experiencing the weight of grief crushing him on the inside, but he was taking the opportunity to help take his mind off it. It also didn't hurt that he would be able to spend some more time with Micah.

In the center of the training tent stood a weapons rack

filled with swords of all different sizes. Bo eyed it warily, but Ace gaped at it in awe.

"Good morning, trainees," Micah said as he and Nathan strode into the tent. "Pick your weapons carefully. Make sure they feel right in your hand, they don't weigh you down, the hilt is not uncomfortable, and eventually, it should feel like an extension of your arm." Micah came to a stop beside the weapons rack. Ace approached the weapons first, trying out a couple before deciding on a sword that was a little longer than his arm with a large hilt that encompassed his hand, protecting it.

"I think this one works for me," Ace proclaimed, swinging it from side to side, feeling it out. Bo stepped up to the weapons and found himself drawn to a sword a little shorter than Ace's, but also a little wider. The hilt was simple and comfortable enough in his hand.

"Great." Micah passed him, close enough for Bo to feel his body heat, and shivers shot down his spine. Micah grabbed a sword for himself and tossed one to Nathan who caught it without even blinking. Bo was pretty sure if someone had tossed a sword to him, he would have at *least* flinched, if he had not run in the other direction.

"Now, Bo, stand over here, across from me." Nathan waved Bo over. Bo glanced at Micah and did as he was told. "Ace, you'll partner with Micah." Nathan showed Bo a few steps and a few different ways to swing the sword to defend against an attack. Bo fumbled through the steps at first, but after repeating them a couple of times, he started to feel a little more comfortable. They practiced these over and over, until Bo was confident in his movements.

"Better," Nathan commented. "Now, let's try something else." He began showing Bo a new set of steps and different ways to attack, rather than defend. These took a little longer for Bo to grasp. Knowing he didn't want to hurt Nathan made his movements more hesitant.

Bo looked over at Ace and Micah who seemed to be moving along at a faster pace. They were already practicing actual fighting. Their swords clanged as they struck one another. They were both careful not to lose control and hurt the other. A pang of jealousy hit Bo as he admired how graceful they were as they moved and wondered if he would ever be at that level. "Bo, don't worry about them, focus here." Nathan seemed to guess what was going through Bo's mind, and he spoke with understanding, rather than annoyance that Bo had been distracted.

"Right, okay." Bo went back through all the motions, and they slowly became more natural. After a few more rounds of this, Nathan held up a hand for Bo to stop.

"I think you're ready to try fighting." Nathan gave Bo a congratulatory smile, knowing he had been waiting to prove himself. "You start, and then we'll go back and forth with attacks and defending." Bo took his stance and breathed deeply, letting his sword do the work. It was a little cumbersome at first, the impact of the swords rattled Bo's nerves. But, as he swung one after another, the swords striking each other affected him less and less. A smile pulled at the corners of his mouth. He had not expected to enjoy sword fighting, but it was kind of fun.

"Now you've got it! Alright, let's take a break." Nathan defended one last blow, and they stopped. Ace and Micah were already taking a break, drinking some water, and sitting cross legged on the grass. Nathan and Bo joined them, grabbing some water from the table beside the weapons rack.

"You're both doing great," Nathan commented. "Much better than I had expected for two guys who've never used a sword before."

"Well, I used to fence," Ace revealed. "It's a lot of the same movements, only you use a foil instead of a sword." Bo felt better knowing the reason Ace had been so much quicker to learn.

Understanding came over Micah's face. "I could tell you had some experience, it seemed to come quite naturally to you. What's your excuse, Bo?" Micah nudged him.

"I guess it's just natural talent," Bo joked, blushing under Micah's gaze. "I mean, I never fenced or anything. I played football in high school."

"Well, that explains how you're so fit, which helps when holding the sword for extended periods of time," Nathan said.

"Football, huh?" Micah raised an eyebrow. "I've always been a sucker for guys in tight pants." Nathan and Ace both rolled their eyes. Bo blushed again but couldn't stop himself from smiling.

"Alright, it's time to wrap this up. Come on, let's switch partners so you guys can practice fighting against different opponents," Nathan suggested, standing off the ground. They all followed his lead. Ace went with Nathan to the other side of the tent, and Bo stood across from Micah.

"Don't worry, I'll go easy on you." Micah winked. Bo thrust his sword forward, stopping short of striking Micah in the chest.

"Unnecessary," Bo said. Micah cocked an eyebrow and knocked Bo's sword to the side. They moved back and forth for a while until Nathan called out they were done for the day. He and Ace put away their weapons and left the tent. Bo tried one last jab at Micah, and Micah spun gracefully, knocking Bo's sword out of his hand, and ending with his face inches from Bo's.

"Nice try." Micah gave Bo his heartbreaker smile. Bo smirked back. He leaned in and kissed Micah. Micah stiffened in surprise at first, but relaxed and dropped his sword. One of Micah's hands pressed into Bo's lower back, pulling him closer and the other hand went to the back of his neck. When Bo pulled away, he was grinning from ear to ear, and he was nearly out of breath. He had been wanting to do that since their first kiss had happened the night of Micah's birthday.

"You guys wanna get lunch?" Nathan popped his head back into the tent.

"Yeah. Sure." Micah picked up both swords and put them away. "Coming, Bo?" Micah held his hand out to Bo, and Bo grabbed it, feeling goosebumps covering his entire body. He felt like he had won the lottery and was soaking in every second of it.

∞

Andy followed Septimus to the clearing for her training session. He had his sword in a sheath that was attached to his belt, as she had hers. He stopped as he reached the bottom of the little hill that separated the woods from the clearing.

"So, did you practice creating your light?" he asked and instead of answering, Andy clasped her hands together and spread them apart, allowing the spark to ignite and grow into a basketball size orb of light. "Very nice." Septimus smiled at her, and Andy smiled back, proud of what she had accomplished on her own. "So, the heavenly fire comes from the same place as your light. Except," Septimus motioned to Andy's sword at her side, "you will use that as a tool to wield the fire." He pulled his own sword out of its sheath and walked a little distance away from her.

Andy watched as he closed his eyes like he had done when he revealed his wings to her the day before, she noticed his sword starting to glow. It started out as a hazy sort of glow. It changed and grew into gold tinted flames. They were blue at the heart of them, and an orange-gold color framed the outer edges.

"How is it not burning you?" Andy asked incredulously. The flames were so close to his hand, she would think it must at *least* be getting hot.

"I'm controlling them, and I make sure they don't burn me. If I were to lose focus, I could lose control of the flames and they could burn me." The flame seemed to move toward his hand, as if in demonstration, but it didn't move past the hilt.

"Alright. Let me try." Andy pulled her sword out of the sheath and closed her eyes as Septimus had done. Thinking about the light, she imagined it turning to the flames that had enveloped Septimus' sword. Andy imagined the flames coursing through her and into her sword. She opened her eyes and let out a gasp. She couldn't help but smile. Her sword was engulfed in the beautiful blue and gold flames.

"Nicely done. It usually takes people a few tries before they are able to get any flames to appear." Septimus had put down his sword, flame-less and dull. "This is the heavenly fire." The flames reflected in his eyes, which appeared even more gold than usual. His face glowed making him look every bit the angel Andy knew him to be.

Andy's hand became hot, and she glanced down, realizing she had allowed her mind to wander from the flames and they had started creeping onto the hilt of her sword. She dropped the sword from the pain as the flames licked her hand. The flames extinguished and the sword was back to its original state. Septimus took her hand in his and examined it causing Andy to blush.

"I got distracted," Andy admitted. "But it doesn't hurt that bad," she lied. It burned like crazy, and a little red spot marked where the flames had touched her.

"It doesn't appear to have done any damage," Septimus commented, still holding her hand in his. "But you did well. It's hard not to get distracted the first few times. It takes practice to keep your mind clear of any distractions and to focus on the task of maintaining the fire." He seemed to realize he was still holding her hand, and he dropped it. "Do you want to try again?"

Her hand felt as if it were on fire and she was a little worried about aggravating it with more heat, but she also knew she needed to practice if she ever wanted to help fight the demons.

"Yeah, let's try again." She picked up her sword off the ground, and Septimus took a step back, giving her some space.

Andy closed her eyes and imagined the light turning into the flames, as she had done before. She pushed the flames out a little farther so they would not be as close to the hilt of her sword. She opened her eyes and the flames lapped around the blade, starting an extra couple inches away from her hand. She grinned in triumph. Septimus held his sword aloft and flames surrounded his blade as well.

"Ready to try using it now?" He took a fighting stance, and Andy mimicked him. Andy thought back to her training with Malachi and scanned through the moves in her mind. Septimus waited for her to make the first move. As their swords collided the heavenly fire seemed to grow, but it also buffered the sound of the clang from blade striking blade.

They continued their back and forth, strike and defend, for a few minutes and then Andy needed to stop. Trying to focus on both keeping the flames controlled and the sword fight was taking a toll on her. She let her sword drop to the ground and she bent over with her hands on her knees. She closed her eyes and took deep breaths.

"It will come easier with practice. Let's call it a day, and you can head back to your tent and rest," Septimus offered, but Andy shook her head.

"Give me a second." Andy straightened, shaking out her arms. Her right arm was sore from holding the sword, but it was not as bad as the first time she had fought with Malachi. "I want to try one more time." She picked up her sword and looked to Septimus to begin.

"If you feel you're up to it." He seemed wary but said nothing more as Andy closed her eyes and began the process again. She noticed Septimus moving at a more moderate pace as they fought. She resented that he thought she needed him to go easier on her and she put all that resentment into her movements. They became quicker and more decisive. Once he noticed this, he picked up his pace to match hers.

Andy could keep up with him for a little while longer, but again, her energy seeped out of her through the heavenly fire. She stumbled and righted herself, but in the process lost her focus on the flames. They licked up her hilt and burned as they grazed her hand. She dropped the sword again and swore.

"Damn it." She shook out her hand, hoping to ease the pain a little. Septimus went to take her hand to examine it, as he had done before, but Andy pulled it away. "No, don't touch it." Tears stung her eyes as her hand throbbed. She had been burned plenty of times before, but never had it hurt like this. She could have sworn the heavenly fire had soaked into her skin and was trying to burn its way back out.

"I won't touch it, I promise, but at least show me the burn." Septimus put out his hand and Andy reluctantly placed her hand, palm down, in his, to show him where she had been burned. The smooth area between her thumb and index finger was bright red, but also ashy, like the fire had dried her skin. "Still not too bad, but we should end our training for the day. We'll get you some cool water to keep your hand in for a little while, to help with the heat from the burn."

Not too bad? Andy could have screamed with the pain that pulsed through her hand. How could it not be that bad? But she didn't want to let on to Septimus how much pain she was in, so she gritted her teeth and took a deep breath.

"Come on, let's go get that water for your hand," Septimus said. He sheathed his sword and picked Andy's up, holding it out for her to take. She cringed, worrying it might still be hot from the flames, but took it anyway. It was no warmer than it had been before they started training. She sheathed it and they started back into the woods.

"How long did you train before you were able to fight with a guard?" Andy asked as they walked, trying to take her mind from the pain in her hand.

"I technically started training when I was eight years old. My brothers were all older, and they were all at different levels in training. I liked to watch their sessions. Sometimes they let me join them and practice my own fighting. By the time I was twelve, I was almost as skilled in combat as my oldest brother."

Andy thought about her own childhood which had been filled with trips to the beach, New York City, and Sunday night dinners at Grandma's house. It was her dad's mother of course; they never met her mom's parents. It made sense to her now, since they were angels, but at the time Andy always wondered what they would be like. She couldn't imagine growing up in a house filled with angels, training to be prepared for combat at any time.

"They let me go out with my first guard on my fifteenth birthday. We took out a group of demons that had been hiding out in a nearby shopping mall. They figured it was a good place to recruit a lot of souls at once." Septimus spoke of all this so nonchalantly, yet Andy couldn't imagine enjoying a birthday spent hunting demons. Although, it was probably normal for him.

"I also went to the mall on my fifteenth birthday, but it

was a much different experience," Andy said, making them both laughed. "I had my mom drop me and a couple of my friends there. We met some boys that one of my friends had invited and I had my first kiss that day." Andy smiled at the memory. They had all been so carefree and thought they were so bad ass for meeting up with boys without their parents' permission.

"Sometimes I forget how human you are." Septimus smirked at Andy, and she nudged his arm with her elbow.

"Hey, cut me some slack. I didn't know I was an angel at the time. I thought I was your average fifteen-year-old girl."

"You are far from average, Andromeda," Septimus said. Andy stopped and gazed up into his eyes. He had stopped as well, and he seemed like he wanted to say something else. Andy could see the tents now, but she and Septimus remained under the cover of the trees. Before she realized what was happening, he was kissing her and she leaned into him, kissing him back. His hands rested on her lower back, and she clasped her hands behind his neck, pulling herself deeper into the kiss. And then just as quickly, he was pulling away from her.

"I-" Andy tried to say something, but she couldn't think straight.

"I'm sorry, I should not have done that." Septimus turned and hurried back to the camp, leaving Andy feeling like she had a whole hive of bees buzzing around inside of her. Every part of her felt alive and all she could think was *so much better than my first kiss at the mall.*

Andy floated into her tent in a daze. Bo laid on his cot, staring at the roof of the tent with a similar dazed look on his face. Ace had his headphones on, and his eyes were closed, so Andy assumed he must be asleep. She collapsed beside Bo and started laughing. He stared at her like she was crazy for a second, and then he joined in.

"Today was..." She thought about everything that had happened and laughed again.

"Today was awesome," Bo finished for her. "It felt so good to learn how to fight with a sword. I never in a million years would have thought I would ever learn that skill."

"Me neither. I learned how to wield the heavenly fire through my sword," as Andy said this, she remembered her burn and the pain of it came rushing back. The kiss with Septimus had distracted her from it and had temporarily relieved her pain. Bo noticed her looking at her burned hand, and he seemed concerned. "It's okay. Septimus said it's not that bad, but it does hurt, like, a lot." Andy winced as the fire burned beneath her skin.

"Don't they have some ointment or something for you to put on it?" Bo asked.

"Well, Septimus and I were on our way to get some water for me to put my hand in, but we got a little distracted." Andy blushed, and Bo's face brightened.

"Don't tell me..." He smirked, and she bit her lip. "No way! I honestly was beginning to doubt it was ever going to happen."

"What about you? You said your day was awesome, what else happened?" She moved the subject away from herself and put the spotlight back on Bo. It helped to distract her from the pain of her burn again.

"Well, I mostly trained with Nathan, but I trained with Micah for a little while at the end of our session, and we may have had a moment, too." Bo pursed his lips, trying to conceal a smile.

"Tell me everything!" Andy turned to face him and propped her head on her arm. Bo copied her movement, and she noticed the grief that had been present in his eyes since the day his parents died was almost unnoticeable. Andy knew it would not last, but it was nice to see him so happy again.

"So, we were fighting, with swords, because I'm pretty bad-ass and can sword fight now, but I digress. Micah did some fancy move and disarmed me, and when we came face to face, I kissed him." Bo closed his eyes and smiled as if he was reliving the moment.

"Annnd... did he kiss you back?" Andy prompted.

"Yes! And it was amazing," Bo swooned. "Now, *I* need details. Tell me all about you and Septimus." He wiggled his eyebrows and Andy couldn't help but laugh.

"Fine, fine. But I don't think it has as happy of an ending as your story," she warned. "We were practicing sword fighting with the heavenly fire in the clearing, and I burned my hand. So, he decided we should stop training, and we started walking back. I asked him about when he had been able to join his first guard, so he was telling me about how he started training when he was eight years old."

"Bad-ass," Bo commented, making her laugh again. "Sorry, continue."

"As I was saying, he was telling me about his training with his brothers, and how on his fifteenth birthday he joined his first guard. So, I told him about *my* fifteenth birthday at the mall with my friends, and how that was when I had my first kiss."

"Oh, good tactic. Make him jealous," Bo joked. Andy pushed him and stuck her tongue out, making him laugh.

"*Anyway.*" Andy let the rest of her story come out in a rush. She could feel the sensation of Septimus' lips on hers all over again and the buzzing started, making her giggle. Bo laughed with her.

"I'm so happy, Andy. I didn't think it was possible after..." he didn't say it, but she knew he was talking about his parents.

"Me too, but we still need to stay focused." Andy had to stay grounded for Lindy's sake, and for Ace's. He needed her to bring his sister back, and she was not planning on letting him down.

"I know, you're right. But, back to you for a second. Didn't you say your story *didn't* have a happy ending? It seems pretty happy to me," Bo reminded her.

"Yeah, after he kissed me, he told me he was sorry and

shouldn't have done it." Andy scrunched her nose and Bo pulled her in for a hug.

"Oh, Andy." He pulled back, and she realized he was laughing. "If you think he *actually* regrets that kiss, you know nothing about men. Don't you worry about that, he'll be back, you wait. In the meantime, I'm going to go take a shower." He maneuvered around her and hopped off the cot.

"Yeah, I should too." Andy stood and grabbed her clean clothes from under her cot. Nathan had given Bo a second set of clothes so he could interchange his clean and dirty, like Sera had done for Andy. The clothes they'd come to the camp in had most likely been burned, or at least, that's what Andy would have done to them.

In the shower tent, they each grabbed a bucket of water and headed to their own stalls. As soon as Andy was behind the curtain, she plunged her hand into the water and sighed in relief. The burning still caused her hand to throb. The water barely touched the pain, but she left her hand soaking in it anyway. She bit her lip hard, causing the skin to break and blood to well up. She wiped it away and continued soaking her hand.

After about five minutes, Andy took her hand out of the water and continued her 'shower.' Bo was waiting for her when she finished. The happiness that radiated off him made him look like a whole different person. He was handsome before, but he had found his confidence, and he looked as much the heartbreaker as Micah, but Andy knew Bo could never break anyone's heart purposefully.

"You know I love you, right?" she asked him as she looped her arm through his.

"Now, Andy, I hate to be the bearer of bad news, but you're not my type." He couldn't help but break out laughing, causing Andy to fall into a fit of laughter too. "Of *course* I know. I love you, too, Andy. Now, come on. Let's go show the world who we really are. The bad-ass, irresistible, sword-fighting duo."

"Bo, I think you're being a little too generous," Andy joked, but she gave him a smolder, which made them both laugh again. They left the tent, arm in arm.

At dinner, Bo and Andy saw Gabby and Sera for the first time since they left for their guard. They seemed in good enough spirits that Andy figured it must have gone well. She didn't ask, though, because she didn't want to hear whether the demons had managed to recruit any new souls. Nathan and Micah were not with them yet.

"Hello, ladies." Bo took a seat. He wore his new confidence well.

"Hi, Bo, Andy." Sera smiled as Andy sat next to Bo. "A little bird told me you finally made your move." Bo normally would have blushed, but instead he glowed.

"I figured it was about time, life's short, right?" He flicked his eyes to Andy as if he was talking only to her, and she took the hint. She scanned the tent, but Septimus wasn't there. She figured she could wait until later to talk to him.

"You're damn right it is." Micah approached their table with Nathan close behind him. He glowed too, and Andy realized that, though she had been warned he was a heartbreaker, he was equally as smitten as Bo in that moment. "Boy, am I glad you realized it." Micah kissed Bo there, in front of everyone, and Andy couldn't help but be jealous that Micah was so happy and proud of their new relationship, that he wanted the whole world to know...and Septimus had regretted showing even *her* how he felt. Or maybe he truly did not like her in that way, and that was why he had apologized for kissing her. Andy slouched in her seat, embarrassed thinking about it.

"Alright, we get it. You're adorable and now the PDA needs to end so I can eat, please," Sera said, unable to disguise her smile. Everyone seemed to be absorbing some of the happiness radiating off Bo and Micah who sat side-by-side, holding hands under the table.

Andy made her decision that she needed to talk to Septimus *now*. She didn't want to waste anymore of her time not knowing how he felt about her. Andy startled everyone at the table as she stood from her seat, except for Bo. He knew what she was doing, and he gave her a nod.

"Good luck," he whispered for only Andy to hear, and she left the tent. She looked around outside first but couldn't see Septimus out and about. So, she walked to his tent. She cleared her throat outside the entrance and waited.

"Come in," he called out as Andy was about to give up.

She pushed aside the tent flap and stepped inside. He sat up and the book he had been reading fell to the ground beside his cot. He glanced at it but made no move to pick it up. "Andromeda..."

"I need to talk to you," she began, but he stopped her before she could say more.

"I'm sorry about before, I should have never kissed you." He repeated his statement from earlier and Andy almost rolled her eyes.

"Yeah, but you did, and I can't pretend it didn't happen," she said.

"I'm sorry..."

She stopped *him* now. "Please, stop saying that." Andy closed her eyes for a moment, thinking about what she was even doing there. He was still regretting kissing her. Maybe she made a mistake in going to his tent.

"I'm s-" He stopped himself. "I mean, okay. I won't say it again." He stood off his cot and took a step towards her. "You need to understand, this is why my father and Malachi didn't want me to train you. I promised them I would not get too close, and now..." he paused. Andy took a step closer to him.

"Well, it looks like you got too close. What are you going to do now?" Electricity filled the air around them as she waited for his response. He took a deep breath, and she wondered what he was thinking. She closed her eyes again and his lips pressed against hers. She wrapped her arms around his neck and pulled him closer. The buzzing began inside of her again, taking over her whole body. Septimus' arms tightened around her. He pulled away after a moment, but his arms were still around her.

"Please don't apologize again," she murmured against his lips, keeping her eyes closed.

"I promised you I wouldn't, didn't I?" Andy opened her eyes and noticed he was smiling. She kissed him again and he pulled her close again. After a few more blissful moments, Andy pulled away from him, and he released her.

"I should get back to dinner." Andy didn't want to leave him, and the others were probably not missing her. However, she wasn't sure she was ready for whatever was happening between them to go any farther. A nagging in her brain kept pulling at her, making her think about the last person she had kissed…Cory. She knew he was alive and well, though he was a demon. She kept trying to push him out of her mind, but he kept worming his way back in. Andy couldn't be with Septimus while Cory dominated her thoughts.

"Okay. One more thing…" Septimus brushed a stray lock of hair behind her ear and kissed her again. "I will see you tomorrow." Andy left without saying anything, but she couldn't get the smile to leave her face. She floated back to the dining tent to find everyone else finishing up.

"It looks like things went well," Bo commented, no one else seemed to catch on and Andy was grateful he had not said anything to them.

"Yeah. Everything's good." Andy brushed her hand through her hair, worrying it might be messed up, but it seemed as tame as it had been earlier.

Everyone except for Bo stood to leave. Bo stayed behind with Andy while she finished her dinner.

"So, tell me... how did it *really* go?" He spoke low, so no one at the tables around them would overhear. They could listen in if they wanted to, but the angels seemed to respect each other's privacy around here; most of the time.

"Much better than before. Let's say he was very unapologetic by the end of our meeting." Andy took a bite of her salad as Bo deciphered this, thinking back to what she had told him earlier. She waited and when it dawned on him, he gave a fake dramatic gasp.

"You are so bad," he joked. "But seriously, I'm glad you went to him. I knew it was going to eat at you until you did. Now we have one less problem to worry about."

17

The Warning

Andy woke in the same cage as before, but she was not alone. Lindy laid curled up in the corner. Andy ran to her and tried to shake her awake, but her eyelids only fluttered and remained closed.

"She will not wake up," a voice said.

"Who are you? What's wrong with her?" Andy yelled at whomever would hear her. She turned every which way, but no one else was in the room with them.

"She is dying, Andromeda. Only you can save her now." The boom of the voice rattled her. She could feel the heat in the room intensifying.

"What do you want?" She knew what the answer would be, but she asked anyway.

"I want you, Andromeda."

Broken Angel

Andy turned back to Lindy in the corner and realized she was fading away. Andy tried to hold onto her, but she was slipping between her fingers.

"No! What are you doing? Lindy! Please, wake up!" Lindy's eyes flew open, and she stared straight at Andy. Andy shuddered at her black eyes.

"Save me, Andy...Andy...Andy..."

∞

Bo lay awake, thinking about the day his parents died, over and over, overanalyzing every move he made. He knew there were so many things he could have done differently. First and foremost, he should have talked Andy out of leaving the angel's camp. His parents would still be here if...if they hadn't been forced out of the angel camp, if he'd made his parents run, if he'd tackled that demon.

Bo went through it all one more time. He remembered something, or rather someone, he had forgotten about; that black-haired demon Andy had been standing with when he had pulled her away. He'd never asked her about that, though he'd meant to. She was sleeping beside him. For as long as he had known her, she'd had nightmares, and it gave her anxiety to wake up alone. He understood that better now. Every day when he woke up, he thought about how he wanted to tell his parents something, and remembered they were dead. It gave *him* anxiety to think about his future without them.

He observed Andy, noticing how her features were

starting to fill out. She had been so thin when he had first met her; nothing but bone and muscle. She had been beautiful then, but she was stunning as she became healthier. He laughed to himself; these were the random thoughts that kept him awake at night.

Andy stirred, mumbling something in her sleep. Bo knew it was one of her nightmares and he knew what would come next: the screams. He shook her shoulder lightly to try to save her from whatever evil pursued her in her dreams. Her eyes opened partway.

"I'm sorry," she mumbled, yawning, still only half awake. Bo smirked as she attempted to rub the sleep from her eyes.

"It's okay. I was already awake," he said, placing his hands beneath his head as he turned to face her.

"What's on your mind?" she asked.

"I was thinking about my parents, and you," Bo answered. Andy took his hand in hers and squeezed it.

"Tell me everything," she whispered. So, he did. He told her all the thoughts that kept him awake. He finished with his question for her.

"Who was that demon- the one with the black hair that you were having a staring contest with when I pulled you away?" Andy blushed, making Bo even more curious.

"My ex-boyfriend," she admitted. Bo gaped at her. "I had no idea he was a demon when we were dating. I mean, it makes sense now, but I had assumed Cory and his family were either in hiding, or dead. I never thought I would see him again, and I was fine with that."

"Wow, he must have been a really shitty boyfriend," Bo commented, and Andy laughed.

"I never wanted to see him again. But seeing him...there's a part of me that was *happy* to see him. Which doesn't make any sense, I hated him at the end of our relationship, and was about to break up with him before he disappeared." Andy put her head in her hands and Bo reached out to grip her shoulder, trying to comfort her.

"Well, you liked him at some point if you were dating him," he pointed out, and Andy sighed.

"Yeah. He was a good boyfriend at the beginning of our relationship. We were together for maybe three months before he disappeared. I always thought he was being aloof, playing hard to get. But I guess he was hiding who he truly was. And then, about a week before he disappeared, he turned into a different person..."

"All I can say is maybe there's a reason he came back into your life. If you never said goodbye, maybe you need closure," Bo said.

Andy scoffed. "The universe wants me to find closure with the demon who was a terrible boyfriend. Great." Andy cringed. "Now I'm wondering if he knew what I was all along and that was the only reason he was dating me."

"You're gorgeous, I can see why he would want to be with you. And he's gorgeous, so I can see why you fell for him." Bo winked and Andy hit him playfully on the arm.

"You thinking about changing sides? You've got an angel, and now you have a yearning for a demon?" Bo pretended to gag.

"No way. I would never be with one of those monsters, no matter how attractive. Besides, Micah is way prettier."

"He is. You caught yourself a winner." They both stayed quiet for a while and Bo began to drift off to sleep.

∞

Andy was still off put by her nightmare and worried about falling back asleep. She'd had a few nights without nightmares, and she had hoped, unrealistically, that maybe they'd leave her alone for a while. But they'd returned, and in full force. As much as she wanted to avoid her nightmare, eventually her exhaustion won out, and she unwillingly closed her eyes again.

Andy opened her eyes and realized she couldn't see anything. It was pitch black. She started screaming, to try to wake herself, and she heard a chuckle. A small winking light entered the room, giving her a glimpse of the cage she had returned to, and the shadow watching her from outside of it.

"You cannot escape from me, Andromeda," the voice growled. "I am inside your head." She shuddered. The room began to lighten even more, and she realized she was not alone in the cage. It was not Lindy, though, that was curled up in the corner, it was her

dad. She ran to him, but as she reached him, he disappeared.

"No!" She screamed for him and her whole body wracked with tremors.

Andy was pulled out of her nightmare before she could find out who the shadow figure was.

"Andy, it's okay. You're okay," Bo said. His arms were around her, and she buried her face into his shoulder. Her whole body trembled.

"I can't go back to sleep," she cried. He stroked her hair, and she relaxed a little.

"We don't have to..." he yawned, "we don't have to sleep."

"Andromeda..." she heard Septimus before she saw him at the entrance to the tent. He was outlined by the light of the moon shining through the trees.

"Go," Bo whispered and released her from his embrace. Andy climbed over him, off the cot. "I'll be here if you need me," he promised, but he was back asleep within seconds. Andy pulled on her boots and her jacket and followed Septimus out of the tent. From the darkness of the sky, she assumed it was still only midnight, at the latest.

"Come on." He held his hand out to her and she grasped it. They walked to the woods and down the path. "You were screaming again."

"Nightmares..." she was still hesitant to tell him about the room she had been seeing, and the figure, who she assumed was a demon. "About Lindy and my dad." She could at least give him that much.

"I am sorry you are plagued by so many nightmares. It takes a toll, not being able to sleep through the nights." He spoke as if from experience, and she wondered what he had nightmares about. His brothers, maybe.

"I don't have them every night," Andy pointed out.

"Yes, but you do have them quite often. We need you to have all your strength if we are going to get Lindy back." She knew he was trying to convince her to go back to sleep, but the thought terrified her.

"I can't...I can't go back to sleep," Andy's voice wavered as the fear crept back into her mind. *You cannot escape me...* that voice seeped into her thoughts and triggered her anxiety as a chill spread throughout her body.

"You don't have to if you don't want to, I'll stay awake with you." Septimus stopped walking and looked up at the moon. "It's beautiful out here at night." Andy followed his gaze and noticed the stars shining down on them. He was right, it was beautiful. It took her mind off her anxieties for a moment, and everything else disappeared.

"Thank you for bringing me out here." She leaned against his arm and squeezed his hand a little tighter. It was hard to be afraid with him standing there beside her.

"Of course. Anytime you need me, you can always come to me. Do not worry about waking me. I'm a light sleeper anyway." Everything about him made her feel safe.

The last of her fear from her nightmare seeped away into the night.

"I think..." she yawned. "I think I'm ready to try to go back to sleep." They turned back towards the camp. When they stopped outside of her tent, she hesitated. Thinking about leaving Septimus, the fear came rushing back, crushing down on her. He noticed the indecision on her face.

"You can come back to my tent with me, if you want, to sleep." He was careful to add on the sleeping part, which Andy was grateful to him for. It only took her a moment to decide, and she nodded to him. They kept walking to his tent.

Inside his tent was his single cot, as Andy had anticipated, but somehow it seemed so much smaller to her now. Bo and Andy fit fine on the cots together but thinking about being that close with Septimus... Heat rose in her cheeks, and she was thankful it was still so dark. He took off his boots and jacket and laid on his side on the cot. He watched her as she removed her own boots and jacket, but she could see concern in his eyes, and knew he was making sure she was okay, rather than expecting something...more.

She sat on the edge of the cot and turned to Septimus. He put his hand on her back and warmth radiated from him. Andy kissed him quickly and laid on her side, leaning back until her back was just touching his chest. He put his arm around her and pulled the blanket over them. A sense of ease came over Andy and she closed her eyes.

Andy woke to the sun in her eyes. She squinted to see someone standing in the entrance to the tent...and she remembered where she was; in Septimus' tent; in Septimus' arms. The person letting the sun in cleared his throat, and Septimus bolted upright, the blanket falling to the ground. Andy shivered with the sudden change in temperature.

"Your father would like to speak with you," Malachi spoke with a harsh tone. Andy sat up and watched as Septimus pulled on his boots and yanked on his jacket. He left without a word or even a glimpse at Andy.

Andy stretched lazily as she climbed off the cot. She felt well rested for the first time in a while. She pulled on her boots and jacket and left the tent. Everyone else was already awake and she realized they all stared at her as she walked from Septimus' tent to the dining tent. Bo and the others sat at their usual table, so she walked over to join them. They all regarded her as if she had two heads.

"I can't believe you did it," Sera commented.

"What, does everyone already know?" Andy peeked around the tent and saw that everyone still stared at her.

"Of course." Sera pointed to her head. "It's all anyone's talking about if you tap into the angel communication network. We want the inside scoop, though." Andy sat down. Everyone waited for her explanation.

"Nothing happened, if that's what everyone's thinking," she prefaced. "I slept in his tent, which I've done before, though last time he wasn't sleeping in the cot with me... so, I don't see why it's such a big deal." She tried to play it off like it was nothing, even though it meant so much more to her than nothing.

"Septimus has never been in a relationship with anyone, ever." Sera glanced towards Gabby, who seemed fine, but Andy wondered if she was upset since she had once tried to pursue him. "It's a big deal here. Besides, what else does everyone have to talk about? The demons have gone quiet again, so we need some form of entertainment."

"Great. I'm sure Ephram is going to be thrilled with me..." Andy could hear the lecture now. She wondered if Septimus was hearing that now.

"Don't worry about it, Andy. You can't change anything, so let whatever happens, happen." Bo gave her hand a reassuring squeeze.

"I know, you're right. Let's talk about something else now." She turned her attention to the food sitting in front of her and started eating, hoping no one would ask her any more questions. Thankfully, their attention returned to their own plates.

"Well, Sera and I will be training Bo and Ace today," Gabby changed the subject. "Thanks to Micah and Bo's little PDA moment yesterday, Ephram thought it best that someone else take over Bo's training, so there won't be any *distractions.*"

Micah chuckled. "I regret nothing." He kissed Bo on the cheek and smiled in triumph.

"Me neither. Besides, it's always good to get a different

perspective on different fighting techniques," Bo said. Andy knew at the very least, that would be the reaction Ephram would have with her and Septimus. She wondered if Malachi would start training her again or if he would still refuse to. She wasn't sure whether she would rather train with Malachi or not at all...

After breakfast, Bo and Ace went with Gabby and Sera to the training tent, while Andy stuck with Nathan and Micah since she had no idea what was going on with her training today. Septimus was still nowhere to be seen, and neither was Malachi.

"Come on, let's go do a border check. They haven't done one yet this morning." Nathan motioned for them to follow him to the outer edges of the camp.

"What exactly are we looking for?" Andy surveyed the surrounding woods and noticed nothing out of the ordinary.

"Any sort of change. Footprints, any shifted brush, anything that seems a little different than the day before. So, for you, how it looks now will be your basis for comparison on your next border check, so take it all in. Every little detail." Nathan scanned the perimeter and Andy did as she was told, taking in everything in her line of vision.

"Everything looks the same today as it did yesterday." Micah sounded a little disappointed. "Except for those bunny prints over there." He pointed off towards a tree that stood about thirty feet away. Andy focused her eyesight and homed in on where he pointed. She could see the small bunny prints.

"Let's check the other side." Nathan led the way across the camp, and they did the same routine. Scanning the area, focusing on a few different animal prints, and finding nothing notable to report back.

"Alright, I'm going to go let Malachi know we did the check. I'll catch up with you guys in a bit." Nathan walked off towards the meeting tent where it seemed Ephram and Malachi spent all their time. Andy wondered if they slept there at night. She assumed that was where Septimus was now, too.

"So, Micah," Andy turned to him, and he looked up from whatever he stared at on the ground. "I'm happy for you and Bo."

"Thanks. I'm happy too." His smile made him glow, and Andy knew exactly what Bo saw in him.

"Yeah, that's good. I wanted to make sure you know, though, if you do *anything* to hurt him, I will have to kill you." She gave him a mock sorry face.

"Bo's lucky to have you looking out for him, but you don't need to worry. I have no intention of hurting him." Andy could sense he was telling the truth, so she caved and smiled back.

"On another note, do you want to help me practice sword-fighting with the heavenly fire? My trainer seems to be missing." She needed to keep practicing if she was ever going to be able to fight demons.

"Yeah, sure. Come on. We can use the clearing." Micah and Andy made their way through the woods and out to the clearing. Andy had her sword attached to her belt, and Micah always had his on him. "I'm guessing you already know how to summon the fire?" he asked, and she nodded. "Alright, let's do this." His sword was engulfed in flames in an instant. He clearly had a lot of practice with this. Andy pulled out her sword, keeping her eyes open, and went through her process of producing the flames. She watched as her sword glowed first and then became engulfed in flames.

Micah did not go easy on her, which she appreciated. She needed to be challenged if she wanted to get any better. He made moves that, if they were in battle, would either seriously wound her or kill her. She became frustrated that she couldn't move fast enough to defend herself, or get her own attacks in.

"Hold on." Micah put his hand up, and she paused. "You're doing fine, but I think you're worrying a little too much about the fire, and not enough about the moves you're making. It's okay to release a little bit of your focus from the fire. As long as it's present in your mind, and you never forget you are controlling it; you can take some of your focus and put it into your movements. Alright, let's continue." He held his sword back up and they began again. Andy tried to do as he instructed and shifted her focus away from the fire, and more towards her movements.

Broken Angel

A few times her hand grew hot, but she was able to get the fire back under her control before it burned her. She was blocking more of Micah's attacks, and although she wasn't quite fast enough to also make her own attacks yet, it was a start. They practiced for half an hour, and by then Andy's arm ached and she needed to stop.

"You're doing much better," Micah praised her as he slid his sword back into its sheath.

"All thanks to you," Andy said. "I can at least somewhat defend myself now, if nothing else." She sheathed her sword as well.

"The rest will come with more practice. Anytime you want to spar, let me know. I love any chance to practice, so I'm always down," he said as they started to head back to camp.

"Can we check in on Bo and Ace? I want to see how their training is going," Andy asked as they neared the training tent. Micah answered by ducking inside the tent. Andy followed him in.

"What are you guys doing here? We're in the middle of some combat training." Sera put her hands on her hips and gave them an annoyed look. Micah raised his hands in surrender.

"Sorry, I wanted to see how it was going," Andy said, stepping up beside Micah.

"It's going well. Now, please leave us in peace so we can finish up here." Sera shooed them out of the tent. Andy gave Bo two thumbs up and he returned the gesture, sticking his tongue out at her.

Sera rolled her eyes at them, and they both laughed. Micah and Andy left and headed towards the dining tent to hangout until everyone else caught up with them for lunch. They sat across from each other at their normal table.

"You know, I'm a little jealous of your relationship with Bo," Micah admitted, rubbing his neck, a slight blush rising in his cheeks. He always seemed so self-assured, Andy was surprised by this, and her face showed it. "I mean, I know you guys are just friends, I'm not worried about that. I mean, I wish I could be as close with him as you are."

"You will be, in time," Andy tried to reassure him. "I mean, Bo and I became close fast, and now he's the only family I have left," she paused, realizing that by admitting this, she was acknowledging her dad may already be dead which caused her heart to ache.

"I get it. I mean, Sera and I used to be close like you and Bo, but things changed once the war started." Sadness sparked in his eyes, but only for a moment.

"I'm sorry..." She knew what it was like to grow apart from people.

"It's whatever. It was all because of a fling she had with another angel, Joseph, and he and I never got along." He pretended to care less than Andy knew he did.

"Angels don't always get along with other angels?" Andy thought there was some unspoken rule that all angels must get along or something.

"We have to be civil with one another, but there's no law saying I have to like everyone I meet," he explained.

"That makes sense. Malachi has hated me since the day he met me." She tried to laugh, but the statement was too true to be funny.

"He doesn't hate you, that's his personality. He's a lot older than anyone else here, including Ephram, and by a lot I mean like at least three hundred years, probably more. So, he acts like he has no time for us younger angels, and I mean, he has so many other responsibilities that's probably true."

"I definitely got that side of him." That helped to explain why he had started out not liking her.

"I mean, he might not like you for real now, because of Septimus. Malachi and Ephram have always been super protective of him because he is Ephram's only remaining son," Micah pointed out.

"Well, I did know that part, and I get it, I do, but he should be allowed to live his life how he wants," Andy argued.

"It's not as simple as that for angels. Our main purpose here on Earth is to protect humans. We are obligated to always put them first. If Ephram and Malachi think Septimus' relationship with you will influence his ability to do that in any way, they can and will do everything to make sure you don't get in the way." Micah seemed concerned for her now.

"That sounds like a threat," she said warily.

"Maybe it is. I'd be careful around them for a while until you figure out whose side they are on. He may convince them your relationship won't be an issue, but for your sake, be careful."

"Well thanks for the warning," Andy said. It irked her that no matter what she did, it seemed like Malachi would always despise her. She didn't want to be living in the same camp as someone who seemed to have it out for her.

"Hey you two. Why so serious?" Bo entered the tent in good spirits and plopped beside Micah.

"Oh, discussing training. Speaking of which, how did yours go?" Andy tried to sound upbeat, but Micah's warning still bounced around in her head.

"Pretty good, actually. Of course, today I had the upper hand, what with my upper body strength from playing football, so I had to go easy on Ace," Bo gloated, trying to impress Micah, though Micah was already under his spell. Andy shook her head, smiling to herself.

Ace, Sera, Gabby, and Nathan, all joined them, and the chatter turned to talk about all the moves Bo and Ace had learned and what Gabby and Sera had planned for the next day; combat combined with the swords. Andy barely listened, still wondering where Septimus was and what Ephram had been talking to him about. She pushed her food around her plate, too anxious to eat, and Bo noticed.

"Is everything all right, Andy?" He took her hand to get her attention away from the food on her plate.

"Yeah...I just...I haven't seen Septimus since this morning and I'm...worried, I guess. He went to talk with Ephram, and he's been gone ever since." Andy dropped her fork and pushed her plate away.

"Everything's probably fine," Bo tried to reassure her, but her nerves still had her leg bouncing under the table. "Come on. Let's go." He stood and held his arm out for her to take. She let him lead her out of the tent, but not before she saw the longing on Micah's face. He regained his composure and continued chatting with the others.

"Where are we even going?" Andy asked, as Bo started leading her towards the woods.

"You need to clear your head." He led her into the woods and over to the fallen tree. They sat observing the sky for a while, not speaking. Andy took some deep, cleansing breaths, trying to clear her head of all the negative thoughts. She peeked over at Bo, wondering what he was thinking about. He noticed her staring. "Do you think my parents are up there? You know, in heaven, looking down on us and all that."

"Septimus told me that originally all people went to heaven, until hell was created. So, I assume that means that still holds true so long as people are worthy or whatever the criteria is. There's no doubt in my mind your parents are in heaven right now," Andy told him. "You could try talking to Micah about it too though, I'm sure he would know more."

"Yeah, you're right." Bo sighed and laid his head on her shoulder. They sat like that until Andy needed to get up and stretch her legs.

"Come on, we should be getting back." Andy held her hand out to Bo and he took it.

While they walked back into camp, Andy noticed Septimus coming out of the meeting tent. Her first instinct was to run to him, but she held herself back. If they had been discussing his relationship with her, whatever it was, she didn't want to make anything worse.

"There he is," Bo said, examining her and most likely trying to gauge her reaction.

"Yep." She wondered if Septimus would notice them staring at him, or if he would go about his day now. About five seconds later, he made eye contact with Andy from across the camp. A flicker of apprehension crossed his face, like he was worried she was going to make a scene or something, and he ignored her, ducking into his own tent. Bo let out a long breath as if he has been holding it the whole time.

"Andy, take my hand." Bo grabbed her hand and squeezed it. "Now, squeeze it as hard as you need to, just please don't break any bones." She searched his face and could tell he was serious. He could sense the anger and pain that coursed through her in that moment. She squeezed his hand, but not as hard as she wanted to.

"He could have at least smiled, waved, something," Andy said through gritted teeth. "But we're nothing, right? We never said this was anything, we're not dating, we're not boyfriend and girlfriend, we're nothing. That's what this is." She tried to convince herself so she would feel less stung by his actions, but it did not help at all.

"You and Septimus are not nothing, Andy. You slept in his bed last night for God's sake! That was *his* doing. He came to *our* tent for you, not the other way around." Bo pulled her into a hug, and she sagged against him. "He's an idiot. That's the only explanation."

"Thanks, Bo." She pulled away from him. "I think I need some time to process my life for a little while. You should go find Micah. I think he would like to hang out with you more."

"Why, what did he tell you?" Bo's eyes widened.

"Nothing, just that he really likes you, and I think he might want to spend some more time with you, because I'm always hogging you." Bo still looked wary, but she realized it was more because he wasn't sure if she should be alone. He worried too much about her and not enough about himself. "I'll be fine. Don't worry about me."

"Okay... but if you need anything, come find me." He gave her hand one last squeeze and walked off in the direction of Micah's tent.

18

The Lake

As Andy laid alone in her tent on her cot, she tried to think through everything that had happened in the last two weeks. She had been separated from her dad by the angels, began training to fight the demons, her dad had been taken hostage by the demons, Bo's parents were murdered, Lindy was abducted, and everything that had happened between her and Septimus.

For the first time in a while, she thought about her mom. She usually didn't allow herself to think about her or Jason, because the memories brought with them too much grief, and Andy needed a clear head to stay sane. But, right now, she needed her mom. Andy closed her eyes and thought back to the last time she'd seen her.

Broken Angel

Angeline leaned against their kitchen counter, talking to Wayne who sat at the bar. Jason was in his room playing video games. Angeline and Andy looked alike, people always mistook them for sisters, sometimes even twins. Andy didn't think her mom had aged a day since she turned twenty-nine. Andy sat at the kitchen table listening to her parents talk about where they could go if they were forced to leave their home. The war began a few months back between the angels and demons, and Andy was way past the point where she could pretend everything was okay. The world seemed to be falling apart around them, and most of their neighbors had already cleared out to head to bigger cities.

"We could always go to an angel camp," Angeline said. She glanced over to Andy, and Andy realized she had something more she wanted to say, but she didn't want to say it in front of her.

"Oh, come on Ang. I think they deserve to know." Wayne regarded Andy too, and she stared back in bewilderment.

"Deserve to know what?" Andy asked. Angeline glanced between Wayne and Andy, biting her lip. Closing her eyes, she let out a long sigh before sitting in the chair beside Andy. She took Andy's hands in hers and looked her in the eyes. Andy had inherited her eyes, blue with flecks of gold in them.

"Andy, sweetie... I need you to understand something. I hoped I would have more time to tell you this, but with what is going on these days, I'm not sure we have that luxury anymore. Your father is right, you deserve to know the truth," she started and paused, glancing down the hall towards Jason's room. "I can tell

Jason after," she said more to herself than to Andy. She took a deep breath. "I'm an angel, Andromeda." Andy gaped at her, not quite sure of the implications of what she was saying, and not believing it either. Andy couldn't quite grasp the concept and all she could do was blink. "You and Jason; you're both angels," Angeline added, causing more turmoil in Andy's mind.

"Oh," Andy managed to get out.

"I wanted you both to live normal lives, so that's why I didn't tell either of you sooner. I had planned to tell Jason on his eighteenth birthday, but I couldn't bring myself to do it, and then his nineteenth birthday rolled around, and you were turning eighteen, and I just... I didn't want to burden either of you." Tears filled her eyes, and Andy couldn't help but wonder why her mom thought it would be a burden to know who they were. Slow clapping sounded in the doorway between their entryway and the kitchen. All of them turned to see who the clapping was coming from.

"That was beautiful, Angeline." A man stepped out of the shadows and Andy noticed his black eyes right away. That was the first time she had seen a demon up close. Angeline and Wayne both froze. "And, Andromeda, you have grown into a beautiful young woman, haven't you?" Andy shrunk back into her chair.

"W-what are you doing here?" Angeline spoke as if she knew the demon who stood in front of them. Wayne started inching closer to Andy.

"Stop," the demon spoke in a harsh manner, directing his words to Wayne, who stopped moving. "This has nothing to do with you, human," he spat out. "As for why I am here, Angeline, you can't have forgotten?" he sneered, and it seemed to contort his face and make him even more menacing.

"How did you find me?" Angeline's voice was still strong, but Andy had a fear deep down in her gut that everything was going to end in disaster.

"We've had your scent for a while, Angeline. The hounds have been itching to come after you, but we had to wait until the time was right." He smirked and Andy could hear a scratching at the front door. Angeline turned towards Jason's room and the demon laughed. "Oh, Angeline, he's been gone for hours. You should keep a better eye on your children." Panic came over Angeline's face, and Wayne ran to Jason's room. Andy could tell by the dread on his face when he returned that the demon had not been lying.

"What did you do to him?" Angeline sounded vicious and was showing a side Andy had never seen of her before.

"Me? I did nothing. I've been here with you. But my colleagues on the other hand... there's no telling what they've been up to," the demon sneered. Angeline lunged at him and started yelling at Wayne.

"Take Andy and go to the camp! Don't come back, just go!" She yelled as she grappled with the demon. Wayne grabbed Andy's arm and yanked her towards the door, she kept glancing back hoping she would see Angeline following, but she was still fighting with the demon. As Andy and her dad ran out the door, she saw the demon draw a knife from his belt, and Andy turned away before she saw anymore. Her dad fumbled with the car keys, and within seconds they were speeding away from their house and towards their new, *nomadic life.*

Andy opened her eyes and noticed the sun had set while she had been daydreaming. Andy's face was wet with tears, and she wiped them away. She always wondered what would have happened if they had left their house sooner. Would they all still be together? Or would the demons have found them either way?

Ace entered the tent and seemed surprised to see Andy there.

"Hey, Andy. You weren't at dinner, are you feeling okay?" He had genuine concern in his voice, and a lump formed in Andy's throat. She was supposed to be saving his sister, and here she was, lying in bed, worrying about a maybe relationship with a guy who couldn't make up his mind.

"Yeah. I'm okay now. I needed a break from all this." She made a sweeping gesture with her hand.

"I get it. It's been a crazy couple of days. Well, I'm gonna crash. Training drains me." Ace yawned and laid on his cot, pulling his headphones and CD player out from under his pillow. Andy decided to get some food, since she hadn't eaten her lunch earlier, and her stomach felt empty.

The dining tent was nearly empty when Andy arrived, so she grabbed a plate of food and sat to eat alone. She found herself thinking about that demon who had been in their house, watching them as they had planned their next move. She wondered how long he had watched them before revealing himself.

"Mind if I join you?" Andy was pulled out of her thoughts, and she peered up to see Septimus standing beside her. He sat before she could answer, and she continued eating without acknowledging him. It was his turn to make the first move. "I should have come to talk to you sooner. I have been doing a lot of thinking."

"So, have I." Andy turned to face him, ready to stand up for herself. "You don't get to treat me like," she thought for a moment. "Like I don't matter." Andy was no longer angry with him, but she needed some answers. Too much else in her life was an unknown right then.

"I know, you're right. I was wrong to avoid you earlier, but my father... he had gotten into my head," Septimus tried to explain, but that was not a good enough excuse for Andy.

"Well, how unfortunate for you," she said sarcastically, jabbing at her food with her fork.

"Andromeda, please. I'm trying to make this right." She could hear the plea in his voice, so she set her fork down and focused on him again.

"What exactly are you trying to make right? What is *this*?" She searched his eyes and saw him struggling with himself to find the right words.

"Well, I know what I want this to be, but I don't want to assume you feel the same way." He was always so careful, sometimes *too* careful, when it came to him worrying about overstepping boundaries. Sometimes Andy wished he would take the leap.

"You're going to make me say it, aren't you? Well, fine. I want to be more than friends. Is that what you needed?" She couldn't help but smile as the words came out of her mouth. She had been waiting for that moment and it was finally happening. "What happened to the 'reckless' Septimus the others warned me about?" Andy teased, and his face grew serious.

"I haven't taken any risks since the last one caused my brother to depart Earth before his time." His eyelids fluttered.

Andy's face reddened from her blunder. "I-I'm sorry," she said.

"Don't be. I'll see him again someday. I'm sorry to have brought the mood down so considerably." Septimus took Andy's hand in his. "Let's talk about something else."

"Okay. So, where did we end up with the whole me wanting to be more than friend's idea?" Andy blushed as she spoke. Instead of answering, Septimus bent his head to Andy's and kissed her, in front of the few people who remained in the dining tent. He pulled back and kept talking as if nothing had changed, and Andy could not be happier.

"So, Malachi will resume training you tomorrow."

"I assumed that might happen." Andy took Septimus' hand under the table. "I wish I could keep training with you, but I'll do whatever I can to make sure he doesn't dislike me anymore than he already does."

"He likes you...well, maybe not so much. But it's not

that he doesn't like you, he doesn't like us being together." He tried to make it seem better than it was.

"I'll win him over, don't worry. I've been told I'm irresistible," Andy joked, remembering Bo's pep talk in the shower tent the night before.

"I would attest to that," Septimus smirked. "Come on, let's get out of here." He stood and held his hand out for Andy to take. He led her towards the entrance to the camp.

"Where are we going?"

"I told you; we're getting out of here. Don't worry, we will be untraceable by the hellhounds," he reassured her. Andy decided to trust him and let him lead her out of the camp and through the trees, back towards the town.

When they came to a little clearing, big enough that you could see the sky and the stars, Septimus stopped walking.

Outside of the camp's boundaries, Andy felt exposed and sensed someone watching them. "How are the hellhounds not going to find me out here in the open?" Septimus answered her by revealing his wings and letting them unfurl from his back.

"Do you trust me?" He held his arms out, and in answer, Andy put her arms around his neck, clasping her hands there. He placed one arm behind her knees and the other supported her back as he scooped her up into his arms. A gust of wind whipped up from his wings coming together and parting again as they rose into the air. Andy held on a little tighter as they climbed higher and higher until they were above all the trees.

Andy could see the town beyond the tree line, and in the opposite direction, she could see the clearing, and more trees stretching on. Septimus took them in the direction of the town. It was eerily dark since no one was currently inhabiting it. They flew over the town, and past another smaller forest until they came to a lake. They began descending and Andy loosened her grip on Septimus.

Once they landed, Septimus set Andy back on her feet and, after regaining her balance, she walked to the edge of the water. They stood on a small beach beside the lake. Andy picked up a handful of sand and allowed it to run through her fingers. She couldn't remember the last time she had been to a beach. Septimus stepped up beside her and she noticed his wings were gone. The stars reflected off the surface of the lake, which was calm and smooth.

"It's beautiful," Andy commented, feeling the sudden urge to wade into the water and let it envelop her, washing away all her worries and fears.

Andy took off her boots and socks first. Septimus observed her, his eyebrows arched in question. She unbuckled her belt, and he looked away, trying to be modest. Andy laughed to herself at this. After her pants, off came her jacket and shirt, until she stood on the beach in her bra and underwear. Septimus still pretended to be occupied with something attached to his belt, and Andy laughed to herself.

She started to wade into the water and a rush of adrenaline overcame her as the water rose to her shins and over her knees, until it met her stomach, which was always the hardest part to submerge. Andy turned her head to see Septimus watching her, still standing, fully clothed on the sand.

"Are you going to stand there or are you going to come join me?" she called back to him over her shoulder. She could feel her hair tickling her below her shoulder blades as she turned her head back to face forward. She played with one of her curls as she waited for a response from Septimus.

After about a minute, Andy heard him wading into the water behind her. She smiled to herself but continued admiring the water glistening in front of her. She passed her hand over the surface, watching as little ripples spread out from the points she touched.

She turned back towards the beach to see Septimus almost beside her. The gold in his eyes was brought out even more by the moon.

"I was beginning to wonder..." she started, but before she could finish, he pulled her into his arms and kissed her. Andy pressed her hands against his bare chest and trailed them over his abs and around to his back. She pulled him closer. His lips traced her jaw and down her neck, to her collarbone. She let her head fall back and closed her eyes. A twig snapped in the distance, and Andy stiffened. "Wait..." she pulled away and Septimus loosened his arms around her.

"Did you hear that?"

"I didn't hear anything," he said.

Andy couldn't shake the feeling they were being watched, and she had the need to cover herself up, but her clothes were a good forty feet away from her, back on the beach.

"Something's not right, I think we should be getting back." Andy decided to trust her instincts like her dad had told her to and started wading back through the water as quickly as she could without making too much noise. Septimus followed behind her, but she didn't dare look back and take her eyes off the beach.

When they reached the sand, Andy struggled to pull her clothes on, since she was still dripping wet. She needed to get as far from there as possible, as soon as possible. Nothing was visible in the woods on either side of the little beach, but she *knew* someone was out there, watching and waiting. She could feel it.

They both dressed and Septimus had unfurled his wings again. Andy let him pick her up and they took off into the air. Once they were above the tree line, she allowed herself to look back down at the beach. A distinct figure stood where they had just been. She buried her face into Septimus' chest and remained that way until they landed back in the small clearing.

When they were back inside the camp, Andy was finally able to breathe again. Everyone else was already in their tents, except for the angels on the night watch. Septimus walked Andy back to her tent.

"Are you sure you're okay?" he asked, his eyes filled with concern. Andy knew he had not seen the figure. He had not looked back like she had, too focused on where he was going. He thought she had made up an excuse to end their moment.

"I'm sure. I just need some sleep." She gave him a smile to try to convince him that everything was okay.

"Sleep well." He kissed her and strolled towards his tent. Andy ducked inside her tent and went straight to Bo's cot. He was asleep, but she needed to talk to him, so she plopped onto the cot with enough force to wake him.

"Ugh..." he moaned. "I'm asleep..." he muttered, turning away from her.

"Nooo," she shook his shoulder, "you're waking up. Come on, Bo." He turned to face her, grudgingly, and let out a long sigh.

"Wha-" he yawned. "What is it?"

"Septimus took me flying, and we went to a lake," she began, knowing it would capture his attention.

"Alright, I'm awake now." He sat up, his eyes gleaming. "This is going to be good; I can tell."

"Well, it was good at first, we went into the lake, and we kissed, but I heard something in the woods," Andy explained. Bo's face changed to a look of concern. "He didn't hear anything, but I knew something was out there, so I made us leave. When we were flying away, I saw...something. A figure, standing where we had just been. Septimus didn't see it, and I didn't want to worry him, so I didn't tell him about it." It all came spilling out, and Bo listened.

"I'm glad you made him leave. Do you think it was a demon?" They both knew the answer, but Andy responded anyway.

"Yes. I think there's a demon following me, but for some reason it hasn't been trying to take me like the other demons." Andy finally spoke the words aloud. Ever since the first night she saw the hooded figure, she worried that might be the case, and then she saw the shadow following them when they were going to the human camp, and again tonight. She knew for sure now. It all made it even more nerve wracking to think that if she was being personally followed, maybe her nightmares were not just dreams...

"I was afraid of that," Bo lowered his voice even further. "Do you think they're out there, right now?"

"I wouldn't doubt it," Andy matched his whisper; wary someone could be listening in on them. She wasn't sure how close to the camp the demons could get; she knew they could at least be in the woods behind them. She shuddered.

"Do you think Ephram and Septimus know?" Bo asked.

"Maybe. If they did, they probably wouldn't tell me, so as not to worry me." Andy rolled her eyes.

"Well, let's worry about all that tomorrow. We both

need to get some sleep." Bo moved back a little, so Andy had room to lay beside him. It was pointless for her to sleep on her own cot, since they both knew they would likely end up together because of her nightmares anyway. She settled in beside him on the cot and listened as his breathing became slow and steady. He was asleep, and it put her at ease. She closed her eyes, expecting to be awoken shortly by another nightmare, but, that night, she slept soundly with no dreams.

19

The Demon

Andy dragged herself to the dining tent for dinner after an exhausting day of training with Malachi. She paused outside, as she saw Septimus sit next to Sera at their usual table. Andy didn't want to interrupt them, so she hung back for a moment and listened.

"It's weird having you sitting with us," Sera commented, and Septimus looked up from his food to face her.

"Why is it so weird?" he asked.

"I mean, you never paid any of us much attention before Andy arrived," she admitted, and Septimus looked a little guilty.

"I'm sorry, I guess I was so wrapped up in the war, I

never had time for anything else." He took a bite of his food, and Sera watched him for a moment before speaking again.

"It's kind of nice having you in our group, the older angels seem to respect us a little more." Sera's statement seemed to surprise Septimus.

"What do you mean? You are one of our best fighters, and your friends are equally as capable as any of the other angels to fight with our guards," Septimus said with complete honesty.

"Well, thank you." Sera blushed a little, which shocked Andy, because Sera never blushed. Septimus and Sera smiled at each other, and it made Andy feel uncomfortable, spying on them like this. She made her way into the tent, grabbed a plate of food, and sat across from them at the table. She didn't feel the urge to sit beside Septimus right then.

"How did training go?" Septimus asked Andy, and she sighed, not in the mood to talk about it. "Is everything alright?" She forced a smile onto her face.

"Yes, fine. Sorry, it's been a long day." It wasn't a lie, she *was* tired. The rest of their group joined them and saved Andy from having to talk anymore. She excused herself before anyone else and made her way towards the woods. She observed the darkness and wondered what monsters may be lurking out there. She jumped when she felt a hand on her shoulder, but she turned to see it was only Septimus.

"Would you like to take a walk before bed?" He offered his hand to her. She considered taking it for a moment, but instead shook her head.

"I think I'm going to turn in for the night." She yawned as if on cue. "But I will come find you if I change my mind." She kissed him and ducked into her tent. Bo came in behind her and looked surprised to see her there, alone.

"Not hanging out with Septimus tonight?" he asked, a little suspicious.

"I needed some time away from him. Besides, I missed you." She winked, and he laughed. Andy laid on her cot, and Bo lay down beside her, yawning.

"I'm not going to be much company." He yawned again.

"I'm wiped too," she admitted, staring up at the roof of the tent. "Do you ever feel like maybe we don't belong here? Or fit in here..." She let her thoughts leak out to Bo. He turned to her.

"I mean, I obviously don't belong here, I'm human and everyone else is an angel," he reminded her.

"That's not what I mean...like everyone here has been together for so long..." Her sentence trailed off.

"People love you, Andy. You can belong anywhere you want to." He tried to reassure her as he rolled over, but it did nothing to quell that growing sense that she wasn't where she was supposed to be.

"I just haven't felt like myself since we've been here. I thought I would finally feel, strong, I guess, but right now, I just more helpless than ever. Or maybe I'm just broken..."

Andy realized Bo had fallen asleep. In her mind she let that word swirl around; *broken*. It seemed to her all the other angels knew exactly where they were supposed to be, and what they were doing. She knew she was new to all of this, and maybe that sense of belonging would come in time. But it was not only that out of place feeling that made her wonder. Her anxiety, her nightmares, and her inability to accept that she was supposed to be fighting with the angels in the war, all made her think something else was wrong with her.

I'm broken. That's why I can't even sleep alone anymore. I'm weak. Her thoughts turned against her. She shook her head to clear it. It was all too much to think about. Andy would try to talk to Bo about it in the morning.

Andy had no nightmares again and woke feeling refreshed, forgetting all about her worries from the night before. She found Malachi after breakfast, and they headed to the clearing.

They started by practicing sword fighting without the heavenly fire. He went easy on Andy at first so she could find her bearings. As they continued, he quickened his pace, using more difficult moves. Andy grew more confident with every swing of her sword. They decided to take a break before they started using the heavenly fire.

"You have improved much since our previous sessions," Malachi commented.

"Thank you, I practiced with Septimus and Micah too,"

she acknowledged and realized her mistake in mentioning Septimus when Malachi's face twisted into a scowl.

"Oh, I know of your sessions with Septimus," he sneered. His sword was engulfed in the flames of the heavenly fire. Andy tried to summon her fire as well, but he was already behind her. He pulled her left arm behind her back and pinned it there while holding his sword aloft in front of her, the fire coming so close she could feel the heat which caused sweat to bead on her forehead. "He needs a clear head so he can be an effective fighter," he said through gritted teeth, and Andy could feel the anger coming off him in waves. Suddenly, his sword dropped to the ground, and he released her arm. She turned to see him crumple to the ground, unconscious.

Behind him stood a demon who looked to be about her age, wearing a haughty grin. He was much taller than Andy, maybe by six or seven inches. His brown hair was shaved close to his head, and his eyes were black, like every other demon she had met. He swung his sword around in his hand and sheathed it in his belt. Andy gaped at him, terrified she was about to be lying beside Malachi on the ground.

"W-what...who...why did you do that?" Andy stammered, grasping the sword at her side.

"A 'thank you' would be nice," he prompted, crossing his arms over his chest. Andy's hand gripped her swords hilt, ready to be drawn at a moment's notice.

"Why should I thank you?!" She was still in shock.

"He was about to hurt you, and I saved you. You're

welcome." He gave a little bow.

"How do you know he was going to hurt me, and he wasn't just trying to send me a message by threatening me?" She studied Malachi. She knew Malachi didn't like her, but he would never hurt her, at least, that was what she had thought.

"Just trust me on that fact, but that's not why I'm here. I'm here to offer you an opportunity to help save your dad and the girl." Andy's jaw dropped.

"What do you mean?" She questioned him, her eyes narrowing.

"I mean, I know where they are right now, and I can take you to them." He sounded a little annoyed that she was asking any questions at all.

"How can I trust you? You're a demon, and I have no idea who you are." Andy crossed her arms over her chest and stood tall, trying to look a little more intimidating.

"Look, we don't have much time before your dad and the girl…"

"Lindy," Andy snapped, interrupting him.

"Fine, your dad and *Lindy*, are going to be unreachable within the next three hours. We need to leave *now* if you want to save them." He pointed to his wrist as if he was wearing a watch.

"Why would you help me save them?" Andy wanted to save the people she loved, but it could all be a trap.

"Well, now that you ask, there may be a slight catch," he smirked, and Andy groaned. "Leave with me now, and I will help you save Wayne and Lindy, but only Lindy will be coming back to this camp. You will be coming with me, boss' orders." He gave her a mock sorry look.

"How is that any better than me going with those other demons who have my dad and Lindy?" Andy asked, exasperated.

"Well for one, I'm not going to kill Lindy or your dad. Where they're going now, there's no guarantee they will survive the night, which is why we need to intercept them on their way," he explained, and Andy felt the urgency he had been trying to convey.

"Fine. I'll go with you. Can I at least say goodbye to Bo and Septimus?" She didn't want to leave them without any explanation, knowing they would both fear the worst.

"We've already delayed too long. We have to leave *now*." He glanced down as Malachi stirred on the ground. "You have five seconds, and then I'm gone."

"No, I'll go. Let's go." Andy couldn't give up her chance to save her dad and Lindy.

"Good." He started walking away, back into the woods, and Andy followed. They walked past the fallen log, and past the camp. Andy craned her neck to try to see anyone who she could tell that she was leaving, but no one was around. She quickened her step to catch up with the demon.

"Quick question," she spoke up as she reached his side. He continued walking at the same pace, not bothering to look at her. "Who are you?" Andy asked, realizing he knew way too much about her and she did not even know his name.

"I guess it's only fair since I know your name, you know mine. I'm Kaden, your guardian angel," he laughed and winked at her. *Kaden...* she flashed back to the demon who had approached her when she was on her way back to the angel camp after visiting her dad. That was the name he had spoken when he had been fighting against himself to get to Andy. So, maybe Kaden *wasn't* lying about trying to help her.

"Why have you been following me?" She tried not to sound out of breath but keeping up with him proved a little difficult.

"Someone has to keep an eye on you. Your boyfriend was clearly not doing such a good job." Andy ignored that comment.

"How long have you been watching me, then?" Andy wasn't sure if she wanted to hear the answer.

"Me, specifically; since you arrived at this camp, but you've been watched since the day you and your father left your house." Andy cringed. He knew the impact his words had on her, and he laughed. "Don't be so upset, darling, we've saved you on multiple occasions." *Darling.* The word rattled her and brought her back to her nightmares. Kaden seemed to sense nothing amiss and continued. "Marcus was the one who saved you numerous times while on the road with your band of misfits."

"What do you mean?" Andy asked, skeptical that anyone had been helping them since those first weeks had been so horrid.

"Remember those howls you heard while on the road? They distracted the hellhounds who were out for angel blood. And that round guy…"

"Patrick?" Andy cut in.

"Yeah him. Marcus compelled him to walk into that store and invite you back to his house. If not for us, your whole group would have never made it to the angel camp." It all made sense to Andy. There were multiple occasions she remembered thinking they should not have made it out alive, but they did.

"What about the hellhounds and demon who showed up at Patrick and Stella's house? They killed everyone in that house!" Andy could not believe people who were supposedly looking out for her would also slaughter an entire household of innocent people. His face became serious.

"We aren't the only demons interested in recruiting you, Andy," he revealed. "They figured out where you were after the hellhound caught your scent when you went exploring Patrick's neighbors' houses. Had Marcus not intervened, they would have caught you that day. They almost got you again when you stupidly went to that human camp."

"Where were you then? I had to fight my way out of that situation," Andy pointed out.

"Don't remind me. The boss almost had my head for that one. I was distracted." Kaden explained no further.

"Okay, distracted by what exactly?" Andy pressed.

"None of your business. I saved your ass when you finally smartened up and headed back to the angel camp. That's all that matters." So, it *was* him that stopped the other demon.

"Why didn't you stop the other demons from taking Lindy? If you've been watching me, you should have seen her when she left the camp," Andy pointed out.

"I can only do so much. If I'd tried to stop them, I risked getting taken myself, and I was needed here to watch over you. Besides, I knew I would be able to get her back."

"Well, why are they transporting my dad and Lindy now? I thought they wanted to use them to get to me." Andy changed the topic away from the attack.

"They were trying to use Lindy and your dad to lure you to them, but since that wasn't working, they decided they could put them to use in other ways. That's why they're transferring them to their main camp now."

"Why do the other demons want me?" She wondered what made her so special that two different groups of demons fought to get to her.

"That doesn't matter, so long as you stay with me, you'll never have to find out." Kaden sounded cocky now, making Andy laugh.

"As if you're going to be able to protect me from a whole horde of demons? How are we even going to be able to fight them all off?" Andy asked.

"Don't worry about that. I have a plan. But for now,

please, stop talking." They had made it to the edge of the woods where a car waited for them. He opened the passenger door for her.

"After you." He slammed the door after she was in the car, and then went around to the other side. Whoever had left the car there for them, had also left the keys in the ignition.

They drove out of town, and Andy focused on the trees passing by her window. It remained silent for a while, and then she turned to face Kaden.

"So where are we going?" For all Andy knew, he could be one of the demons who had taken her dad and Lindy, and she had doomed them all.

"Can you last more than ten seconds without asking a question?" he groaned.

"Can you last more than ten seconds without being cruel?" Andy retorted.

"I'm cruel because I'm a demon, and it's in my nature. And, I like playing with people's emotions, especially humans. They're so easily manipulated," he sneered, unaffected by her anger.

"But you have a soul, so you have the capability to actually care, and maybe not be so cruel," Andy pointed out.

He cocked an eyebrow at her. "Who says I have a soul?"

"I know the story of the original demons, who were angels that fell from heaven. They were angels and they had souls, yet they were capable of the same kind of cruelty that you've shown me. You don't have to be soulless to be cruel." Andy couldn't help her curiosity about demons, especially since she was now being brought directly to them, as she'd promised she wouldn't let happen. Guilt swirled in her gut, causing it to roil with nausea. She pushed the feeling down for the moment so she could focus on what Kaden was saying.

"We have souls, they just don't necessarily belong to us," he admitted. "Lucifer has command of our souls, at least those of us who enter his servitude willingly. I, on the other hand, was born a demon. So, my soul is mine, until I choose to give him the reins."

"Huh. So, you're telling me, not only do you *have* a soul, but you control it? Yet, you still choose to be merciless and help Lucifer steal other people's souls." She clucked her tongue in disapproval.

"I guess, but it's not stealing if they willingly give them up." He smirked and continued watching the road ahead of them.

"I thought it was uncommon for demons to be able to have children," Andy stated, wondering if he would give her any insight on the issue.

"My mom used to be an angel, the daughter of a ruler. Then, my parents got lucky, and now, you get to benefit from their luck by being graced with my presence." Andy rolled her eyes.

"I get it now. You were spoiled as a child, weren't you?" It would explain his holier-than-thou attitude all the time. He slammed on the brakes and turned to her.

"Let me make this perfectly clear for you, we are not friends, I have no desire to *be* friends, no matter how hard you try, and don't you ever assume anything about me or my childhood." He turned back to face the road and they were off again. She had done it; she had pushed the right button. She turned to look out the window and smiled to herself.

"You know, I don't want to be friends with you either." Andy turned back to Kaden, determined to keep him talking. The more he talked, the more useful information he may reveal. "I'm not sure where you got that impression, but now I'm thinking *you do* want to be friends. Isn't that how it goes? The boys are always mean to the girls they like. Reverse psychology." She tried to stay nonchalant, even though she gagged as she thought about being friends with a demon. "Besides, you're the one who sought me out in the angel camp."

"You don't shut up, do you?" he grumbled.

"Fine. I'll be quiet." She started drumming her fingers on the armrest and humming a random tune. She could tell he was getting annoyed as his grip on the steering wheel tightened and his jaw clenched.

"Please, stop," he grumbled through gritted teeth.

"Please? So, your parents *did* teach you manners. Huh. Weird." She stilled her hands and stopped humming. Her sword started to dig into her thigh, and she tried to adjust in her seat to get comfortable, but it was too cumbersome.

"What's wrong with you?" Kaden glared at her like she was being ridiculous.

"It's my sword. Can I put it in the back? I promise not to take it out of its sheath or anything." Andy knew to still be careful. She still didn't entirely trust the claim that he was helping her.

"Fine," he snapped.

"Thank you. I guess they don't expect you to be in a car with this thing on." She unhooked her sword from her belt and laid it across the back seat. "That's much better." She settled back into her seat and wiggled her coat off.

"What are you doing now?" He was becoming paranoid.

"I'm taking off my jacket. Chill. It's hot in here." She threw her jacket into the backseat on top of her sword. She readjusted in her seat and hugged her knees to her chest.

"How is *that* more comfortable for you?" He gaped at her in disbelief.

"Don't judge." She leaned back and he shook his head.

"You are ridiculous," he said, and she noticed a smile playing at the corners of his mouth.

"At least I'm not a jerk who takes pleasure in messing with other people's emotions," Andy countered.

"Lash out at me all you want. I can take it."

"What makes you think I need to lash out at you?"

"You're mad at me because I'm the one who took you from your friends," he guessed.

"I'm not mad at you, well maybe a little, but not because of that. You're following orders, and you're taking me to save my dad and Lindy. I don't care what happens to me after that. If I'm mad about anything it's that I live in a world where I have been forced to make the decision to give up my happiness or have people I love be killed and be unhappy anyway. I'm mad both of my parents have been forcibly removed from my life, and I'm mad my mom waited *eighteen years* to tell me I'm an angel. I'm mad I never got to go to college and become a teacher," Andy paused; she had never put much thought into what her life would have been like had the war never started. "But, no, I'm not mad at you."

"It must be nice to have so many things to be mad about," Kaden said, and Andy turned to him, confused. "My life now is pretty much the same as it was before the war. I am given orders, and I follow them without question. Although now I have to deal with you. So, I guess I can be mad about that," he joked.

"Ha, ha. Very funny." She slow clapped for him. "I guess I'd rather have things to be angry about, because at least that means I have something I care about enough to get angry at." She wondered whether he had ever had anyone he cared about, other than his parents. Although, she was not even sure he cared about them all that much.

"Well, I'm glad you've come to that realization." The sarcasm was obvious. Her stomach started to grumble.

"You don't have any food by chance?" she asked,

sheepishly. Her stomach growled even louder.

"That's almost worse than your humming. There're some crackers in the glove box." He reached over and opened it for her. She grabbed the sleeve of crackers and started eating them.

"Do you want any?" she asked, her mouth full, and held the sleeve out to him.

"No," he answered. After that, Andy stayed quiet for a while. She thought about Bo and Septimus and wondered whether they were upset with her for leaving, or if she would ever see them again.

"Are you allowed to tell me why your boss is so keen on having me? Why not kill me, like all the other angels you come across?" She broke the silence again.

"I could tell you, but I like surprises, and telling you would spoil all the fun." He winked at her.

"*Of course* it would." She crumbled up the empty cracker sleeve and tossed it onto the floor. She crossed her arms and looked out the window. There were no more trees, but fields now.

"Don't get all pouty on me now, it doesn't suit you."

"What do you care?" She continued staring out the window.

"I don't."

"Right. Got it." Something shifted in one of the fields and Andy tried to focus on it. The tall grass hid whatever it was too well, though, and she still couldn't see it properly.

"There's something out there," she commented, trying not to let him hear her intrigue or else she knew he wouldn't tell her anything. He slowed down a little, observing the tall grass.

"Would you look at that?" He grinned and Andy knew it could not be anything good. Its head popped out of the grass, and she understood why Kaden smiled. It was a hellhound, out in broad daylight. "We could stop and say hi if you want, I'm sure he'd love to get a little taste of you..."

"You're vile," Andy spat out. "Let's just go." She turned away and glared out the windshield. Kaden resumed his normal speed, and the hellhound was soon far behind them. Andy wanted nothing more than to sit in silence for the rest of the ride, however long that would be. However, curiosity got the better of her and she broke the silence once again. "I thought hellhounds only came out at night."

"Things are changing, darling. They've never *not* been able to go out in the daylight, but it was new to them, so they've needed time to get used to it. It seems like they're finally coming out of their shells." He laughed, though nothing about that was funny to Andy.

"Why do you always call me *darling*?" She hated it and it sounded so much worse coming from him, who claimed to not be one of the demons trying to harm her. Yet, whoever had been invading her nightmares had called her the same thing. She was not about to tell him this, though, and give him any insight into her mind.

"Don't tell me you don't find it endearing, even a

little." He winked at her and she shuddered. "Oh, come on, am I really so repulsive to you?"

"After everything demons have done to me and my family, are you surprised?" Andy wondered if he had any guilt at all for all the harm and pain he and his fellow demons had caused.

"So, if I had been a little nicer, maybe a little more heroic, like your boyfriend, you might be attracted to me?" He taunted her, fishing for some kind of validation.

"I guess we'll never know, now, will we?" Andy would not give him what he wanted. She was there to help save her dad and Lindy. "How much longer until we get to where we're going?"

"I feel like I keep having to repeat myself. I told you I'd let you know when we're close. You don't listen well, do you?" Andy leaned her head back against the headrest and closed her eyes. If she was going to have to deal with Kaden for the rest of the day, she was going to need a nap.

20

The Plan

Andy tried to sleep, but a pounding had started in her head, and it was getting worse as they drove. She glimpsed the clock on the dash that said it was three o'clock. The sun shone brightly in the sky, and they had yet to reach their destination. Trees lined the sides of the road again, and Andy felt safer, without all the openness the fields offered. She could see houses through the trees and wondered if anyone was living in any of them, or if they had all been abandoned, their owners fleeing towards the safety of the cities.

"I have to pee," she announced, stretching her arms out in front of her.

"You are a needy one, aren't you?" Kaden said, but he pulled the car to the side of the road. "Go ahead." Andy opened her door and walked deeper than necessary into the surrounding woods.

When she returned to the car, Kaden still sat in the driver's seat, waiting. Before she climbed in the car, he stepped out and announced he had to go too. He strolled into the woods.

Andy did some stretches while she waited, her body had been cramping from sitting in the car for so long. Her head was still pounding, and it steadily worsened. She let her hair out of its ponytail, trying to relieve some of the pressure building. It barely touched the blinding pain now throbbing in her skull. She put her head in her hands and tried massaging her temples, but even that wasn't helping. The pain continued to gradually increase. Andy fell to her knees, keeping her head in her hands, squeezing it as if it would explode otherwise.

"What's happening here?" Kaden was back and he crouched beside Andy.

"Make it stop," she whimpered. "Please, make it stop."

"What's wrong?" Andy heard an actual hint of concern in his voice, emphasis on the hint.

"My head," she croaked. Bile rose in her throat, the pain so severe it turned her stomach. She threw her hands to the ground in front of her as the crackers came back up. She heaved until there was nothing left in her stomach. Tears streamed down her face, and she realized Kaden was holding her hair back. She turned her head to him. "What's happening to me?" Her throat was raw, and it hurt to talk.

"We're closer than I thought to crossing into demon territory. It's a mental trick demons use to keep out angels and I've seen it before. There must be a demon nearby to be able to get into your head. Come on, we should keep moving before they show up." He grabbed one of her arms and helped her off the ground. She leaned on him and let him practically carry her back to the car. He opened the door to the back seat, moved her sword onto the floor, and helped her inside. She lay curled up on the seat, clutching her head in her hands. The car lurched forward, and they sped away.

It was a solid ten minutes before the pain started to subside in Andy's head. She waited until it was a dull ache to sit up.

"Ugh." Her mouth felt like sandpaper and tasted even worse. She ran her hands through her hair, trying to brush out some of the snarls that had formed from lying down.

"Feeling any better?" Kaden watched her in the rear-view mirror.

"I guess…I need some water or something though," her voice cracked.

"I've got some in the trunk, hold on." He pulled the car over again and hopped out. He was back in a few seconds holding two water bottles, one for Andy and one for himself. Before they pulled away, Andy opened the car door, swished some water in her mouth, and spit it onto the ground. She drank half of the bottle of water before Kaden pulled the car back onto the road.

"Thank you." She leaned forward onto the center console, so she was somewhat beside him.

"Whatever, it's just water." He tried to play it down, and Andy leaned back. "Which, you should slow down with, by the way. You're going to have to go to the bathroom again if you keep drinking it that fast." He put on his annoyed voice, and Andy grabbed the water bottle and started chugging it.

"You mean, like this?" She finished it off. "Ah, so good." He smirked in the mirror. "I already have to pee again anyway. But I'll let you know when it's serious." She leaned forward again.

"You are ridiculous."

"Ridiculously amazing? Or awesome? Or all the above?" She laid her head on her arm, watching him and gave him an *aren't I hilarious* smile.

"I stand by what I said: simply, ridiculous." She let out a dramatic sigh and leaned back into her seat.

"I'm coming up front," she announced, beginning the awkward climb over the center console into the passenger seat.

"W-what are you..." Andy dropped into the seat with a huff. "Actually, you're insane." Kaden shook his head, and Andy laughed. "Next time, I can pull over and you can get out and back in like a normal person."

"I thought we established that I'm not normal." She smirked. He started slowing the car down.

"We're here," he announced. Andy examined the area

around them, but nothing out of the ordinary stood out. Kaden pulled the car to the side of the road, and into an alcove Andy had not noticed before. He concealed the car behind a well-placed grouping of trees. "I had someone scout the area while we were on our way," he said.

"Now what?" Andy whispered, though she wasn't sure why.

"All you need to do is be a distraction," he told her, and Andy gaped at him.

"What do you mean? I came all this way to be a *distraction?* I'm not even going to be able to fight?" she exclaimed.

"If everything goes as planned, we will be out of here with both your dad and Lindy within ten minutes from..." he focused on the clock, waited a moment, and said, "Now."

"I'll believe it when I see it." Andy opened her door and stepped out of the car. Kaden followed suit and they made their way to the side of the road.

"All I need you to do is stand here." He steered her closer to the road. "You're going to wave down the SUV that is about to be coming around that corner. Once they pull over, walk back over there." He pointed to the tree line. "And wait until my friend over there." A tall, blonde, man waved to her from behind a tree on the other side of the road. "Gives you the signal to walk back to the car. I will meet you there with your dad and Lindy."

"Who is he?" Andy asked, indicating the man across

the road.

"That is Marcus, the one who was looking out for you before me. He is one of my boss' right hand men. He is here to make sure everything goes off without a hitch. If anything appears to be going wrong, he is going to get you out of here safely." Andy gave Kaden a worried look. "Don't worry, everything is going to go as planned."

"It better," she mumbled.

"Now, I have to hide, but remember the plan." Kaden left her alone on the side of the road, disappearing behind the trees. Marcus was gone, too, leaving Andy feeling *abandoned*. Even though she knew they were just out of sight, she could not shake that eeriness.

As Kaden had said, an SUV came zipping around the bend in the road a minute later. Andy did as she was told and waved her hand at the SUV. The driver slowed as they neared her and pulled towards her side of the road. She tried to push down the fear that was creeping up on her.

"Well, what do we have here?" Andy heard as the driver rolled down his window and gave her a sly grin. He licked his lips as he checked her out, leaning further out the window. "What's a pretty little angel like you doing out here all alone?" Andy took a step back, and another.

"I-I need a ride," she said, taking a few more steps back. "I'm lost." The demon cackled and turned to his companion in the passenger seat. Andy took the opportunity to take a few extra steps back towards the tree line.

"What do you think?" the demon asked. The demon in the passenger seat leaned forward, staring at Andy a little too intently.

"I think that's her." His eyes widened. "That's the girl he wants." The driver whipped his head back around, with an even wider grin spreading across his face.

"Oh shit. You're right!" He started to open his door, but it slammed shut forcefully. "What the-" he fought with his door. Andy had not seen Marcus yet, but she had also not been watching for him. She may have missed his signal.

A hand clamped onto Andy's arm, and another covered her mouth, stifling her scream. She was pulled backwards, under the cover of the trees. The hands let her go once she was out of sight of the SUV.

"What were you doing?" Kaden whispered harshly. "I never told you to *talk* to them!"

"What was I supposed to do, stand there looking like an idiot? I had to say something!" Andy whispered back, throwing her hands up in exasperation. "Where were you anyway? What kind of plan was that? They're still in there!" She pointed back to the road, and Kaden groaned.

"Everything went exactly to plan, except for *you*." He gestured to the car where Marcus hurried her dad and Lindy into the backseat. Andy squealed in surprise, and Kaden glared at her.

"Be quiet! They are still out there. Though, they'd be gone if you'd kept your mouth shut." Andy ignored him and ran to her dad. He pulled her into a tight embrace. "Everyone needs to get in the car. Andy, come with me," Kaden commanded. Wayne let her go, and she walked over to stand beside Kaden. Everyone else climbed into the car.

"What now?" Andy grumbled.

"We need to fix your mistake." He took her hand and led her back out towards the road, where the SUV was still idling. The two demons, though, were on the other side of the road seemingly searching for her.

"I think I have what you're looking for," Kaden spoke calmly, and both demons turned to look at him. Their eyes lit up when they saw Andy. A cold fear seeped through her bones as she grasped that Kaden was about to hand her over to these demons. "Remember, don't say a word," he muttered to her under his breath. Her gaze flicked from Kaden to the other demons hurrying towards them.

"Thanks mate." The driver gave Kaden a nod. "We'll take her and be on our way." He walked over to them and went to grab Andy's arm, but before he did, Kaden pulled her backwards. The demon shockingly did not seem to notice and seemed to think he had her in his grip, because he was leading an invisible being back to the SUV.

The other demon opened the back door, allowing the invisible being to be put inside, and then they hopped back into the SUV and took off.

"What the…" Andy was at a loss for words. "How did you do that?" She gazed up at Kaden in awe, but he didn't respond. Marcus pulled the car out to the road and Kaden jumped into the passenger seat, leaving Andy to climb in the back with Lindy and her dad.

"You came for me!" Lindy hugged Andy tightly.

"Of course I did," Andy told her. Lindy pulled back and Andy noticed her eyes were still a deep black color, but she seemed to be herself again.

"Where's Ace? And Bo?" Lindy asked.

"You will be back with your brother soon. I promise." Andy glanced at Kaden in the front seat, and he gazed back at her in the mirror.

"We have another car stashed around this corner. Marcus will take Lindy back to the angel camp," Kaden explained, and relief washed over Andy knowing that Lindy would be reunited with her brother in a few short hours.

Marcus started to slow the car and pulled to the side of the road. A small sedan waited ahead of them. Marcus hopped out of the car and opened the back door for Lindy. She looked at Andy anxiously.

"Can you come with me?" she asked, and it broke Andy's heart knowing that she couldn't.

"I'm sorry, Lindy…I promised Kaden I would go with him," Andy told her, and Lindy's eyes filled with tears.

"I'm scared," she whispered.

"I'll go with her," Wayne said, and Andy turned to look at him.

"Are you sure, Dad?" Andy worried if they split up,

she may lose him again. He gave her a reassuring smile.

"I'll make sure she gets back to Ace safely, and then I'll come back to you," he promised, and Andy hugged him.

"Let's pick up the pace here, those other demons have noticed their cargo is missing by now and will be catching up shortly. I cut their brakes, so it may be hard for them to stop once they find us but let's not test their determination." Kaden switched to the driver's seat while Wayne, Lindy, and Marcus loaded into the sedan. Andy hugged Lindy one more time.

"Dad, can you let Bo know I'm alright? I didn't get to say goodbye, and I don't want him to worry about me." Andy wished she could go back and tell him herself, but she'd made a deal with Kaden.

"Of course. I'll see you soon, kiddo." He kissed her forehead, and they went their separate ways.

Once Andy and Kaden were back on the road, a weight lifted off her. Lindy and her dad were safe. She settled into her seat and closed her eyes. When she opened them again, she checked the clock on the dash and realized she had slept for two hours.

"Nice nap?" Kaden asked, glancing over at her. Andy stretched her arms out in front of her and cracked her neck.

"Not really. My neck is killing me now." She rubbed it and flinched at the pain.

"That will happen when you sleep with your head at a right angle. Also snoring tends to happen when you sleep like that. Not the most enjoyable sound to listen to for two hours."

He laughed and Andy's cheeks reddened.

"Whatever. Are we almost there?" she asked, looking around at the surrounding fields. There were some farmhouses in the distance, but nothing that appeared occupied.

"About three more hours," he told her.

"What am I supposed to do for three hours?" If Bo were there, they would be playing I-Spy or some other children's game. She smiled at the thought of it.

"You could sit there quietly instead of pestering me with your questions," he suggested, and Andy scoffed.

"Speaking of questions, I think we should play twenty questions," Andy smirked as Kaden groaned. "I'll go first, how did you get my dad and Lindy out of the SUV without anyone seeing?"

"Magic," he answered, irritated.

"Come on, tell me the truth."

"Fine, I can manipulate people's minds to make them think they are seeing something else. So, I made them think their hostages were still sitting pretty in the backseat of their SUV. I did the same when they tried to take you, I made them think they had you," he explained, and Andy gaped at him.

"That's insane. How do you do that?" She was impressed, even though she should probably fear his ability. He could make her think she was safe when she wasn't, or maybe everything that had happened *was* a mind trick.

"It's an ability only some demons possess. But I have

been practicing since I was a kid, so I've gotten pretty good at it. It's a lot harder to do to more than one person, which is why when you started talking to them, the façade of who I had made them believe you were, faded, and they recognized you. I can only make them believe so much."

"Sorry about that," Andy mumbled, embarrassed she had nearly ruined the whole rescue mission.

"So, you asked me *two* questions now, do I get a turn?" he pointed out and Andy laughed and shook her head.

"I get to ask *all* my questions, and then it's your turn," he groaned, and Andy laughed again. "So, are you taking me to a demon camp?"

"Kind of."

"That's not much of an answer."

"You never specified how I had to answer the questions."

"Fine. Are your parents at this demon camp?" Andy noticed him flinch.

"No questions about my parents," he snapped.

"It's a simple question, yes or no will suffice," Andy pressed him, and he gripped the steering wheel tighter.

"My turn. Do you ever shut up? How on Earth did your perfect prick of a boyfriend ever deal with your incessant questions?" he snarled, and Andy shrank into her seat. She remained silent for a while after that.

The trees passing by the window gave Andy something to watch as she tried to look at anything *but* Kaden.

It had been an hour since either of them spoke, and they still had two more hours to go.

After another half an hour, Kaden broke the silence for once.

"You're awfully quiet over there."

"I don't have anything to say." Andy continued staring out her window.

"That's a first." Andy didn't respond. If he wanted her to talk, he should've never yelled at her for asking a simple question. She watched the signs they passed, and noticed they were in Massachusetts. After another hour, they passed the *Discover Beautiful Rhode Island* sign.

Kaden did not try to engage with Andy again until they turned off onto a narrow dirt road and he announced, "We're here." The road was winding and bumpy. After a few more minutes, they pulled up to a gate. He pressed a button on a remote he had pulled out of the cup holder and the gate opened.

Once they passed through the gate, it closed behind them with a loud clang. They drove for another minute before they pulled up to a light blue mansion. Beyond another gate, Andy could see a large fountain encircled by a dirt walkway. She couldn't help but gape at it as she stepped out of the car. Kaden came around to stand beside her and made to take her arm.

"Don't touch me." She shook him off and stepped forward, he didn't react and went to open the gate in front of them. They walked past the ornate fountain that spewed water, the mist tickling Andy's skin. Up the stairs at the too-white front door, Kaden used the knocker that was shaped like a lion's head and the door opened, revealing two demons.

"Welcome, Andromeda. Thank you for bringing her, Kaden." The tall man on the right said. The shorter man on the left remained statuesque, simply observing.

"Come in." The tall demon stepped to the side so they could walk past him into the house. They stepped into a foyer with three archways, one in each wall, leading to different areas of the house. Through the one straight ahead, Andy could see a wrought iron spiral staircase that had intricate designs on the railing. It reminded her of the one in Patrick and Stella's house and her heart ached for them as she imagined their final moments. The front door shut behind her and she turned back to the others.

"My name is Cairn," the tall demon introduced himself. "And this is Jackson. We will show you to your room and then we will take you to dinner." Andy felt more like a hotel guest than a captive, and it made her uncomfortable. She followed Cairn and Jackson as they led her towards the spiral staircase. Kaden headed off in another direction. *Good riddance,* Andy thought.

Andy was led up the spiral staircase, which was in a room made up entirely of white marble. It was almost blinding to behold. At the top of the stairs, they continued down a corridor with large oak doors lining each side, but they did not stop until they reached the door at the end of the hall.

"This is it," Cairn announced. "We will wait out here until you are ready." Andy stepped past them and opened the door. She gazed into the room in awe. A king-sized bed with a canopy stood straight ahead, and two wardrobes on either side, both so tall they touched the ceiling. There was also a mahogany desk in one corner with a large plush armchair in front of it.

She closed the door so she could have some privacy. At first, her head seemed to buzz with the sound of silence. She had been surrounded by noise every minute of every day since she and her dad left their house. Even when they weren't themselves making any noise, the cicadas chirped, or the wind rustled the leaves, never leaving complete silence as she heard in that room. It made her feel *sick*. She took deep breaths as she leaned against the door and closed her eyes. That helped to slightly ease the anxiety creeping in, and she opened her eyes.

There were two other doors, one on each side of the room. She went to the first one, on the right side, and discovered a closet filled with beautiful gowns and party dresses. At the back of the closet, Andy noticed a rack full of shoes: heels, boots, and flats. She closed the closet and went to the other mystery door and opened it to find a bathroom. A shower with a waterfall shower head filled one wall, and a vanity stocked with every kind of makeup you could imagine took up the other wall.

Andy started the shower, relieved to have some white

noise filling the hollow silence once again. Before getting in the shower, though, she went back into the room to pick out a change of clothes. A simple black dress had been laid out on the bed and she grabbed it, assuming it was put there on purpose. It was long enough to touch her knees, and it had long sleeves with a slight V-neck. She remembered owning a dress identical to it before she had to leave everything behind.

Taking a *real* shower, for the first time in weeks, made Andy feel raw. The water beat down on her as she scrubbed away all the layers of dirt that the buckets of water from the angel camp just could not touch. She stayed in there for twenty minutes before deciding she should be getting ready. She put on a fuzzy robe that hung on the door and sat in front of the vanity. She blew her hair dry and left it wavy. Examining the makeup left her overwhelmed. She had never been good at doing her makeup. She scrutinized herself in the mirror, for the first time in almost a month, and she was surprised at how different, but the same, she looked.

She turned to examine herself at all angles. She had lost weight in some areas but gained muscle in others. She probably looked a lot worse when she first made it to the angel camp. She still seemed a little unhealthy, but the new muscle she had gained helped to balance her out. She figured a few more weeks eating as she had been, and she would be back to normal.

Staring into the mirror, overanalyzing, Andy broke down. Her breath came in gasps; she was hyperventilating.

She braced herself, gripping the edge of the vanity as her whole body was racked with tremors. It was all too much. The quiet gave her brain nothing to distract itself with. All her traumas were parading across her mind.

"Go away," Andy pleaded with herself. A knock echoed through the room. "Just a minute!"

Andy hurried to put on mascara and a little blush and called it good. She had not worn any makeup in so long, even that little bit made a big difference. She pulled on the black dress and picked out a pair of flats to wear and then opened the bedroom door. Cairn and Jackson still waited there for her. They did not say a word but began walking back down the hall and she followed them.

Once they were downstairs, they led Andy to a dining room. A long wooden table that sat at least twenty people took up the whole room. No one else was in the room and only one place setting had been laid out, in front of which was a tray of food. Andy sat and dug in. After thoroughly emptying her stomach earlier, it welcomed the nourishment.

"When you have finished, we will take you to meet the boss," Cairn announced. The thought of meeting whomever was responsible for Kaden bringing her here turned Andy's stomach, making her lose her appetite.

"I'm ready." She followed them back to the room with the spiral staircase. As they walked through the room, she heard Kaden talking as he descended the stairs. As he came into view, Andy noticed he was not alone. Andy did a double take when she saw who Kaden was talking to. His honey-blonde hair that curled over his ears, tall lean build like her own, and cock-eyed grin...

"Jason..." she breathed. Her knees weakened and every instinct inside of her was screaming it wasn't possible, he couldn't be real. Kaden must have been messing with her mind.

"You're finally here." Jason's voice...when he spoke, she knew it was *him*. Something inside her broke and she collapsed in a heap on the floor; tears flowing uncontrollably down her cheeks.

"Jace," she croaked. He was beside her now and gathered her into his arms. "How...?" She held onto him as if he would disappear if she let go.

"I've been here, waiting for you," Jason said.

Andy pulled back and studied Jason's face. She noticed he was the same, but his eyes had changed since she had last seen him. They used to be the same as hers – blue with gold flecks, but the golden flecks had disappeared and a ring of black encircled his bright blue irises.

"Is it really you? How is this possible?" Andy blubbered.

"Obviously it's me, Andy. The demons brought me here." Jason wiped away her tears and Andy pressed her cheek against his hand, convincing herself that he was *real*.

"They told me you were coming too, but it was taking longer because you had run away."

"Jason, why did you let them take you away from us?" Andy searched his face for any fear, or any sign he did not *want* to be there, but he seemed content.

"They didn't take me away from you. I chose to go with them. I've been here, the whole time. Why didn't you come sooner?" He flipped the question on her.

"Did they not tell you what happened after they took you?" Andy looked at him with envy now. He had been living unburdened by the weight she had been carrying around.

"You ran away when they asked you to go with them."

"Fine, yes, I ran away, but not before Mom gave her life to make sure Dad and I were able to get away. They killed Mom, Jason, and I thought... I thought you were dead too." Tears filled Andy's eyes again from her grief. Jason looked at her like she was crazy. "Do you even care?"

"Of course I care, Andy! But Mom's not dead." He let out a small laugh that soothed all her pain in one moment. A nearly unbearable weight lifted from her, and she could have shouted with joy.

"What do you mean, she's not dead?" Andy asked, still confused, and she tried to sense whether he was lying to her, but as far as she could tell, he seemed to be telling the truth.

Jason seemed a little taken aback. "I mean, Mom is fine. I saw her a few hours ago."

"C-can I see her?" Her heart tightened as she thought about being able to see her mom's face again, when she had thought she was gone forever. Jason did not answer right away, so Andy went on. "What about Dad? Is he here yet?" Her mind started whirling.

"Yes, everyone's here. Come on, I'll take you to our father." Andy's heart soared. Her whole family was alive. Everyone was here, everyone was okay. She hugged Jason one more time.

"I'm so happy you're okay. I never thought I would see you again," Andy said. Jason laughed and she released him. "Let's go." Jason helped her up from the floor. Her knees almost gave out again, but she was able to remain standing with Jason beside her. She wiped away the tears on her face and found that she couldn't stop smiling.

Cairn and Jackson were still in the room, waiting for them. Somehow, Andy ended up walking beside Kaden as Jason caught up with Cairn and started talking with him.

"Such a happy family reunion," Kaden remarked, and Andy was unsure whether he was mocking her or stating a fact. Either way, the smile disappeared from her face.

"Oh, sorry, you probably know nothing about that kind of thing, what with you not caring about anyone but yourself." Her voice was laced with the lingering anger that she held towards him.

"Oh snap. You're still mad at me I guess." He chuckled, which caused her to despise him even more. Jason fell back to walk between them.

"I trusted Kaden to bring you to us, Andy," Jason said. "I had to choose who to send to keep an eye on you and to escort you here once you decided to come along, and I chose Kaden. He's the first friend I made when I came here." Andy gave him an incredulous look.

"I find that hard to believe," she scoffed. "Kaden is incapable of being a friend." Jason nudged Andy.

"Cut him some slack, he didn't grow up human like we did." Andy rolled her eyes, that changed nothing about how he was acting now.

"Yeah, cut me some slack," Kaden smirked.

"He's the one who explicitly stated we were not friends, and we would never be friends," she reminded Kaden, and Jason raised an eyebrow at him.

Kaden ran his hand over his head. "She's a difficult travel partner." Jason inclined his head in agreement and Andy smacked his arm.

"Really, Jason? I'm your sister, you could at least be on my side." Even though she was annoyed with him, happiness flowed through her, washing away every other care as she walked along beside him.

Cairn and Jackson stopped, and Andy saw they had reached a large double door at the end of the hall. The door was double the size in height as all the others in the house, reaching the tall ceiling. The mahogany-colored wood had whorls carved into it that resembled flowers, though Andy couldn't tell what they actually were.

"Wait here, we will announce you to the boss," Cairn said, slipping into the room behind the doors, closing them before Andy could catch a glimpse of what, and who, was inside. Jason had said before they were going to see their parents. Andy wondered if her dad had been able to relay her message to Bo. Jason took her hand and gave it a reassuring squeeze. Cairn came back out and beckoned them forward.

"He is ready for you." He pushed open both doors.

21

The Revelation

Andy stepped into the room and everyone else hung back. She viewed the room around her in awe. It reminded her of a throne room in a castle. A man sat on a throne-like chair on a platform at the back of the room, and rows of benches faced him, filling the rest of the space. Four pillars supported the ceiling which was vaulted and made of glass. The sky was dark, and the moon shone down on them. Andy's parents were nowhere to be seen.

"Welcome, Andromeda," the man on the throne spoke, his voice reminded her of the voice she had been hearing in her nightmares, but she knew he was not the same man. This man spoke more casually, though the authority was not lacking. "I'm so glad you could finally join us here." He smiled at her and Andy felt drawn towards him.

"Why *am* I here?" she asked, still looking around, so as not to make eye contact with the stranger sitting in front of her.

"Of course, of course." He beckoned her forward. "Come sit and we will have a chat. All of you, come along." Jason took Andy's hand and led her down the aisle to the front bench where they sat beside each other. Kaden sat on the bench across the aisle, while Cairn and Jackson stood guard outside the door. "I can imagine you are full of questions, my dear. I hope to answer as many as I can for you now." His eyes were black, and for some reason it did not put Andy off like it usually did. There was something familiar about him. She studied him for a moment, noting his shoulder length dark brown hair that feathered out at the bottom. He had a tall, lean build, but his muscles were defined. There was no way to tell how old he was, as all other demons, he looked no older than thirty. Andy pulled her attention away from him and remembered why she was here.

"I do. I have a lot of questions," she began. "But first, Jason told me we would see my dad, where is he? Has he not returned from the angel camp yet?"

"Ah, of course, Jason misunderstood you. Your dad is not here. He is still with Marcus, though, so do not fret." He clasped his hands in front of him, resting his elbows on the arms of his chair.

"What about Lindy? Did she make it back safely?"

Andy asked. She wondered how Jason could have misunderstood her, but she had a promise to keep with Lindy that she would make it back to Ace, and that would be her priority.

"Yes, yes. Everyone is safe, and as promised, Lindy is with her brother now. No harm done." He acted as if Andy should trust him even though he was a demon, and she had no reason to believe *any* of them.

"I will be wanting proof of that. But now, I need to know why I am here. Why did you want me to come here?" It was time for Andy to finally find out the truth. No more guessing. He smiled warmly, and she felt as if she should smile back, but her better senses knew to be wary of all demons.

"I'm surprised you have not figured that out on your own yet, you have always been so smart, my dear." He regarded her with familiarity in his expression, which only brought more confusion for Andy. He talked as if he *knew* her, but she had never seen him before in her life.

"How do you know whether I'm smart or not?" She remained guarded.

"I've been keeping an eye on you, Andromeda. I could not let anything happen to you, of course," he grinned. "I think you *do* know why you're here."

"I promise you, I don't." Andy became frustrated he wouldn't tell her what this was all about. The guessing game was becoming more infuriating by the second.

"Oh, my dear Andromeda. You haven't wondered why you've been dreaming about demons? Why we can talk to you through your mind?" he probed. "Think, Andromeda. It's right there. Remember when you burned yourself with the heavenly fire? If you were only an angel, it would have stung a little and faded. But it didn't, did it?" Andy thought back to her burn and how it had burrowed into her skin, trying to burn its way out, and lasted through to the next day.

"It's the same reason your brother misunderstood you when you asked if your father was here." In her head, she knew what he was telling her, and it all made sense, but she fought against the truth. She did not want him to say it out loud. She wanted to pretend none of it was happening. "I am Ronan, I am your father, Andromeda. Your *real* father." Once the words were out of his mouth there was no going back.

Also by Holly Huntress

The Broken Angel Series:

Broken Angel
Condemned Angel
Forsaken Angel

The Unbound Series:

Unbound
Disgraced

About the Author

Holly Huntress is a self-published author and content creator. She graduated from the University of New England in 2015 with a bachelor's degree in English, but she has been writing stories since grade school. She is driven by the desire to share her writing with the world and to encourage others to do the same. All her books are currently available on Amazon and Barnes and Noble. If you want to connect with Holly on social media, find her at the handles below!

TikTok: @authorhollyhuntress
Instagram: @hollyhuntressauthor

Made in the USA
Columbia, SC
15 May 2023